PRAISE FOR *IF YOU CAN'T STAND THE HEAT*

"Prima donna chefs, restaurant secrets, family warfare, and murder. Welcome Poppy Markham, health inspector and Michelin-star-deserving sleuth!"—Gillian Roberts, author of the Amanda Pepper mystery series

"Robin Allen delivers big time, with colorful characters and an intriguing plot that keeps you turning the pages. Can't wait to see what Poppy Markham cooks up next."—Ben Rehder, author of the Edgar Award finalist *Buck Fever* and other Blanco County mysteries

"Poppy Markham hits the mark! This fast-paced tale of an aspiring eatery, an insufferable Michelin chef, and the crew of Texas hipsters, hotheads, and raw talent that keep the kitchen going is great fun, rich with character and conflict."—Nadia Gordon, author of the Mystery Writers of America Mary Higgins Clark Award-nominated *Lethal Vintage* and other Napa Valley mysteries

If You Can't Stand the HEAT

ROBIN ALLEN

If You Can't Stand the

HEAT

POPPY MARKHAM
CULINARY COP

MIDNIGHT INK
WOODBURY, MINNESOTA

First Edition
First Printing, 2011

Book design by Donna Burch
Cover design by Kevin R. Brown
Cover illustration © Desmond Montague
Editing by Connie Hill

Midnight Ink, an imprint of Llewellyn Worldwide Ltd.

Library of Congress Cataloging-in-Publication Data

Allen, Robin, 1964–
If you can't stand the heat : Poppy Markham, culinary cop / by Robin Allen.
— 1st ed.
    p.   cm.
ISBN 978-0-7387-2607-6
1. Women in the food industry—Fiction. 2. Murder—Investigation—Fiction.
3. Restaurants—Fiction. 4. Austin (Tex.)—Fiction. I. Title.
PS3601.L4354I37   2011
813'.6—dc22

                                                                        2010052309

This is a work of fiction. Names, characters, places, and incidents are either the product of the author's imagination or are used fictitiously, and any resemblance to actual persons, living or dead, business establishments, events, or locales is entirely coincidental.

Midnight Ink
Llewellyn Worldwide Ltd.
2143 Wooddale Drive
Woodbury, MN 55125-2989
www.midnightinkbooks.com

Printed in the United States of America

ACKNOWLEDGMENTS

Writing is lonely work, but ideas, information, inspiration, education, encouragement, feedback, friendship, access, suggestions, and kicks in the butt come from many other people. From the very deepest place of my heart, I would like to thank Tina Neesvig Pfeiffer, Letty Valdes Medina, Camille Kimbro, Teresa Kenas, Pat Aborn, Jackie Kelly, Lorie Shaw, Regan Brown, Karen MacInerney, Winter Prosapio, Cappy Lawton, Paul Allen, the Austin Writer-Grrls, the Writers' League of Texas, the Heart of Texas chapter of Sisters in Crime, my agent Kimberley Cameron, my editor Terri Bischoff, and my yogis.

Detective Brian Miller with the Austin Police Department and former Austin/Travis County senior health inspector Susan Speyer, RS, owner of Safe Food 4 U in Austin, Texas provided expert information when I asked for it, but I didn't always ask and I didn't always listen, so any errors or inconsistencies are my own.

When people reach such an apogee of glory and arrogance, their decline is near, and that is precisely what happened.

—from *Larousse Gastronomique*

ONE

"AND JUST WHERE HAVE you been?" Ursula yelled when I walked into the kitchen.

"Up to my elbows in rancid chicken at a taco trailer on the east side." I swung my backpack full of cook's togs over my shoulder. "And don't start. I'm doing you a favor tonight."

She thwacked a small animal with a meat cleaver, severing body parts. "The favor is for Mitch, not me."

"So fire me," I said.

"How about if I wait for you to quit again?" *Thwack!*

Ursula York is my stepsister and the chef at my father's restaurant. Whatever had her so agitated couldn't have anything to do with me. Ursula was an of-the-moment kind of girl and we hadn't shared any moments for the past six months. "Seriously, Ursula, can't you give it a rest tonight?"

Before she could respond, Évariste Bontecou, the Michelin-rated chef my father had flown in all the way from his exclusive restaurant, *Le Château Azul* in Monte Carlo, for Markham's grand re-opening, burst through the swinging doors, red-faced and twisted tight about something. Évariste was a short man. If I said he stood about four feet tall and two feet wide and resembled an oversized, undercooked chicken drumstick, I would be exaggerating. But only by a few inches. His bright red chef's coat made him look even more like raw poultry.

Évariste's brilliant modern interpretations of recipes in the classic 1938 French encyclopedia-cookbook, *Larousse Gastronomique,* earned him respect, but his tantrums made him famous. The evening promised fireworks, which was one of the reasons I had agreed to help out in the kitchen. No way would I pass up a chance to see the Wicked Witch of the Southwest mix it up with Europe's *Enfant Terrible.*

"Stupid reporters!" Évariste shouted. "When I say I 'ave a Michelin star, he ask if eet is from the tire people."

Will Denton, the restaurant's general manager, trailed Évariste through the doors. "Reporters love to joke," he said.

"Cretin!" Évariste roared, ignoring Will, or perhaps responding to him. "I will not be aggressed with stupidity!" He poked his finger into the air, grazing Will's chest. "Everyone knows what a Michelin star is. No more interviews."

I had heard firsthand reports about Évariste's flare-ups, but that was my first time to see him in action. I tried to catch Ursula's reaction, but couldn't see enough of her face to tell if she was fuming that he had brought his gripes into the kitchen or smirking that it was Will, not her, who had to deal with them.

Will's fading smile dropped completely from his face. "Évariste," he said, smoothing his voice, "this is an important night for you and for Markham's. I need you to speak with these reporters."

Évariste waddled over to a cooling tray of silverware by the dishwasher. He selected a handful of spoons, then took his time walking across the thick rubber floor mats to the stove. He began tasting the sauces and soups simmering in huge silver pots, aware of his audience, but not acknowledging us.

Will was right. My father had a lot riding on this night and we couldn't afford a tantrum so early. I have a way with chefs and knew just what to say to calm him down and send him back to the dining room. "Évariste," I said.

He spun round. "Chef!" he barked. "You call me as 'chef' een my kitchen!"

"Okay, chef—"

"Chef Bontecou," Will interrupted, "you are the star of the evening."

That's not what I would have said, but it worked. Évariste stopped shoving spoons between his pink lips. He turned and looked up at Will, then tilted his head, inviting him to continue.

Will stepped closer to Évariste. "*We've* gone to a lot of trouble to bring you here and to promote your Texas debut. Important people will be here tonight. As a successful businessman, surely you can understand that we need you to do what you're good at."

"They are stupid," Évariste said, softening but still petulant.

"Yes," Will agreed, "they are stupid. But even a stupid reporter can write a good story."

"*Pft*," Évariste said, lifting the lid on another pot.

Uh-oh.

Ursula's special pot. The pot she uses to experiment with, to perfect her famous soup recipes. The pot everyone in her kitchen knows not to touch.

Ursula looked up from the frog legs she had been cutting off at the ankles, glared at Évariste, then returned to the business of defooting frogs. I doubted she had started inviting critiques of her cooking. She had once fired a cook who tasted one of her soups and then suggested that her crawfish bisque "felt grainy on the tongue." I considered that she had learned to control herself, but that seemed just as unlikely.

We crowded around Évariste to watch him work, but even standing on his tippie-toes, he couldn't see inside the pot. "Get him a step-stool," I said.

Ursula's sous chef, Trevor Shaw, stood closest to the stock room and in moments produced one. He held on to Évariste as the little chef ascended the steps. Évariste sniffed the pot, looked as if he had smelled nothing more enticing than boiling water, then lowered his head and sniffed again. "This is not mine," he said.

"It's Ursula's," Trevor said. "Venison stew. She's been workin' on the recipe for a few days."

Ursula looked up, her face as hard and white as horseradish root. Her cheeks flared crimson when Évariste poked a fat, hairy finger into the pot then into his mouth. He clicked his tongue, snapping the flavors around, then held out his hand. "*Verte* peppercorns." He said it with such authority, I expected them to materialize in his fleshy palm.

"*Verte?*" Ursula asked in perfect French. He had finally thrown her witch switch. We all turned to look at her, as quiet as boxing fans waiting to see if it's a true KO. "I have asked you many times to speak English in my kitchen."

That was it? Speak English?

Évariste stared into the pot as if looking for the translation rising in the steam. "*Verte*," he murmured, then looked up. "Grin!" he exclaimed. "Grin peppercorns."

I reached around to a shelf behind me and handed him a canister of green peppercorns. The look Ursula gave me could have singed a yeti bald. I should have felt bad about cooking with the enemy, but after making me miserable for months as her sous chef, she had run up quite a tab. That night was my first and maybe only chance at settling up with her. Besides, Ursula cooked better when she was ticked off.

Évariste shook two tablespoons of the peppercorns into his hand, brought them up to his face for a sniff, then rubbed them together in his hands and let them fall into the pot. "Eet weel be good in thirty meenoots."

Trevor helped him down from the stool, a look of awe on his face. "You're amazin'," Chef. One taste and you knew exactly what it needed."

Will broke up the love fest. "Chef, please, the reporters are waiting."

Évariste turned to me and pointed to his hat. "Is eet straight?"

I looked at the foot-high pleated cylinder atop his rotund body. He looked like a pudgy exclamation point. "Straight enough," I said.

"Straight as a shark's fin," Ursula muttered.

Will escorted Évariste out the swinging doors, setting off a lightning storm of flashbulbs and thunderous cheers among the reporters. Ursula returned her attention to the frog legs, her anger beginning to settle into a simmer.

Ursula's kitchen used to be my kitchen and then our kitchen until I quit and became a public health inspector. My father understands why I chose that traitorous occupation, but he hasn't forgiven me for leaving the family restaurant in the first place. The fact that I had agreed to be an extra pair of skilled hands in the kitchen during the rush that night gave him hope that I might return. I was going to disappoint him again.

I don't like Ursula, but I love my father and I love the restaurant, so I needed to get along with the chef. Even though she had been the one to yell, I decided to apologize for being late. I tapped her on the back and she turned to me, finishing a thought she had started in her head. "You know, my guys won't give me so much as an 'attagirl' when food critics add a fifth star to their restaurant rating system just so they can award it to me, but that Monaco midget adds one little spice to a pot of deer meat and they turn his step-stool into a pedestal."

"Just ignore him," I said, knowing she couldn't. *Wouldn't.*

She pulled a teaspoon from her apron and dipped it into a container of something one of her cooks had set on the counter. "That's what Mitch tells me," she said, sipping from the spoon. "But how am I supposed to do that? The only reason I'm going through all of this is because of that Gallic grunt. Big flippin' deal he can cook camel's ribs. My meat supplier's still laughing from when Évariste tried to place an order for them."

She dipped another spoon into the container then hovered it in front of my lips. I sipped something much too salty. "Tastes like the Gulf of Mexico," I said.

She pitched the spoon across the kitchen with expert precision, landing it in the bus tub with a hard clink. "I am so sick of men telling me what to do."

"Then why don't you tell me what to do," I said.

"Get changed and you can field-dress the rabbits. Évariste swears we'll sell out."

So that's how it was going to be. She knew I was a vegan. If I didn't eat animals, why would I want to flay them? Why couldn't I peel potatoes or pre-plate salads? But grousing about my assignment would send both of us into the ring, and we had too much prep work to do.

"No problem," I said. I swung my backpack off my shoulder and hugged it in front of me with both arms, taking up as little space as possible as I veered around prep cooks slicing fresh beetroot and chiffonading parsley.

When I pushed through the swinging doors into the wait station, I stopped dead.

The main dining room, usually cool and serene before service, churned with people and activity. The French Fox, as American food writers had dubbed Évariste—not for his looks, but for his business acumen—held court in front of dozens of journalists. I recognized a lot of the Austin media, but also saw film crews from other cities and even a few with foreign identifications. All at Markham's. And all because of Évariste Bontecou.

I caught sight of a woman in a perfectly coiffed platinum-blond bob standing next to a tan, handsome, bald man. My stepmother Nina and my father Mitch. I hardly recognized my father anymore. He had been a cradle-to-grave hippie until Nina sunk her acrylic claws into him. She was more interested in how people looked than in who they were, and Mitch became a victim of her shallow upgrades. When he cut off his wispy ponytail and traded his full Hemingway beard for a trim goatee, local newspapers wrote stories on his "transformation."

Not one to pass up an opportunity to get her name in the paper, Nina had parlayed the interest in Mitch's makeover into more publicity by making over the restaurant. She had coerced Mitch into transforming Markham's Bar & Grill, the casual eatery he had started with my mother before I was born, into an upgraded white-linen restaurant with an upgraded name, Markham's Grille & Cocktails, the extra 'e' completely unnecessary and pretentious. Between husbands or when she's bored, Nina works as an interior designer, and I had to admit that the restaurant's sleek new look deserved to be celebrated.

I moved closer to the podium and waved across the crowd to get their attention. Mitch's face lit up when he saw me, but Nina scowled. *The feeling is mutual,* I telegraphed with my own scowl. She said something into Mitch's ear and his answer made her frown. *Yes, Nina, I will be here all night.* They turned back to the reporters volleying questions at Évariste, then to Évariste lobbing answers back to them.

"Chef!" a reporter called. "What's your favorite beer?"

"Free ones."

"Chef, what's your impression of Austin?"

"Ow-steen reminds me of home, but *les filles* at home, they wear no tops on the beach."

Ursula slammed through the kitchen doors just as a reporter asked, "Chef, do you like the Longhorns?"

"Eet depends on how you cook them."

Ursula uttered a forceful, "Ugh!" over the laughter and stomped past me.

The night was bigger than Ursula and bigger than me. If I was going to put up with her, she could put up with Évariste. I followed her to the women's restroom, ready to tell her to cowgirl up, but when I opened the door, what I saw shut my mouth before I even opened it.

TWO

Tears.

I had never seen Ursula cry before. Never even suspected she had tear ducts. She always handled everything with the grit and efficiency of an army battalion commander.

Whether due to my shock at her unprecedented display of human weakness or my sudden regret at helping Évariste earlier, I had the urge to pull her to me for a hug. But I stopped myself. Being that nice to Ursula would be too weird. Then she sniffed like a little girl and I gave in. She resisted, but I held on and she finally dropped her head onto my shoulder.

Ursula and I are both in our thirties, but that's about all we have in common. She's five foot seven and all leg, thin and elegant with long red curly hair and intense blue eyes. I'm five foot four, muscular and athletic with blond hair and green eyes. She attended private schools and cotillions. I went to public school and was in the Girl Scouts, until I set two Brownies on fire while going for my Camping badge. I did, however, earn the Poking Her Nose

Where It Doesn't Belong, Too Big for Her Britches, and Conclusion Jumping badges. Ursula is creative and manic, while I tend to be logical and calm.

She pulled away and ran cold water from the tap. "That should be me out there."

"I know," I said, slipping into the handicapped stall to change.

I had been zapped too many times by Ursula to feel sorry for her, but I understood what she was going through. The things she could do with food filled Markham's dining room every night and won her many awards, but the amount of media coverage she had received in her entire career was only a fraction of what Évariste had received in the past two weeks. Seeing all of those reporters wooing him with bouquets of microphones and candied words in the dining room while she butchered amphibians in the kitchen would be to dream of retribution.

"Look," I said, "I know Évariste is a jerk, but—"

"That culinary carbuncle is jeopardizing my career!"

Stealing the limelight, yes, but he was not having dire and long-term effects on her career. Unless she meant her career as the world's most difficult chef. They were neck and neck for that designation. I unwrapped my rubber clogs from their plastic bag and dropped them on the floor. "Don't you think you're being a bit dramatic?"

"No, I don't. And I don't think you appreciate the gravity of this situation."

Any situation that rides counter to Ursula's wishes is always grave or tragic or dire or some other description of a Victorian-era heroine's world view. She couldn't see me roll my eyes, so I put it into my voice. "So the Food Channel loves him and he has a Michelin star. Big deal. Half those reporters out there don't even know what a Michelin star is. They're used to covering boring political scandals and the Keep Austin Weird campaign. They're just looking for a little spice."

I came out of the stall pulling on my old chef's coat. Below the restaurant's logo, it too was embroidered with *Executive Chef* and my name, *Poppy Markham.*

Ursula glanced at my coat.

"Don't say anything," I said. "It's the only one I could find." I turned on the faucet to wash my hands.

Her face hardened. "I could strangle that little quisling, Trevor. He doesn't know anything about food I didn't teach him."

The only reason I knew that a quisling is a person who aids an invading enemy is because I looked it up after Ursula called me that when she found out that I had become a health inspector. After I left Markham's, Ursula appointed Trevor her second in command. Trevor is young and cocky, moody and unpredictable, and a great cook. I respected him for performing so well in Ursula's shadow, and in spite of their off-and-on romantic relationship.

"I thought y'all were getting along this week," I said.

"He's been sucking up to Évariste like a turkey baster. Everyone is. I can't stand it!"

And now we had come to the ultimate truth of this situation. It wasn't about talent or ability. It wasn't about gender or age. It wasn't even about food or her career. It was about Évariste Bontecou getting more attention than Ursula York.

A sharp rap on the door startled us. "You in there, Ursula?" Trevor called.

"Just a sec," she said. She turned to look at herself in the mirror, tucking errant strands of curly auburn hair into her white beanie, then tossed her head and put her hand on the door handle. She turned to me and said, "There is no way Évariste Bontecou is taking over my kitchen."

During my daily rounds inspecting restaurant kitchens, a lot of what I do is point out the obvious. "I'm sorry to be the one to tell you this, Ursula, but he already has."

Évariste's press conference had ended by the time Ursula and I walked back through the dining room. Nina stood near the front door speaking with one of the *Austin American-Statesman's* lifestyle columnists who scribbled in her notepad. When Nina saw Ursula, she abandoned the woman in mid-sentence and hurried over to us, her heels against the tile floor sounding like a firing squad.

Nina grabbed Ursula's hand. "Come with me, honey."

"Oh, Mother, I'd love to give an interview, but I have no time."

"This will take no time."

"Hi Nina," I said.

She didn't even look at me. I don't know what my father sees in that salon-processed media hound. She is the exact opposite of my late mother, an easy-going flower child.

Instead of returning to the reporter, Nina led Ursula through the second dining room toward Mitch's private office, a 7x10 nook that doubles as the wine cage for Markham's more expensive vintages. The determined look on Nina's face brought to mind the day she married my father. I followed them in case Mitch needed backup.

He looked up from his paperwork and beamed as the three most important women in his life marshaled in his doorway. He stood up and held out a hand to Nina. "Hello, Duchess, I thought you were going home to make yourself even more beautiful before the party."

Mitch could charm a queen bee out of her royal jelly.

"Sit," Nina said.

Except this queen bee.

She had directed the order at Ursula, but Mitch sat too. I have always resisted following Nina's one-word commands and remained on guard in the doorway. My father threw a "what's going on?" look at me. I shrugged. Whatever Nina was leading up to, it would be amusing.

Nina placed a bony hand on her bony hip. "Why is Évariste Bontecou's name on the marquis and Ursula's name is not?"

Ursula stared at her, Mitch opened and closed his mouth, and for the four-hundred and twenty-ninth time, I was glad I had left Markham's when I did. Before she met my father, the closest Nina had come to being in the restaurant business was when she judged her gardening club's annual Pansies and Piña Coladas contest. But when she became Nina Hall York McNally Markham, she suddenly had opinions on top of suggestions on top of ideas. They were mostly ridiculous and easy to dismiss, but once in a while she had a good one. That idea qualified, but her timing was suspect.

"You're just now noticing?" I asked.

"No," she said to me, but stared at my father. "Ursula is the executive chef of Markham's. Her name should be on the marquis."

"That sign has been up for a week and you thought the best time to bring this up is two hours before the start of one of the most significant nights of our lives?"

"It's okay, honey," Mitch said.

I left my post and stepped onto the battlefield. "No, Daddy, it's not okay. As usual, Nina thinks her precious daughter is in danger, so she's wasting everyone's time trying to make herself feel better and get whatever attention she can. She could have said something a long time ago."

"Can we talk about this later, Duchess?" Mitch asked. "Our daughters have a lot to do before we open and I still have to talk to the *Chronicle*." He hadn't taken my side, but that's how Nina would see it.

"We can talk about this right now," Nina said, an even sharper edge to her voice. "Ursula cooked Mexican food for President Bush, while he was *president*, not *governor*—as if we didn't know—" and she cooked for that William Nelson last month."

"Willie," I said. "Willie Nelson."

"So," Nina said as if that settled things, "when are you going to fix this?"

Mitch leaned forward and placed his forearms on the desk.

"I've explained this to you before, love." I heard a strain in his voice and thought it best to back off and let him rein in his wife.

She arched one perfectly plucked eyebrow and said frostily, "Obviously I'm not understanding it, *love*. Please explain it to me again."

Mitch sighed, then said in his talking-to-the-foreigners voice, "Evariste Bontecou is a world-famous Michelin-rated chef who has come here from his one-star restaurant in Monte Carlo."

15

"Aha!" Nina cried, advancing toward the desk. "Ursula has three stars."

That woman is as dense as a dirt clod.

Mitch tapped a pencil against the plastic box that enclosed his prized baseball signed by Babe Ruth. "It's not the same rating system. Ursula has three stars from the Mobil Travel Guide. Évariste has one star from Michelin." To the blank look on Nina's face, he said, "It's the difference between triple-A baseball and the majors."

Nina probably didn't understand that analogy, but she pretended to. Along with color coordination, Nina has a special gift for pretense.

"Then you can put Ursula's name on the marquis, too," Nina said.

Ursula had been fidgeting while we discussed her worthiness, anxious, no doubt, to see what kind of disturbance Évariste had caused in her absence. She stood up. "That's fine, Mitch," she said. "Mother, I really need to get back to the kitchen. Are you wearing your new purple Chanel tonight?"

Listening to women talk about their outfits rates right up there with listening to heart patients talk about their bypass surgeries. I escaped out of the office, Mitch close behind me. We stood just inside the kitchen doorway and Mitch motioned to Amado, the dishwasher, who had been spraying hot water into a greasy pan. Mitch pulled a 3x5 card from his shirt pocket, printed Ursula's name on it, then handed it to Amado who darted into the storage room.

"Why do you always give in to that woman?" I asked.

"Honey, there are two kinds of people in this world. Those who do what Nina asks and those who sleep in the guest cottage."

"I know Nina would never make you sleep in the guest cottage."

"Then you also know that I don't always give in to her." He looked around the kitchen, nodding in satisfaction that everything seemed to be under control. "In this case, Nina has a point. Ursula is the best chef in Austin and I don't make a big enough deal about her. There's room for both of them on the marquis."

"But is there room for both of them in the kitchen?"

Ursula and Mitch passed each other through the swinging doors.

"All taken care of, hon," he said to her, then to me, "Play nice."

"I will if she will," I said sweetly.

In the few moments it took her to walk to the kitchen, Ursula had reverted from helpless daughter to head chef. No longer hon, but Hun. Her eyes lasered in on Trevor melting butter in a saucepan, a prep cook dicing onions, and a waitress navigating through the kitchen to the walk-in.

"Good thing there's no 'e' in your name, huh?" I said, trying to lighten the mood. "Évariste hogged them all on the marquis."

"Speaking of swine," Ursula said.

"*Excuse moi.*" Évariste had to turn sideways to pass us. "I must geeve another interview."

He pushed open the door and smacked belly-first into Belize, one of the early-on waitresses. She dropped a metal container on his foot, scattering yellow quarter moons of wet lemons across the floor.

"Dammeet!" Évariste screamed, rubbing his forehead where it had connected with her chin.

"Oh, Chef!" Belize said. "I'm so sorry." She crouched and began picking up the wedges.

"Is everyone een Texas an idiot?"

"Hey!" Trevor said, balling his fists and starting toward him.

"You don't need to talk to her like that."

Ursula stepped in front of Trevor. "Remember what we talked about," she warned.

Before Évariste could answer Trevor or Trevor could answer Ursula, Belize answered Évariste. "It was an accident, Évi," she said, standing up, her dark eyes boring into his. "They happen."

"Go away," Évariste said, pushing past her.

One of the guys in the kitchen snickered and pointed at Shannon, a big-boned, shaggy-haired prep cook. "You called it, man," he said.

"Called what?" I asked.

Shannon said, "Do you think he really is this much of a jerk?"

"Dude," said Trevor, "haven't you been payin' attention these past two weeks?"

"Yeah, but he just seemed, I don't know, irritated with everyone. Like he's testing us and we don't live up to his standards."

Shannon scooped up a handful of scallions and threw them into a plastic container. "But tonight he's different."

I hadn't spent any time around Évariste, but from the rumors I had heard—and rumors are the only way information is circulated in restaurants—he had spent his days at Markham's issuing orders, giving interviews, and investigating the availability of ingredients, and his nights in the downtown bars investigating the availability of "wine that has fermented longer than sauerkraut."

"He has a reputation to live up to," I said. "Big dramas mean big stories in the paper."

Ursula rapped tongs against the countertop. "We have three hundred people to cook for in the next five hours, we're behind schedule, and"—she shot a meaningful glance at the swinging doors—"we're short one cook. Back to your stations."

Ten white hats bent in unison, twenty hands moved with expertise, and the kitchen resumed its hum of food preparation. I could put off my task no longer.

I had never skinned a hare before. Or any animal for that matter. The meat I cooked at Markham's Bar & Grill had been wrapped in plastic and delivered in boxes. Did I leave the head on? What did I do with the ears and paws? Save them for rabbit stock? I became a vegan years ago for health reasons, not because of animal rights, but I shuddered at the thought of handling their lifeless little bodies. Ursula had plenty of other cooks who could do it, and I decided to politely request a different assignment. But my request would have to wait.

Évariste pushed through the swinging doors and stopped in front of Ursula. She looked up at the kitchen clock. "Have your interviews concluded?"

"I 'ave a few more to geeve," he said. He puffed out his chest to stand as tall as he could, but still reached only to Ursula's collarbone. "But now I must cook. *Où sont l'escargots?*"

Ursula stood as tall as she could, giving her another inch on Évariste. "As I reminded you thirty minutes ago, in fact every day since you've been here, we speak English in my kitchen."

Évariste took a deep breath, preparing himself, I thought, for another clash. Instead he said, "Where are the snay-ulls?" Then added, "Dood."

"Dammit, Évariste!" she said, brandishing her knife at him. "It's two hours until service and we're eight hours behind on prep. I've had it up to my hairline with your asinine antics." She pointed her knife toward the back door. "Help or leave."

Trevor left his sauté station and stood as close to the portly chef as Évariste's generous stomach would allow. "Dude, are you makin' fun of me?"

Évariste looked up at Trevor, then said, "*Pf*," dismissing Trevor, Ursula, and the entire situation with a wave. "I do not 'ave time for this." He waddled to the walk-in, only his toque visible as it glided past the hunched shoulders of Ursula's cooks.

Ursula went back to dressing the frogs, guillotining their tiny webbed feet with an intent thwack of her knife.

"No one in Austin can get snails," I reminded her. "There's a quarantine at Lone Star Supply."

"Duh, Poppy." Ursula lined up a few more speckled green legs. "He'll be in there a good five minutes before we have to listen to him again." *Thwack!*

Duh, Poppy? Okay, family restaurant and grand opening be hanged. It was time to collect partial payment on her tab. "He put a cigarette in his mouth just before he stepped inside," I said.

Ursula stopped chopping, then flicked the stumpy legs into a container. "He what?"

She stormed to the walk-in and threw open the door, me right behind her to make sure she didn't stiff me. Knives, pans, and tin containers clanged as Trevor, Amado, and most of the crew literally dropped what they were working on to witness the showdown. They surrounded the open door and Shannon parted the octopus—the vertical plastic strip curtain that dangled just inside the door—to reveal Évariste resting in thoughtful repose on a large tub of sour cream, a lit cigarette dangling from his lips.

Ursula's knuckles whitened around her knife handle and her face turned as red as Évariste's coat. "What are you doing?"

Évariste looked up through a haze of smoke at all the faces staring down at him and grinned. "I could not locate *l'escar*...the snells." He looked like he enjoyed all the veins bulging on his account.

"So you're smoking in my walk-in!" She swept the knife toward me. "Poppy is a health inspector. She could close us down right this minute!"

Not true. Such a violation would only take a few points off their health score. But I would correct her later.

Évariste pursed his lips. "Oh, Ursoola, you are so full of the dramatics," he said, waving his lit cigarette toward us, "bringing your posse for a gunfight at the O.K. Corral." He took a final drag on his cigarette and jutted out his bottom lip to blow the smoke up into Ursula's face. He dropped the butt to the wet floor where it hissed out, then he toed it down the drain.

Shannon grunted. "That explains the slow drain."

Ursula pointed her knife at Évariste again, her eyes louvering into slits. "I wouldn't need a gun or a posse. You smoke out back like everyone else."

"What's going on here?" At the sound of Will's voice, the spectators scattered, leaving me, Ursula, and Évariste in the walk-in.

Will parted the octopus and surveyed the scene. "We're going to be filled to capacity tonight and you two are in a pissing contest? Let's stay focused, people."

Évariste heaved himself off the sour cream, then turned sideways and scooched past Will. "Thank you, Weel, but I do not need you to fight my battles."

"Me either," Ursula said, following behind Évariste. "Pay attention to the front of the house and keep your Florsheims out of my kitchen."

"What was that all about?" Will asked me.

"Irresistible force just went *mano a mano* with immovable object."

Will left and I stayed in the walk-in, hunting wabbits. Did they come in a box or a crate? What if their bodies weren't lifeless? What if they were in cages? I had just found a box with fur in it when I heard a clatter of metal on the other side of the door. I dashed out to see Évariste backed against the wall, Trevor holding a meat cleaver to his throat.

THREE

"TREVOR!" URSULA SCREECHED, SCATTERING frog feet in her rush to the deadlocked duo. She held up her hand to stop the rest of us from following, but we ignored her. Both men exhaled hard, eyes intent and unblinking. "Look at me," she said.

She meant her words for Trevor, but Évariste turned pleading eyes to her and let out a whimper. Trevor leaned in closer to Évariste, forcing the little chef to look up at him.

Ten minutes ago, Trevor had been drooling over Évariste's brilliance, and now he looked ready to dispatch his idol to the great galley in the sky. That was bad enough, but defying Ursula was worse. A kitchen crew is highly tuned to the sound of their leader's voice, acting on the words without thinking. It should have been second-nature for Trevor to look at Ursula when she told him to.

I became concerned for what Évariste's severed jugular would do to Markham's grand opening. "Trevor, please," I said, "drop the knife and I'll buy you some ice cream."

I couldn't see Trevor's face, but he let his arm fall to his side and the cleaver drop to the floor. He turned and stalked toward the back of the kitchen, karate-kicking the waist-high safety bar on the back door. Ursula couldn't afford to lose a cook, much less her sous chef, especially since I was the only one with enough experience to replace him, and I hadn't cooked meals in the hundreds for almost two years. I wanted to follow him outside, but the only thing I could think to say to him started with, "Grow up," so I stayed put.

"Show me your neck," Ursula said. Surprisingly, Évariste complied, turning his face toward the ceiling exposing a bold red line from jaw to Adam's apple. "It's just a scratch," she said. "You'll live."

Évariste straightened. "I heet some pans down getting out from his way," he said. He rubbed his forearm, then circled his wrist dramatically. A knife to the throat got him no sympathy from Ursula, but he thought a boo-boo on his arm would? She had once broken two of her fingers on a busy Friday night and didn't see a doctor until after Sunday brunch.

"Back to work, guys," Ursula said.

And that should have been that. We should have all gone back to our respective tasks and tried to forget that Trevor almost killed one of the most famous chefs in the world.

But that famous chef wasn't ready to move on. "What kind of villains are een your kitchen?"

So now it's Ursula's kitchen.

"You, Évariste Bontecou, are the only villain here," Ursula said. "For two weeks, you've antagonized everyone within hearing range, started jobs you never finish, and left me and my cooks to

24

get the work done while you get in our way. Monday cannot come soon enough."

Évariste responded with a grunt as he bent down to pick up his chef's hat which had been knocked off during the ruckus and lay on its side. Multiple layers of rich food and expensive wine in the form of his belly prevented him from bending over more than four inches. After his third swipe, I picked it up and handed it to him. He inspected it for damage, sniffed it, then placed it back on his head.

Trevor came through the back door, sending Évariste scurrying toward the swinging doors, saying he needed to speak with Weel. Trevor walked up to Ursula, but before he could speak, she put her hand on his chest and looked him in the eye. I didn't think it was possible for the kitchen to get any quieter. Everyone must have stopped breathing.

"Trevor Shaw," she said, "you are the best cook I have ever had in my kitchen. But if you do anything like that again, you're gone."

I didn't know what Trevor expected her to say, but his stony face said that threatening to fire him hadn't been on his mind.

"Right," he bit out.

"Good," Ursula said, then louder, "Back to work, everyone."

In any restaurant kitchen, there are two places a cook can go to take momentary refuge from the absurdity of cooking with other people for other people. Like Évariste, I prefer the walk-in. With the door closed, it's like a tomb where you can boil over with rants and indictments of all things food, and no one can hear you. The dry storage room is also good. Warmer, but noisier and more open, it requires you to maintain a low simmer.

The dry storage at Markham's doubled as the linen room. I pulled an apron from a folded stack on a shelf inside the doorway, then sat on a large sack of white flour. I had been inspecting restaurants since five o'clock that morning and my muscles throbbed out their opinion of doing this favor for my father. I agreed with them.

I looked around the small room at all the spices and rice, canned tomatoes and dried beans. These things knew how to get along. The sugar didn't think it was better than the flour. The dried oregano didn't antagonize the curry. They didn't aspire to be anything, except maybe a sweet tart or a savory sauce. They simply worked together in harmony.

But kitchens are hot, miserable places where harmony melts in temperatures that can reach as high as a hundred and thirty degrees near the grill, with the rest of the kitchen only a few degrees cooler. Throw in a dozen random personalities, then arm them with sharp implements and put them under pressure, and things happen. Bad things, mean things, messy things. But from that springs a passion that empowers all of those miserable people working in an impossible situation to transform a few simple ingredients into a sophisticated feast. It doesn't bring out the best in a person, but it brings out the best in a cook.

I stood and slung the apron over my head then reached behind my back to criss-cross the apron strings. I stopped when I felt someone take them from me. "Chocolate or vanilla?" Trevor asked, his soft Texas drawl filling the small space.

I turned round to face him and looked up into his blue eyes. I couldn't tell if he had settled into a trot or escaped the corral. "Rocky road," I said.

He laughed. "My favorite." He leaned in close, then reached around my waist and pulled the strings too tight in front of me. A little flirting to help rebuild his ego.

I didn't mind.

"You cookin' tonight?" he asked. He stood close enough that I caught a whiff of patchouli under the wood smoke.

"You know what they say about too many cooks," I said. "I'm just here for the dinner rush, then I'll presto-chango into the owner's daughter and join the party."

"Lucky Popstar," he said as he tied the strings into a double bow.

I untied the bow, loosened the strings, and retied them. "What happened in there with Évariste?"

He looked through the doorway into the kitchen. "Nothin' happened. It's just a lot of pressure tonight. I guess I lost it for a minute."

Poor guy, caught between his loyalty to Ursula and his admiration of Évariste, but it wasn't nothing. "Trevor, you almost severed his windpipe."

He wiped his sleeve across his forehead. "It's over, Poppy. Let it go."

"Were you protecting Ursula's honor?"

"Ursula's not the one who needs my protection."

I followed him out of the room to ask what he meant, but Shannon snagged him and I lost my chance.

We had about an hour until the first guests began to arrive, and I felt the familiar charge of adrenaline I used to feel when I worked

27

in the kitchen. That is my favorite hour. When the waiters start clocking in to stock the wait stations and set up their tables, and the bartenders uncork bottles of house wine and fill the ice bins, when the fragrances of grilled meats, baked bread, and sautéed garlic arise from pots, pans, ovens, and grills. The kitchen throbs with life, and it feels like the point of no return. But it's a precipice you enjoy teetering on. Everyone is focused because if everything doesn't get done in the next sixty minutes, you're in the weeds from the very first order and it's well-nigh impossible to recover.

Évariste did not return from his meeting with Will, apparently choosing to leave rather than help, which forced Ursula to shuffle duties around. She made Shannon skin the hares, a job he attacked with such relish, you might think he viewed it as a promotion. By the time I finished stemming a box of asparagus and washing two boxes of artichokes, the first orders had started rolling off the printer.

That was when I was supposed to exchange my clogs and sweat for sandals and a smile, but having no Évariste meant we had no expeditor. I was standing in the wait station calling out orders as fast as they machine-gunned out of the ticket printer when he stumbled back into our solar system. Sweat poured down his neck, forming a dark stain on the front of his coat, and he wore an inane grin on his pudgy face.

He looked in my direction, then pushed off with one foot and barreled toward me. I had no room to move and the impact pinned me between the countertop and his pillowy stomach. When he realized he had quit moving, he relaxed his body, then laid his head against my chest and cast unfocused eyes up to my face. "*Bon soir*," he sang.

Sweet fancy Moses, the man was drunk!

And this toad was the only person who knew how the plates should be dressed before the waiters served them to customers. Important customers. Restaurant critics and congressmen. Maybe even local celebrities like Matthew McConaughey or Sandra Bullock. The expeditor conducted the kitchen's symphony, but Évariste couldn't stand erect, much less read and call out orders, make sure they were prepared correctly, garnish plates, and chivvy waiters to get hot food to the tables.

"What's going on out there?" Ursula asked as she placed two roasted rabbits in the window. They had no paws or heads, which resolved one of my curiosities that night.

Évariste had lost his skyscraper hat somewhere in his travels, which made him too short for Ursula to see over the pass. "Nothing," I said. Hands down, the biggest lie I had ever told. "I need to find Évariste so he can show me how to dress this hare. Back in a sec."

Ratting on Évariste smoking in the walk-in just to issue a little payback to Ursula was one thing. But she would become dangerous if she caught Évariste soused. I had to protect Markham's.

I shoved Évariste away from me, spun him around, then prodded him the few feet into Will's office. I closed and locked the door then pushed him into a chair. He started giggling and pitched his head back.

I seized his sweaty head with both hands and forced him to look at me. "Évariste!"

He blinked then focused his eyes on my face. "Alo *cherie*."

Gin.

"What goes on the rabbit?"

"Rub eet?" he asked, the suggestion creeping into his eyes. Euw. "The hare. What goes on the saddle of roasted hare?" He hiccupped.

I squeezed his head. "Focus, you drunk little demon!"

He winced. "Uh . . . lemon, beerut, water . . ."

Someone rattled the door handle, then knocked. "Will?" Belize said. "Those friends of yours are asking for you."

"He's not in here," I called.

Back to the rummy. "And the frog legs?"

He blinked slowly. "I like *les mademoiselles* with the blond hairs." Then he went limp.

"Argh!" I dropped his head.

Évariste started snoring as I flew out of Will's office, slamming the door behind me and rushing to the wait station. I shot my hand into a plastic glove then threw lemon, beetroot, and watercress on the plated hares just before a waiter swept them into the dining room.

"Where's Mount Everest?" Ursula demanded.

"Taking a break in Will's office," I said. "I can take over as expo. He can't reach the ticket printer anyway, even if we put him on a milk crate." That was not a lie, and not just because he had passed out.

"A break from what?" she asked. Then the printer jumped to life, redirecting our focus. I tore off a string of paper chits and called out, "Ordering. Five frogs, four tournedos medium, three with mushrooms, one with artichokes, three stuffed artichokes, two cheese plates," sending the cooks into battle.

All busy nights are exactly the same. Ninety-five things happen at once and any one of them can throw you off your game. It could be a waiter who screws you up by forgetting to turn in an order and taking another waiter's food, or you run out of the nightly special in the first two hours and have to eighty-six it, or every customer inexplicably orders soup and you run out of bowls.

That night everyone would point to the dishwasher, Amado, but he didn't deserve the blame. The second dishwasher didn't show up for work, leaving Amado with the Sisyphean burden of keeping the line supplied with clean dishes when every dish in the restaurant was at a guest's table in the dining room.

"I need those frogs for table seven," I called to Ursula.

"Ready," she said, reaching under the stovetop for a warm bowl and coming up with nothing. "I need a bowl, Amado."

"One minute, Miss," he said.

"I don't have one minute!"

"Put it on a plate," I said. "This rabbit's dying."

"Bowl. Now." Ursula hovered the pan over the flame and waited for Amado to power rinse and dry a bowl. It seemed to take forever. Everything takes forever when you're so busy that time loses any meaning. She poured the frog legs into it then slid it to me and I put it up in the window next to the rabbit. "Order up!"

For every order that left the kitchen, four more came in. Waiters ran back to let me know which orders would be eaten by VIPs. "Those bunnies are for the mayor's table." "The congressman's wife wants her meat discs extra rare." "Table four wants rice instead of veggies." I knew Mitch loved having all the wattage in the restaurant, but their pickiness was killing our ticket times.

31

Will came up to me. "Where is Évariste?"

"In your office," I said in a low voice. "Passed out."

"Perfect," Will said. He looked calmer than I would have if I had a major disaster brewing with very few solutions. Without word or expression, as if he had done this dozens of times before, he pulled a loaf of bread from the warming drawer and a full pot of coffee from the burner, then opened the door to his office.

About half an hour later, Évariste walked out unattended, and wearing his hat. He looked more tired than drunk, so I figured Will's mission had been a success. As the night wore on, Évariste occasionally wandered back to the kitchen trailed by an expensively dressed couple or a gaggle of tipsy girls who twittered at everything he said. They would stand just inside the swinging doors while Évariste explained how the kitchen worked and what each cook was doing. I wanted to flog him with asparagus every time he gave the kitchen a thumbs up and said, "Kip up the good works, guys," before he toddled back into the dining room.

A couple of hours later, orders for *Petit Fours* and *Tarte aux Figue* started to replace the heavy demand of appetizer and dinner orders. Shannon took over as expeditor so I could start my third job that night entertaining Markham's guests. Between inspecting restaurants all day and working at Markham's all night, I felt like I had been inside one kitchen or another for twenty-four hours straight, but it was probably only twelve or thirteen hours.

I had just untied my apron when Évariste busted through the kitchen doors, chased by a flawlessly made-up woman. A tight cream silk dress set off glossy raven hair, her face severe and desperate. She walked on the balls of her feet, expertly hovering her four-inch heels over the holes in the floor mats.

She screamed something at Évariste in French and he spun around to face her. "*Merde!*" he cried, then let loose a tirade punctuated with hasty hand gestures and emphatic facial expressions. They yelled over each other, neither of them listening to the other. Then in two long strides, she was in front of him, slapping him hard across the face.

FOUR

If Évariste wasn't completely sober before, he was now. As a bonus, he was also speechless. If only someone had slapped him earlier. I leaned into Trevor. "*Madame* Bontecou, I presume."

He rested his forearm on my shoulder. "BonBon does not live up to the sweet promise of her name."

Évariste backed up, keeping his eyes glued to the silk-clad cyclone. Blood tricked from a scratch at his temple. She looked around the kitchen, pointing her heavily ringed fingers first at Ursula then at me, still yelling in French.

Évariste shook his head. "*Non, cherie, non.*"

It didn't take a private eye to figure out that BonBon thought he had been unfaithful to her, and with one of the only two women in the kitchen. Ursula shook her head along with Évariste, for once in synch with him. BonBon took another step toward him and he raised his arms to protect his face against another blow.

Évariste's savior came through the doors wearing a bright smile. "Ah, BonBon, there you are," Will said merrily. "I've been looking everywhere for you."

When BonBon turned around, Évariste scampered into the dry storage room.

"The governor and his wife are waiting to meet you," Will said, taking her by the elbow. Derailed from her intent and now without a target, she allowed Will to steer her out of the kitchen.

Ursula told Trevor to watch a pan of artichoke hearts simmering in butter, then she peeked around the doorway of the dry storage before stepping inside. It wasn't a good idea for even Cujo to be alone in a room with Ursula, so I followed her.

"I really don't need you to look after me, Poppy," she said.

Ingrate. "Actually, I'm looking after Évariste."

He stood in the center of the room, pressing a white linen napkin to the cut at his temple. Ursula stepped in front of him, hands on hips. "I'll thank you to keep your domestic squabbles out of my kitchen."

"Eh?" Évariste responded.

"Fight with your wife somewhere else," she said, then went back to work.

I opened the first-aid kit on the wall, then tore open an alcohol packet with my teeth. "What did you do to Trevor to make him attack you?" I asked.

Évariste crossed his arms. In his red chef's coat he looked like an inverted, exploded Roman candle. "What did *I* do? I ask heem to order truffles and oysters for tomorrow and he yells obscenities at me, tells me he is not my boy yet. If he aggresses me like that een my own kitchen, I will sack heem on the spot."

35

I began to swab his cut. "Then it's a good thing he did it in Ursula's kitchen."

"*Sacrebleu!*" he bellowed, recoiling from the sting.

He couldn't be serious. I pointed toward the door. "Most of those cooks out there have second-degree burns on their hands, and they're still working. If this were a TV show, I'd hire Anthony Bourdain to make you go bobbing for French fries to show you what real pain feels like."

He stood still and I applied the alcohol more gently. "Why is your wife so upset?" I asked.

He squinted at the name on my coat. "You are Meech's daughter?"

"Poppy Markham," I said, extending my hand. "Nice to meet you."

He turned his head, examining a shelf of silver chaffing dishes. "You weel leave me alone."

"Fine. Do it yourself?" I threw the alcohol pad at his chest, then pulled my apron over my head. It was stiff and filthy from butter, hare grease, beet juice, melted cheese, sweat, and the hundred other things I had wiped on it the past few hours. A sharp contrast to Évariste, his pants and coat spotless, even though he hadn't worn an apron the entire night. He hadn't cooked, so he hadn't needed to.

"You're unbelievable," I said.

He turned to me, smiling, as if I had paid him a compliment.

"I came in here because I wanted to help you, but you don't deserve it. Ursula is right. We do all the work; you complain. We make you look good; you insult us. Our hands are full of burns and cuts, and you whine about a tiny nick on your face."

Évariste looked out the doorway into the kitchen. "You are right."

"Huh?"

"I do not need your 'elp." He toodled his hairy Vienna sausages at me. "You weel leave me alone now."

I scrunched my apron into a tight ball and aimed for his face. He looked me in the eyes and smiled again, daring me to do it. It would have felt good to me, but better to him, so I threw it in the bag of dirty linen. Then I snatched my backpack from a hook near the door and left. As I pushed through the back door, I admired Ursula's self-control. I would have killed him already.

As soon as the door clicked shut behind me, I felt like I had been released from prison. My lungs ballooned with fresh oxygen and my mind relaxed as sounds faded to tolerable decibels. I unbuttoned my chef's coat and let the breeze, still in the upper eighties, cool the sweat on my body and face.

Amado backed through the door, dragging two plastic bags of trash. He hadn't seen me, and it would have been so easy to slip behind the dumpster and let him struggle with the bags alone. But he would do this two or three more times before the end of the night, while the heaviest thing I'd lift would be a glass of champagne. I grasped the top of one of the bulging bags and dragged it to the dumpster. It felt filled with wet sand.

"*Muchas gracias*, Miss Poppy," he said after we heaved the bags over the top.

"You did a great job tonight, Amado."

He dropped his eyes shyly and tucked both hands inside his wet apron.

"Mitch really appreciates how hard you work. Ursula too."

37

He looked up at me and displayed a grill of silver teeth behind chapped lips.

"See you later, *amigo*," I said.

"*Adios*, Miss."

I started to tell him that I would be right back, that I wasn't abandoning everyone. I was just going to my car to get a change of clothes and had hours of work ahead of me, too. But he had already disappeared into the restaurant.

Mitch hired a valet service for the guests, but employees were told to park a few blocks away in a residential neighborhood. I walked up the sidewalk, taking long strides to stretch and revive my muscles. My feet, legs, and back were on fire from hours of standing, squatting, spinning, and reaching, and I could smell myself. That's when you know you really stink. Gallons of sweat, steam, and grease had seeped into the fiber of my clothes, into the cells of my hair and skin.

I slowed my pace to enjoy this short reprieve from hostilities and surveyed the dreary landscape of "Closed" and "Going Out of Business" signs that had quietly shown up in the windows of neighboring businesses. For years, south Austin had done a good job of laying low while over-coiffed developers rumbled into town on sleek black bulldozers hauling in troughs of cash, reconfiguring the rest of the city in the name of profits and growth. But the scourge had started to flow south. Just dribbles at first, a gas station here, a taco stand there, eventually consuming strip malls and entire square blocks. Protestors barely had time to organize before a construction crew shored up a formerly tree-lined embankment with rebar and concrete.

One of the great perks of living south is opening your front door to a rough and ready world teeming with danger and entertainment. But when all of the cool old buildings that house noodle shops and all-night video stores are razed to make way for generic high-rise condos and chain drug stores, what would be the point of living there? Choices would be limited, experiences would be managed, and everything would look exactly the same. I didn't believe Austinites wanted such homogenization, but it's what greed and resigned acceptance has gotten us.

I picked my way around dirty orange pylons and chunks of concrete, glad that Mitch had declined the dozens of offers to buy the restaurant over the years. Even if I was no longer part of the daily operations, Markham's was still a part of me. I grew up there, first bussing tables and prepping food in high school, then waitressing and cooking in college, eventually managing the restaurant. I became head chef when my father's ancient chef, Rolly, suffered a heart attack in the middle of a Valentine's Day dinner rush.

But as much as I loved Markham's, I did not want to go back inside to make small talk with people I barely knew. It would be so easy to jump in my old green Jeep, drive to my placid little house, pour myself a fat glass of meritage, and watch *The Big Lebowski* for the hundred and thirty-ninth time. In ten minutes, I could be far away from crazy cooks and their bloated egos, watching the Dude try to get his rug back.

I didn't have that choice, however. As the owner's daughter, what I did have were capital-O Obligations. Nina would buzz around the more prominent guests, meaning her country club cronies and Lance Armstrong if he showed up, but Mitch counted on me to make the B-listers feel like A-listers. The more important people feel, the more money they spend.

It was later than I thought, 9:07 PM according to the Jeep's dash clock, one of two extras that still worked. The other was the "Check Engine" light. I grabbed a second backpack that held my hostess clothes and a few toiletries, then headed back to the restaurant. I could at least look forward to changing my outfit and brushing my teeth.

I wondered how much trouble Évariste had caused, and whether I had missed anything good. He had seemed calmer when I left him nursing his head, but he could have taken that time to stew about Ursula's constant combat, Trevor's bizarre attack, and BonBon's hostile allegations. I hoped he had returned to the dining room where people didn't know him personally and would be glad to see him.

As I neared the back of the restaurant, I heard cars honking, policemen blowing traffic whistles, women laughing, and the staticky babble of valet guys calling to each other on walkie-talkies. Guests were still arriving and it looked like my fourteen-hour work day had a good chance of going the distance to twenty-four.

Crossing the gravel parking area, I noticed movement at the top of the dumpster. A herd of cats clawed at the garbage bags to reveal the tasty delicacies of rabbit ears and slimy frog feet inside. I ran toward the cats, waving my arms. "Scat cats!" Most of them bounded into the darkness, except for a yellow tomcat that had prevailed over worse than me, if his empty eye socket and patchy fur were any indication. He looked up and twitched his whiskers, then returned to his feast. I walked around to the back of the dumpster and pushed over one side of the heavy lid. With a disgruntled yowl, he leaped off the edge, landing among his hungry comrades on the other side of the fence.

When I came around the side of the dumpster, there at my feet, on his back in the sparse grass between the dumpster and the fence, lay Évariste Bontecou, a knife sticking out of the Markham's logo embroidered above his little cinder heart.

I heard a police whistle and started toward the street. That's what you do when you stumble upon a scene like that, right? You tell the nearest policeman. But then I stopped. Because maybe, just maybe, Évariste was still alive.

I tiptoed to the edge of the gravel until the toes of my clogs barely brushed the grass. "Évariste," I stage-whispered. "Are you—" And then I saw it. What I mistook for the dark shadow of Évariste's stomach cast by the moon, was a pool of blood. A lot of it.

Yes, the man was dead.

I should tell a policeman, but then what? Police cars would converge from all directions, lights twirling, sirens screaming, announcing "an incident" at the restaurant. Then the television crews covering the party inside would rush out and film Évariste's body as it lay undignified in the grass.

There was only one thing to do.

FIVE

Just in case Évariste had a soul, I commended it into the care of Saint Macarius, the patron saint of chefs, then ran through the back door. Nothing had changed inside, except that Amado looked even more behind on dirty dishes. I watched Trevor pick up a filet from the grill and flip it in the air, wink at me before catching it mid-fall with his tongs and place it back on the flames. How could anyone be in a good mood at a time like this?

I ducked through the swinging doors ignoring Ursula's demand to come back and help.

Filled with pulsing, overindulged bodies, the dining room gave no relief from the heat of the kitchen. A buzzing congregation of voices rose above tinkling laughter and clinking glasses at the perfect party. Ursula had outdone herself.

But Évariste would steal her limelight one more time.

I had been on autopilot for the last couple of minutes, but what I had just seen began to sink in. Évariste Bontecou was dead. Murdered in the time it took me to walk to my car and back.

I scanned the dining room, desperate to find Mitch, and caught sight of his bald head on the other side of the dining room. He sat at a corner table talking to three men I didn't recognize. Mitch wore the biggest grin I had seen on his face in months, but the men looked about as happy as the statues at Easter Island. Mitch had probably just finished one of his "you had to be there" stories.

I weaved through the tables, feeling like a fraud as I smiled and nodded at people without really seeing them. My mind hadn't caught up with my instincts and I didn't know how I would tell my father. Would I blurt out the facts or drag him out back and show him?

I had almost reached Mitch's table when I bumped into a man's very wide, very hard chest. "Poppy, my dear," Will said, "this is a major social event." He looked down at my clogs and worked his way up to my faded Achiever t-shirt beneath my stained chef's coat. "Surely you're going to put on something more appropriate."

"I need to talk to my dad," I said, trying to step around him.

He put his hand on my arm. "Mitch has been on his feet all night. Get changed and give him a few minutes to relax, okay?"

Every second Will delayed me was another second someone else had to wander back to the dumpster and discover Évariste, then come running through the restaurant screaming bloody murder.

And then Belize came running through the restaurant scream-ing bloody murder.

The homicide detectives were like a live personality test, asking the same question in varied and off-center ways to see if they could catch you in an inconsistency. They finally questioned me around midnight, then I helped the wait staff serve coffee to the Markham's guests who had been detained until they could give a statement.

I hoped I wouldn't be questioned again because I knew that the police would finally break me and I would confess that I had discovered the body first. Then I would have to answer perfectly valid police-type questions about why I didn't go straight to an officer, and—in light of my silence on the subject over the past few hours—why I didn't mention it sooner. I couldn't have given any other answer except, "I don't know," which was the truth. How could it matter anyway? I didn't see the murderer or disturb the crime scene. But something niggled at me about what I had seen.

Around 5:00 AM, just when I had figured out how I could assemble a comfortable bed with two tables, a tablecloth, and a bag of wild rice, things began to wrap up. I had been awake and working for a little over twenty-four hours and felt as abused as Apollo Creed after Rocky's second wind. Even the blisters on my hands couldn't muster the effort to finish forming. I felt sorry for the detectives draining their last cups of coffee and the news crews packing away their cameras and microphones. They still had hours of work ahead of them.

Despite Nina's insistence that the publicity would be good for Markham's, Mitch decided to close the restaurant for the weekend out of respect for Évariste. Will sent the wait staff home after they did their checkouts, telling them to come back in a few hours to finish cleaning up, not even waiting until they protested before promising them free food and triple pay.

After Mitch and Nina received final instructions from the police and saw them out the door, Mitch stepped behind the bar and

Nina sat on the other side. They leaned across the bar, engaging in a quiet but intense conversation.

They pulled apart when I sat down next to Nina. I thought Mitch would pour his customary rum and orange juice, but instead he started putting away the olives and limes, bevnaps and straws. "No tasty beverage tonight, Daddy?"

"No," Nina answered without looking at me. "Your father has stopped drinking." It sounded more like an edict than an explanation.

"Has he stopped speaking for himself, too?" I asked.

Mitch ran a wet towel over his sweating face. "I've cut back."

Nina stood and reached across the bar for Mitch's chin. She pulled him to her for a kiss on the lips, then said, "Ciao, darling," using her thumb to wipe at the dark red smear of lipstick she had branded him with. "We'll figure this out later." She looked as fresh as she had earlier when she complained about Ursula's name missing from the marquis. Except she wore her purple Chanel.

"Goodnight, Duchess," Mitch said. He made quick kissing sounds in the air. "I'll be home soon."

"You look terrible, Poppy," Nina fired at me on her way out the front door.

"Thanks for noticing." I stood on the stool's footrest to get a better look at my reflection in the new mirror behind the amber bottles of Chivas Regal, Crown Royal, and Grand Marnier. "I don't look that bad."

"We hired a lighting consultant for the renovation," Mitch said. "No one looks bad in here."

45

"Thanks … I think." I sat down on a shiny leather swivel bar stool that had replaced the scratched, creaky wooden ones. I liked those old bar stools.

Mitch threw the towel over his shoulder. "What'll it be, Miss?"

"Did Nina really cut you off?"

"Back, not off." He filled two highball glasses with ice, then mixed equal parts of dark rum and OJ into them. He slid one of the drinks to me, then lifted the other in a toast. "To cutting back."

"And going home." I clinked my glass against his and he drained half of his drink before I swallowed my first sip. "I was afraid Nina had taken all the fun out of your life."

"She's doing what she thinks is best."

"For who?"

"Whom, not who." He came out from behind the bar and picked up two cups of cold coffee and an untouched fig tart from a dirty table. He balanced two more plates on the first one and carried the dishes to the bus tub in the wait station. Then he pulled a large serving tray and tray stand from against the wall and set them up in the dining room next to the closest four-top. Given the choice between bussing tables or going home to Nina, I would have chosen the dirty dishes too.

I knew he wouldn't take a break until he either fell asleep on his feet or he had cleared every table. If I stayed and helped, we could be done in an hour. My bed could wait that long. I left my drink at the bar, then set up a tray at the table next to his and placed empty glasses and crusty silverware on its cork surface.

"This is just about the worst thing that could have happened," Mitch said.

"What did the police say?" I asked. "Do they have any idea who killed him?"

"They think maybe it's a panhandler looking for drink or drug money." He laughed. "As if it were that simple."

"What does that mean?"

He looked up at me, then opened his mouth to say something, shook his head, then said, "It means I need to rethink a few things," and went back to stacking dishes.

I raised my arms overhead and stretched and yawned as I looked around the quiet restaurant. "How much did this renovation cost? And bringing Évariste all the way down here? Can you afford to close for the rest of the week and make good on Will's promise to pay the entire staff triple to clean up?"

"Don't you worry your pretty little head, Penelope Jane."

Penelope Jane isn't my real name, but my father uses it the way any parent uses their child's full name. Which didn't bother me. Neither did the condescension in his tone. It was the "pretty little head" comment that got me. If I had been close enough to him, he would have patted my head to make sure I got the point. He must have wanted an argument if he had taken a hammer to that particular nail. "Don't talk to me like that, Daddy. I'm just concerned about the restaurant."

"If you were so concerned you would have stayed."

Or that nail.

"I did stay! For months, until I couldn't stand working under Ursula another second. And the day I quit, you didn't even bother to call me."

Sweat trickled down his face. "And say what? That I'm proud of you for sticking it to your old man?"

"You married Nina, then hired Ursula behind my back and demoted me to sous!"

"You couldn't get it together after Drew left you. I had no choice."

"Drew left both of us, Daddy. And the situation you created with Ursula gave me no choice."

"You should have stayed," he said, sounding more disappointed than angry. He had to feel as fed up as I did arguing variations on an old theme. We were both right and both wrong, but the hurt would never go away.

"Well, I didn't," I said, too tired to raise my voice again. "And I'm glad. I was never a great chef, but I'm a great health inspector. So great, in fact, they made me the only Special Projects Inspector. I'm a SPI. Get it?"

He dropped a stack of plates in the center of his tray. He didn't like talking about my job. Each story I told him, each success, took me further away from Markham's. Not so long ago, we both believed I would take over operations one day, but that didn't seem likely anymore, and neither of us knew how to relate to each other easily without this common ground.

"I'm proud of you, honey," he said.

"Thanks, Daddy."

And with that, our worlds tilted back into place.

We cleared more tables in silence, loading our trays with what should have been considered signs of success, but had been recast as relics of a disaster: half-finished entrées, ramekins of sauce on the side, lipstick-smudged wine goblets. If Mitch had it in him to keep moving an inch, he would keep going.

I was as strong and determined as my father, but my feet hurt. "Let's let the wait staff do this in the morning," I said. "It's late…or early…and we're both knackered."

Mitch crouched down and scooped his right shoulder under the dish-laden tray, then dead-lifted it. "I still got it," he said.

And then he fell, crashing his head and the tray onto the tile floor.

"Daddy! Are you okay?"

"I think so," he said, trying to sit up.

"You're bleeding. Don't move. I'm calling an ambulance." I ran to the hostess stand for the cordless phone.

"I don't need an ambulance," he said. "I need another drink."

He tried to sit up again, but I was back, kneeling beside him and dialing 911. "Don't make me sit on you, Daddy."

I grabbed a couple of bread rolls from the nearest table and arranged them under his head to cushion it against the hard tile as I told the emergency operator what happened.

"That's what you came up with? Sourdough pillows?"

"Try to relax, Daddy. And try not to make fun of me. The ambulance will be here in a few minutes."

"At least give me some butter."

I laughed as much from his silliness as from relief at the wail of a siren coming closer. Would this have happened if we had both listened to Nina? If Mitch had downed plain orange juice instead of juice laced with rum? I had been feeling smug about winning this small battle against Nina and her wet-blanket campaign, but

49

was it really a victory? I leaned down and kissed him on the forehead. "I'm sorry, Daddy."

The EMTs who arrived were the same Barbie and Ken team who had taken Évariste away earlier. They rolled a stretcher through the front doors, entering cautiously, both of them with a not-another-dead-body look on their faces.

"Over here," I called, standing up between the tables. "My father fell."

"I didn't fall," he said, "I slipped on this tile floor, which could use a good scrubbing now that I'm down here so close to it."

Ken began questioning Mitch about his general health and the medications he took. "None," I answered for him. Mitch was the healthiest senior citizen in Austin. But my father corrected me, speaking another language as he told Ken about dosages and daily schedules. When had his health become so tenuous? He didn't take medication before he married Nina. That much I knew.

Barbie hooked him up to a portable machine and ran some tests, then nodded in agreement when Ken suggested Mitch go to the hospital. "You've got a wicked contusion on the side of your head and may have a concussion. And your blood pressure is low."

"Hey," Mitch said as the EMTs gently transferred him to a gurney, "did you hear the one about the ambulance and the Aggie?"

"Right behind you, Daddy," I said. "I'll call Nina."

The restaurant phone rang as they wheeled him out the front doors. I answered on the fifth ring. "Markham's Bar and, uh, Grille and Cocktails. How can I help you?"

"Put your father on the phone." Nina sounded panicked about something, probably that one of her mollycoddled dogs had stopped eating again.

"Nina, Mitch is——"

"Go get him!" she demanded. "Ursula has been arrested."

S I X

"Arrested? For what?"

"For killing Évariste!"

"What? How? Why?"

"I don't know. Ursula just called me, hysterical, and now I'm calling your father. He has to meet me at the police station."

Nina would be useless at the police station, and frankly, I would rather she stay with Mitch to make sure he didn't fall through the medical cracks. She began to cry when I told her about Mitch's accident. I assured her that he would be all right, that the EMTs took him to the hospital only as a precaution.

"I'm closer to the police station," I said, "so I'll check on Ursula and you check on Mitch. They're taking him to St. David's."

I hung up and raced for the front door, but didn't have my keys. I had stuffed them in my backpack, along with my chef's coat, which I remembered tossing into the dry storage room, what, eight hours earlier? I turned the lock on the front door, ran through the dining room, grabbed my backpack, then shot out the back door and into a line of bright yellow police tape. A young uniformed policeman looked up from his notebook. I held my breath, waiting for a lecture about contaminating a protected crime scene.

"How's your dad?" he asked.

"How did you—"

He pointed to his police radio. He probably knew about Ursula, too.

"Just a little bump on his head," I said. "He'll be back soon."

"I'll keep a good thought for him."

"Thank you," I said, then with transparent nonchalance, "I know it's early in the investigation, but did y'all find anything you can use tonight?"

"Just the knife in the guy's heart," he said, as if such a discovery happened on every one of his shifts. Maybe it did. He rubbed his eyes. "We'll look again as soon as it gets light."

"Thanks," I said, offering a quick salute before maneuvering around the cordoned area to my Jeep.

I threw my backpack in the front seat, then put the key in the ignition. The sky had turned from inky black to charcoal gray, and the blobby outlines of cars, trees, and houses began to take on definition. The previous morning had started out the exact same way. I dropped my forehead to the steering wheel. How had so much gone so wrong in a single day?

During the police interviews, while refilling coffee cups, I overheard several Markham's employees telling the detectives about Ursula locking horns with Évariste, but that couldn't be enough to arrest her for murder. Nina had to be mistaken. She usually missed important parts of a story because she paid more attention to herself than to the storyteller. She could have missed the part about Ursula being taken in for questioning because she left the restaurant before she could give a statement, or she could have missed the part about Ursula confessing to the murder.

I took off for the police station, wishing I had thought to ask the officer the quickest way there. It's one of those places you pass on your way out of downtown or while looking for a place to park for a concert at Stubb's. Was it on the corner of I-35 and 7th or 8th? Darn Ursula.

By the time I pulled into the parking lot under the bridge on I-35, the dark gray sky had pulled the pants off the crack of dawn. I crossed the access road, dodging early morning commuters, and took the steps two at a time into police headquarters. My presumption that I would announce my purpose and be escorted straight to Ursula turned out to be a delusion. Several people crowded into the small foyer and I had to take a number and wait my turn—on my feet because every chair held someone desperate for information. Darn Ursula.

In the fullness of time, I spoke with a desk officer. He confirmed that an Ursula York had been arrested, but unless I was her attorney or a detective on an official visit, I couldn't see her. He told me that because Ursula's last name started with Y, I had to wait until the T through Z public visiting hours on Friday at 6:00 PM. I doubted Nina had spoken to Mitch's attorneys, and I didn't want to wait until the next night to see my troublesome stepsister, so I tried a bluff. I dug in my backpack and flashed my health inspector's badge. "I'm official," I said, disappearing it before he could get a close look.

Of course it didn't work. "Ma'am, this is the wrong place for con games. If you really want to come in here"—he looked toward a side door—"I'll gladly take you in." He moved his hand to his lower back. I had seen enough episodes of *Cops* to know that his gesture implied handcuffs.

Did they handcuff Ursula when they arrested her? She probably resisted and made things worse. I would have resisted, too.

"Sorry, sir," I said. "I've been awake for twenty-four hours and not thinking straight. Can you please tell me what's happening to her?"

It wasn't a good story. After being questioned by detectives at headquarters, Ursula had been taken to the county's central booking facility on 11th Street, which was where she would stay until she was released on bail. He assured me that I could not contact her. So until she called me or Nina, I would have to use my imagination about her overnight lodgings and state of mind. I hoped she had kept her mouth shut and asked for a lawyer. Even if she hadn't, this mistake would be corrected soon. Ursula may have all the tender sweetness of a seasick crocodile, but I couldn't believe she murdered Evariste.

So who did? Yes, Evariste was infuriating enough to want to kill. I myself had flirted with that sentiment. But to actually go through with it?

And then I had a sickening thought. Could this be my fault? Had I provoked Ursula past the point of all reason? I had simply been having a bit of fun making sure their paths collided once or twice, but had I gone too far?

No, I wouldn't believe Ursula did this. Even if she had motive and means, she didn't have time to do it. She was slammed all night. Everybody was.

Back in my Jeep, I called Nina's cell phone to check on Mitch, but she didn't answer. Every dehydrated cell in my body, every frazzled hair, every ragged fingernail wanted to go home and sleep. I had already fulfilled my end of our deal by going to the police station. My house and my bed were so close. But my father was more important.

The information lady at St. David's told me that Mitch had been admitted to the fourth floor. I found Nina asleep on the couch in the waiting room, a garish fence of chip bags, soda cans, and candy trash on the table in front of her. Ursula had once told me that her mother ate junk food when she felt stressed out, but after watching Nina regularly nibble on toast and coffee for breakfast, salad for lunch, and skinless chicken for dinner, I had found that hard to believe. I had to believe my own eyes, though. How could she sleep with all that sugar in her?

And how could she look so good? She had changed out of the silk suit she wore at the party and dressed in white cotton pants and a navy blue twin set, a ruby red pashmina shawl draped over her feet. I still wore my cook's clothes, the same ones I had been wearing for the past fifteen hours, and felt especially grungy against the contrast of her freshness. She had probably even brushed her teeth.

I left her to whatever dreams aging socialites dream about and found my way to Mitch's room. My father lay in the far bed, face up, head back, mouth open, reminding me of how he looked when I was young enough to be fascinated by the sight of my father napping. But his body looked small and frail under white sheets and ugly blankets. A clear tube connected his nose to a machine and a pulse monitor clung to his finger. He looked much older than his sixty-two years. I sat in the chair next to his bed and held his hand.

He snorted, waking himself up, then he opened his eyes and raised his head.

"Hey, Daddy," I said.

"Hey, honey." He squeezed my hand. "Long time no see." He dropped his head on the pillow.

"I just now finished bussing all those tables."

He smiled weakly. "Don't expect overtime."

"When are they letting you out of here?" I asked.

"Today or tomorrow. Nina's making me listen to the doctors."

"Nina is right," I said.

He turned his head slowly and looked at me. "I'm counting on you to keep an eye on things."

Fury stirred inside me. That was all he cared about. That bloody restaurant! I opened my mouth to remind him that I had a job and that he had a general manager. But when I looked into his weary eyes, the words evaporated. My father was sick and needed to get better. It wouldn't be too difficult to help Will look after Markham's for the weekend, especially since we would be closed.

He squeezed my hand again. "Do this for me, Penelope Jane."

"Sure, Daddy."

"That's my girl." He released his grip and closed his eyes. "I feel better already."

Before he asked, I said, "I can't see Ursula at the jail until tomorrow night, so I don't know exactly what's going on."

His eyes flew open and he jerked his head to look at me. "Ursula in jail?"

"They arrested her a few hours ago. Didn't Nina tell you?"

"Arrested." He started coughing, then gasping for air.

I ran toward the door as one of the machines beeped out an SOS, summoning a male nurse into the room. "It's okay, Mr. Markham," he said gently. He helped Mitch sit up and the coughing subsided. Mitch drank water from the cup I handed the nurse, then laid back, breathing hard.

The nurse checked the machines then readjusted the oxygen tube. "Only happy words today, okay?" he said to me on his way out.

I leaned down and kissed his forehead. "Get better and don't worry about anything."

He nodded, but didn't speak.

I felt as tall as a baby carrot. "Sorry, Daddy," I said.

When I walked out the door, Nina was at the nurse's station talking to Mitch's nurse. He pointed at me, then said something to Nina. She pinched her lips together so tightly, her mouth looked zippered shut. It wouldn't stay that way for long.

I was in no mood or age range to get lectured by her. I kept my head down as I walked past her, but she followed me into the waiting room. "What did you do to him?" she said.

"Why didn't you tell him about Ursula?"

"Because I knew it would upset him." She placed a trembling hand on her chest. "And I was right."

"It's his restaurant, Nina. You can't keep something like this from him."

"Not with you around."

She sat on the couch and adjusted the shawl around her thin frame. "Did you see Ursula? How is she?"

I sat down next to her and she scrunched up her surgically perfected nose. I lifted my arms to fix my hair, a childish attempt to offend her further with my *eau de kitchen*, and she scooted to the other end of the couch.

"I couldn't talk to her," I said. "She's being processed through central booking right now and we have to wait until tomorrow night at six for visiting hours." Nina's lower lip quivered. I have a genetic aversion to helpless emotions, so to preempt any waterworks, I said, "Has she called you?"

"No." She checked her cell phone to make sure. "Ursula doesn't belong in jail with all those disgusting criminals!" She slapped her fist on the couch which made a light plopping sound. Hardly the punctuation such a statement deserved. "You have to get her out of there now!"

Nina has no concept of time. Everything has to be done *now*— speeding tickets are dismissed *now*; weight is lost *now*; wrinkles are erased *now*. Ursula should be out of jail *now*.

I scraped something brown and crusty off my pants. "That's not really possible, Nina. It's up to the police to let her go."

She scooted back over and took me by the shoulders. "Then you have to convince them!"

"Sure, Nina. Right after I convince a class of sixth-graders that cauliflower is good for them."

She sniffed. "There's no need for sarcasm."

"Then please listen when I say that the police have to go through a process. It takes time." I leaned against the back of the couch and caught the flickering light of a television in the corner

59

of the room. A color publicity photo of Évariste filled the screen. When they showed the video of his sheet-covered body being loaded into the ambulance, I shifted my eyes back to Nina. "Why are the doctors keeping Mitch?"

She told me that Mitch had a slight concussion and low blood pressure so they wanted to keep him overnight. Nothing different from what Barbie and Ken had said.

"Your father told me about the terrible things you said to him at the restaurant," she said.

I looked up at the ceiling. "It's an old argument, Nina. I didn't say anything to him tonight that I haven't said before."

"You've been back less than twenty-four hours and already you've upset him." Nina stood. "Twice." She began to pace the waiting room, arms crossed, hands clasped around her elbows.

She had me there. I was sure Mitch hadn't told her we'd had a drink together or she would have thrown that in too.

I felt more tired than I had ever been. Not even as tired as the weekend I staked out a cock fight, the losers of which were suspected of becoming the "*pollo loco*" taco special at several street stands on the east side. It's not against health code to cook and serve fighting cocks on a tortilla with pico de gallo and guacamole, but the birds need to come from a USDA-approved supplier.

My brain had stopped working, so it couldn't tell my muscles to move my limbs. I watched Nina walk in circles, looking like a stir stick agitating a martini.

I must have dozed off because the next time I saw Nina, she was looming over me with a cup of coffee in one hand and a candy bar in the other. "They gave your father a sedative," she said, accusation dripping from her words. "Why don't you go home and see what you can do about getting Ursula out of jail."

Of course Nina hadn't listened to me when I said I couldn't help Ursula. And of course it never occurred to her that I might want to sleep when I got home. But that was not the time to help her improve her listening and comprehension skills. "If Ursula calls you, ask her to call me next," I said. I could at least get her story firsthand.

I had more than just dozed in the waiting room. It was 10:00 AM when I left the hospital so I had slept for about three hours. I felt better and decided to swing by Markham's on the way home to fulfill my promise to my father.

When I drove up Lamar past the front of the restaurant, I saw Will leaning into the open passenger window of a black sedan. I braked hard then gunned the Jeep over the curb into the parking lot, coming to a stop by the front doors. Will waved to the car as it pulled away and I reached over to throw open the passenger door as he approached.

"Lost tourists looking for Zilker Park," he said.

I nodded. "Mitch is in the hospital and Ursula is in jail." I assumed he already knew, but told him to let him know that I knew everything too.

"I just got off the phone with Nina," he said. "I asked her to assure Mitch that I would handle everything and not to worry." He patted my hand on the passenger's seat. "You either."

"You're a gem, Will," I said, because that's what he looked like in his obsidian pants and sapphire shirt: a sparkly, well-rested gem.

He knocked on the dashboard then shut the Jeep door. I turned my car around in the parking lot and saw Amado coming around the side of the building, an empty plastic trash bag in his hand. He usually washed dishes at night, but occasionally came in during the day to work on special cleaning projects. The parking lot was littered with flattened cups, straws, paper napkins, and cigarette butts. The blacktop had been resurfaced for the party, so the debris stood out like dandruff on a tuxedo. Seeing Amado there made me feel even better about going home. No matter the mess, he would get it cleaned up. I waved to him, suddenly okay with Will paying everyone triple-time.

Before I could exit, a dark blue minivan pulled in and parked in a clearly marked handicapped space by the front entrance. Five young men with carefully sculpted bed hair and precise facial stubble filed out and began unpacking cameras, lights, tripods, cords, and canvas bags. All of the television stations had gotten their stories last night, so they could have come back to get file footage of the front of the building. But five people?

This portended something more.

SEVEN

A BANTAM MAN WITH a very long neck that exaggerated his Adam's apple strutted toward Will. I pulled the emergency brake then hopped out of my car and reached them seconds later. The man looked at the building, his eyes seeming to both assess and condemn it at the same time. He addressed Will in French. Will turned to me for help.

"The only French I know is what I learned from Évariste," I said, "and I don't think insulting this man's provenance or cooking abilities is appropriate here."

The man nodded vigorously. "*Oui*! Évariste. *Où est* Évariste?" When neither of us answered him, he placed his hand on the top of his head then raised it high into the air, indicating either a toque or Évariste's inflated ego. "*Le chef*," he said, his voice rising. "*Où est le chef?*"

"How can he not know?" I asked Will.

Will shook his head, then said slowly, "Évariste is dead."

The man rubbed his stubble. *"Comment?"* It sounded like, *"Como?"*

I looked over at the group of guys who had stayed by the minivan, smoking cigarettes and pouting like a bunch of bored underwear models. "Does anyone speak English?" I asked. They mumbled amongst themselves and shrugged their camera-laden shoulders.

Amado had worked his way to the front sidewalk, which gave me an idea. Something I had done a few weeks earlier when I investigated a flea-infested convenience store whose owners spoke only Portuguese. "Amado, please ask this man if he speaks Spanish."

Amado addressed the man in Spanish and the man nodded. They exchanged a few words, then Amado turned to me and held up a half-inch of space between his thumb and forefinger. "A little bit," he said. Using Amado as interpreter, we asked the man, who we learned was named Jean-Michel Laroche, to send his crew into the restaurant for coffee, then took him to Mitch's office.

Jean-Michel told us that he and his men had traveled to Austin to film part of a documentary about Évariste Bontecou. They had flown in from France just that morning. He looked distressed as he conveyed that flight delays in New York had caused them to miss Évariste's debut. His eyes flitted around the room and he seemed anxious to be done with this conversation that had nothing to do with anything.

He was one of the only people in Austin who didn't know Évariste's fate, but it couldn't be kept from him any longer.

As Jean-Michel processed what Amado explained to him, wet rims formed around his brown eyes. *"Mon ami,"* he murmured,

64

slumping back in his chair. His Adam's apple worked up and down as he choked back tears. He wanted to know how he died. A heart attack?

"No," Amado said, then told him Évariste had been stabbed. Jean-Michel didn't seem to understand, so Amado curled his fingers around an imaginary knife and made a stabbing motion toward Jean-Michel.

"*Sacrebleu!*" the Frenchman exclaimed, his hands flying to his chest. "*Et BonBon?*"

I had forgotten about BonBon until that moment. I hadn't seen her after she slapped Évariste in the kitchen and she hadn't come back to the restaurant after the murder. She may have decided to be done with him and hopped on the first flight to France. More likely she had gone out partying and was waking up to the news that her husband had died. I asked Amado to tell the distressed filmmaker that BonBon was probably at her hotel.

Jean-Michel bolted out of the chair, and we followed him into the restaurant. He clapped his hands quickly and yelled something at his crew. Did every Frenchman act as if he ran the world? Within two minutes they were packed up, through the dining room, and out the front door. Will and I followed them out and watched their minivan lurch into the street.

"American foodies report every time Évariste Bontecou trims his nose hairs," I said. "You'd think news would travel the other way just as fast. He's still the lead story on CNN."

"Good thinking to get Amado involved," Will said. "Mr. Laroche won't soon forget his dramatic re-enactment."

"It got the point across."

"Indeed." Will took in my mussed hair and ragged outfit. "You look exhausted and I need to get back inside. I've done nothing but field phone calls all morning."

"Better you than me," I said, shielding my eyes against the sun.

"I can't stand talking to reporters."

"Neither can I, but a lot of customers are calling to ask if we're open and whether we're taking reservations."

"Are you serious? What are you telling them?"

"That we're closed for the weekend and we'll re-open our usual business hours on Tuesday."

The police had asked the restaurant to close until they released the crime scene, which they said usually took anywhere from twelve to twenty-four hours. Closing for the entire weekend had been Mitch's decision, but I didn't see the wisdom of that. Business and profits slowed in the warmer months as people preferred picnics in the park to porterhouse steaks. We couldn't afford to lose what little business we had, especially with all the money Mitch had spent on the upgrade and grand re-opening. And if customers still wanted to eat at Markham's . . .

"Are the police still looking for clues?" I asked.

"They're working right now and expect to be finished this afternoon." He checked the time on his watch. "What are you thinking?"

"We both know Markham's can't afford to be closed for four nights. I know my dad's heart is in the right place, but I think we should open. Especially if so many people want to make reservations."

Will put his hands on his hips and looked up at the marquis. Évariste's and Ursula's names had already been removed from the sign, replaced with "Closed Til Tuesday." Will's stance emphasized his slim waist building into a broad back. He had nicked his chin shaving, which made him look human. I knew he was going to say no.

"With the police gone," I continued, "there's no good business reason to stay closed."

"You're forgetting that we don't have a chef?" He looked at me, one eyebrow raised. "Unless you'd like to take the helm."

Will didn't know it, but his simple request tested my commitment to Mitch and to Markham's. The restaurant needed to open, but was I prepared to do the actual work? For a couple of days, maybe, but I didn't know how long Ursula would be out and I couldn't do it for the foreseeable future. On top of that, did I still have what it took to run a kitchen? Wednesday night had just about killed me, and I hadn't even been on the line. I shifted my weight from one foot to the other and they both flared in agreement, giving me the answer: no. But I had promised Mitch I would watch over things. "Sure," I said.

Will must have heard the hesitation in my voice, or maybe saw the pain on my face. "Actually, I have a better idea." He seemed to be running through the idea once more, then nodded as he saw it working in his mind. "Never let it be said that Will Denton shied away from a challenge."

"Whatever you want to do has my blessing," I said.

"But if Mitch takes issue with us opening, it was all your idea."

"Of course."

"If I can get a crew together, we'll open tonight," he said and went inside.

Out of curiosity about the crime scene, I walked around to the back of the restaurant. A company of serious men and women picked through garbage, grass, and gravel. A crime scene photographer took pictures of little plastic triangles with numbers on them that I assumed identified evidence. In the spotlight of the sun, surely they would find something that pointed to Évariste's real killer.

My cell phone rang. "Markham," a voice growled, "be in my office within the hour."

I had almost forgotten I had another job. "Olive, how nice to hear from you."

"You're supposed to be here for a face-to-face."

Olive hadn't been my boss for very long and we were still feeling each other out. Well, I did most of the feeling. She stayed busy scheduling an excessive number of meetings to make sure I was "cooking at the same temperature as everyone else."

"I don't suppose you'll cut me some slack because a famous chef was murdered at my father's restaurant last night, my stepsister is in jail, and my dad is in the hospital."

She swallowed whatever she had been masticating, then said, "Yeah, I heard something about that. Sorry. But Kowsaki's leaving this afternoon and we need to get some stuff straightened out."

"I've been up for thirty hours and I smell like a meth addict going through detox."

"You can spare a few minutes. Then you can have the rest of the day off."

She hung up before I could respond. I had planned to take the day off anyway, but since it was Olive's idea, maybe she wouldn't leave me a thousand messages asking my whereabouts. Besides, I had gotten used to my own smell.

My tummy grumbled, reminding me that I hadn't eaten anything except for a few sautéed artichoke hearts Trevor had given me during the rush. I stopped at Whole Foods for a veggie sandwich and tangerine juice, then feasted on the way to the offices of the Austin/Travis County Health and Human Services Department.

Olive's door was shut, so I went to my desk to check email and vmail messages.

"You look like you've been through the spin cycle a few times," Gavin Kawasaki said as I dropped my keys on the desk next to his. It isn't unusual to see an inspector, or Registered Sanitarian, which is our official title, in the office during prime inspection hours, but I hardly ever see Gavin. I would see even less of him in the next two weeks because he was going on vacation.

I slung my backpack to the floor, then sat down in the most uncomfortable chair in the office, which somehow always ends up at my desk. "At least ten spin cycles."

"Hey, did you hear about those naked people in Nashville awhile back?" he asked. Gavin collects bizarre restaurant stories and gives them a new ending.

"Tell me," I said as I turned on my computer.

"This couple is staying at a no-tell motel near a waffle house. The man gets drunk and decides to seduce his woman by choking her. She gets away somehow and runs next door to the waffle house in her birthday suit and hides in the bathroom."

"That is *exactly* what I would do," I said.

"The guy, thinking she's playing hard to get I guess, hightails it after her, so now there's two naked people in the waffle house." He sat back in his chair and tapped his pen on the desk. "Would you shut them down or just take off points?"

"Were the lovebirds cooks or waitresses or anything like that?"

"Just naked people passing through town."

"It wasn't the waffle house's fault the girl chose their place to hide from Johnny Loverocket, and it's not against health code to serve customers not wearing shirts or shoes, or, uh, pants or underwear, but something like that should be addressed. I guess I'd do a page two."

A "page two" is what we call the second page of the inspection sheet where we document noncritical violations, which is anything we can't officially ding the restaurant for, but they need to fix or improve. Stuff like the personal hygiene of the staff or leaky bus tubs or the manager not being vigilant about catching naked patrons before they run onto the premises.

"After getting hitched by the same judge who assessed a two-hundred dollar fine on the couple," Gavin said, "the bride's mother was quoted as saying 'I'm so proud of my baby marrying a famous man with money.'"

"You should write romances," I said.

"No thanks. And don't forget you're covering for me next week."

"What's happening next week?" I asked, pretending to look for my desk calendar. Gavin started reminding me about his vacation three months earlier after he planned a two-week visit to Florida to visit family. My email inbox showed five new messages from Gavin with the subject line of "My Vacation."

70

He stopped moving and I looked up. "I heard about that mess at Markham's on the news," he said. "Were you involved?"

If you counted finding Évariste's body first and not telling anyone about it, then yes. "Not really," I said.

"Everything will turn out okay." Gavin stood and grabbed his inspector's vest from the back of his chair. "I'm off to see sun, sand, and sisters. Be nice to my restaurants."

Olive's door banged open and she shot out, coughing frantically. She ran to the water fountain and slurped like a hound after a hunt until her normal breathing resumed. She was dressed in her usual personal uniform of black polyester pants and one of several short-sleeved shirts from golf courses throughout the United States. That day's shirt came from the Useless Bay Golf and Country Club. We call her Golferina, although I doubt she would have the stamina to play a round of miniature golf, much less go a full eighteen holes. Flabby and pale, she often came to work with an Ace bandage binding an elbow or a knee.

Olive looked around the room, water dribbling down her chin. She caught my eye, then invited me into her office with an epileptic jerk of her head. I nodded an acknowledgment, then took a moment to prepare myself for our face-to-face.

Olive would be a good boss if she could wrap her nine-to-five sensibilities around the helter-skelter nature of my SPI position. I don't have an assigned division or set schedule like everyone else. I work on special projects and my responsibilities and working hours change depending on where I'm needed. Most inspectors work regular daytime hours and concentrate their inspections during breakfast or lunch. Sometimes they do nighttime inspections, but it's rare, and weekend inspections are even rarer. Who wants to work their day job at night? I do, it turns out. I spent most of my life working those odd hours at Markham's, so it's comfortable and familiar to me. Plus, no restaurant owner or manager expects a health inspector to show up in the middle of the dinner rush.

Rather than trust that I'm a dedicated employee who knows the job, Olive keeps constant tabs on me. She calls me whenever she feels like it, often waking me up after an overnight stakeout that I reminded her about in advance several times, the idea being that she wouldn't call me and wake me up. After I spend a long night in the field, she demands to see my paperwork immediately, but gives the other inspectors days to turn theirs in.

At first, I tolerated her hands-on management style because my position was so new. I reasoned that eventually she would figure out that I would have a better chance of preserving the public health against *Salmonella*, *E. coli*, and *Scombroid ichthyotoxicosis* if I spent more time in the places where the good citizens of Austin would likely come into contact with these foodborne pathogens. But after three months, she hadn't figured out anything.

I stopped for a refreshing drink of water, but noticed food residue in the basin and kept walking. I stood just inside the door to her office, a smile pasted on my face. "Yes ma'am?"

Two corn chips disappeared into her mouth as she said, "You know you're covering for Kowsaki next week."

"Kawasaki, yes, starting tomorrow. He's taking a month-long Alaskan cruise through the Congo, right?"

"Visiting family in Florida," she said, batting crumbs off the front of her shirt and onto her desk.

Now that we had caught up, I waited for the real reason Olive wanted to see me. Even Nina knew that I was covering for Kawasaki.

"Valdes will inspect Markham's," she said, inserting one, two, three chips into her over-glossed lips. "If necessary."

I took a deep breath and let it out slowly. That was why I had to drive over? I never inspected Markham's, even when it was in my district. Then when I became the Special Projects Inspector and started working all over the city, Gavin took over my district. He had recently inspected Markham's and they had scored a perfect one hundred, as usual, and wouldn't be up for another random inspection for several months. This unnecessary reminder, and one she could have made on the phone when she called me, must have come out of the "Micromanaging for Maximum Exasperation" mail-order course she had been studying in secret.

I said, "Regardless of who inspects Markham's, it'll pass."

Olive snorted. "Even with a dead stiff out back?"

I narrowed my eyes at her. "Anything else?"

"I don't need any more phone calls from you in the early AM hours."

The previous week, I had called her at 4:30 after a stakeout to make a lengthy report about black market beef that turned out to be horse meat. "I thought you wanted me to check in after every inspection." I reminded her. "You insisted on it, actually. If I remember correctly, you said, 'If you don't call in after every inspection, Markham, you're fired.'"

"Yeah, well, now I don't." She swept crumbs off her desk and into her lap. "Go home, Markham."

As I walked to my Jeep, I pulled my phone out of my backpack to call Nina to check on Mitch, but the screen lit up with an incoming call before I could dial. I answered the way I always do when I don't recognize the number. "Go."

The most odious, intolerable, insulting sound came through—an automated voice. Before I punched the End key, I heard, "from an inmate at the Travis County Jail."

EIGHT

I PUT THE PHONE back to my ear and was told that I could accept the charges or listen to what the charges were. It took me a moment to figure out that the fake operator meant the phone charges, not the charges against Ursula. I had to pay to talk to her?

I punched the right numbers then said, "Ursula?"

"Oh, Poppy! Thank goodness." Her voice quivered. "I've been trying Mom and Mitch for hours. They're saying I murdered Évariste!"

"So I've heard," I said. "But, that's impossible. You were in the weeds all night."

In a flash, her tone went from desperation to indignation. "You think being busy is the only reason I couldn't have done it?"

"No, but there are laws that prevent the police from making arrests without a good reason."

"They say they have proof."

"What proof?"

She hesitated, then started crying. I heard a woman in the background say, "Don't be wastin' the phone on tears, girlie. Git on wicher business and git off." I pictured a large black woman, wild hair bleached red, kicking Ursula's heels and bumping up against her back as I had seen women do the one and only time I was in jail.

A couple of months earlier, I had inspected the kitchen at the jail when I covered for another inspector who had been arrested for DWI. Out of curiosity about the workings of a jail, and hoping to catch a glimpse of my shamed colleague, I asked if I could see where they housed inmates.

A female guard escorted me to the women's jail. Small cells ringed a large room where the inmates spent the day watching television, making phone calls, and occasionally fighting over what to watch or how much time someone spent on a single call. Each woman stayed on the phone as long as the patience of the other inmates would allow. After a few minutes, the women turned rowdy, forcing the talker off the phone and to the back of the line. With all those dead-end calls Ursula made trying to get in touch with Nina and Mitch, she must have waited in line for hours before she finally reached me.

I softened my voice and asked again. "Ursula, what proof?"

She sucked in a breath and whispered, "Evariste was killed with my knife."

I tried to picture where Ursula's knives had been in Markham's kitchen the night before. She wailed to cover the dead air. "Ursula, listen to me. The police must have made a mistake."

"They won't set bail."

"Can they do that?"

"I don't know!" Women cackled in the background. "Poppy, I am so scared and everything is happening so fast." She choked out another sob. "I can't spend another second in here. Has Mom called Ari Gross?"

"She didn't say, but I'm sure she did. Ari and Ira were at the party last night, weren't they?"

"What, are you a cop now? I wouldn't know if they were at the party because I was cooking in the kitchen all night!"

"Okay," I said, "if it really was your knife, then someone might have done this just to set you up."

"I thought about that, but the only person who hated me was Évariste."

What kind of deluded life had Ursula created for herself that let her believe that she was liked and admired by everyone? Even the Dalai Lama has detractors, and Ursula is no Buddhist monk. "Really, Ursula? You can't think of anyone else who might have a grudge against you? Maybe a cook you fired for giving you cooking advice? Or a waiter whose orders you screwed up on purpose because they complained once about long ticket times? Or a supplier you stopped using because you found out they gave another restaurant a better deal?"

"What are you talking about?"

Yes, she was deluded. She had done all of that and worse.

I told her what happened to Mitch and that Nina had gone to the hospital to be with him. "That's probably why they didn't answer when you called."

"Is Mitch okay?" she asked.

"He will be."

77

"What was he doing lifting a tray of dirty dishes, anyway? The heaviest thing he's lifted lately is a nine iron."

I laughed, glad she wasn't too distraught for a tease about Mitch's new hobby. "Mitch doesn't know he's a senior citizen," I said. Then I told her about the gang of French guys arriving at the restaurant to film Évariste.

"Oh!" she said, tapping her fingernail against the mouthpiece, which had the same effect as rapping tongs against a countertop. "Call Jamie!"

Ursula could do brilliant things with beef, chicken, and vegetables, but her brilliance ended there. Jamie Sherwood ran a foodie website and had actually made up words to describe Ursula's cooking. "Ursalicious" came to mind.

He is also my ex-boyfriend. We had parted ways three months earlier and while I hadn't stopped thinking about him, I had avoided all contact.

"You've been charged with murder," I said. "How is a restaurant reviewer going to help you?"

"He writes other stuff," she said. "He has connections at the paper and on the police force. He can vouch for me."

Not for the first time, I wondered if she had a crush on him.

"You know it doesn't work that way. This isn't Mayberry."

"You just don't want to call him because you're still mad at him."

"Yes, I am. If I thought Jamie could help you, I'd call him, but he can't. Let's let Mitch's lawyers work on this, okay?"

I heard more cackling in the background, then a woman barked, "Time up Victoria Secret."

78

"Please call Jamie," Ursula insisted. "I don't know exactly what he can do, but he can help somehow. I can't stay in here, Poppy."

"Okay, I'll call him," I said, having no intention of doing so. All of this would be cleared up if I had to find the real killer myself.

"Thank you," Ursula squeaked before the line went dead.

It wouldn't be a good idea to call Nina either. If I updated her on Ursula's new situation, she would insist again that I get her daughter out of jail. Ursula had just used up all my nice and I couldn't trust myself to be tolerant of Nina's ludicrous demands. It looked like Ursula would be in jail for at least the weekend, and Mitch was in good hands, so I fired up the Jeep and turned toward home. Seven miles and ten minutes the only two things between me and my bed.

I pulled up to my house and cursed when I saw a blue car parked in my driveway. Not just any blue car, but a blue car that had parked there regularly for two years until the owner of the car decided to park somewhere else one night.

I left the Jeep on the street so he could leave as soon as I told him to, which would be the first thing out of my mouth.

He hopped out of his car to follow me to my front door. Dressed in faded jeans and a gray t-shirt, he looked harmless. He didn't fool me, though. I caught his familiar scent of shampoo and shaving cream. The scent of a rogue. "I don't want to talk to you, Jamie."

"It's not about us," he said. "It's about the murder."

We arrived on the front porch at the same time. Had Ursula conjured him somehow? "What does a food writer care about a dead chef, except to joke about him in cyberspace?"

Jamie examined his fingernails, which prompted me to look at my own rough hands. Just one night back at the restaurant had done so much damage. "I'm tired, Jamie, and I don't have time for your little boy games."

"This isn't a game," he said. "And you know I write about—"

"Everything food, amusing or not," I said flatly, reciting the tagline on his website, Amooze-Boosh.

I unlocked my front door and left it open as I dropped my backpack on the floor, kicked off my shoes, and flopped onto the couch. Jamie took it as an invitation to keep talking. "I want to do a story on the murder at Markham's and I need you to be my inside source. I'll keep you anonymous, of course."

He said "the murder at Markham's" as if the headline of his story had been turned into a Broadway play. I wanted so badly to close my eyes, but if I did that, I would become sleepy and vulnerable. I needed to get him out of my house before he talked me into doing something stupid. "No, Jamie. Go away."

He shut the door, leaned his back against it, and put his hands in his front pockets, staring at me in that way he had. Jamie's t-shirt clung to his muscular chest and showed off new biceps. And his hair was longer than usual. He looked beautiful.

His voice dropped an octave. "You look good, Poppy." He smiled, revealing one perfect dimple in his left cheek.

I had to be strong. "No, Jamie."

He raked a hand through glossy dark curls. "Why not?"

Good question. Why not let someone with sympathies toward Ursula and Mitch write about the tragedy? Jamie had access to many more sources of official information than I did, so he could use his contacts to keep me informed about the investigation. And

I could make sure he didn't report anything too ugly about what happened. I knew he wouldn't leave my house until I gave in. I could change my mind later when I came to my senses.

"It must be the thirty umpteen hours of no sleep," I said. "But okay."

He actually rubbed his hands together. "That's more like it."

"First exclusive quote: Ursula York did not kill Évariste Bontecou."

"Wait." His hands stopped moving and his brown eyes glimmered. "The police think Ursula killed Évariste?"

"Oy," was the last thing I remembered saying before I closed my eyes and passed out.

I woke up around 4:00 in the afternoon to find that Jamie had put a pillow under my head and tucked me into the couch with my favorite afghan, the psychedelic one my mother knitted for me the Christmas before she died. I had a crick in my neck from sleeping wonky, and man-oh-man, did I need a shower. I wouldn't have blamed Jamie for wearing gloves when he lifted my head onto the pillow.

My thoughts yo-yoed between sheets and shower, but as soon as I walked into my room, sheets won. I changed into pajamas then dove under the covers, savoring that first touch of warm cheek to cool pillow.

I had just closed my eyes when the hammering started.

NINE

WHEN THE REAL ESTATE boom hit at the turn of the current century, price rather than location dictated where people bought homes, turning neighborhoods upside down. Young families walked their dogs past the beer can-strewn front yards of unofficial frat houses. Widows in white clapboards cultivated herb gardens next door to multimedia artists in purple brick homes with hair to match. And my quiet evenings in my eight-hundred-square-foot pre-war chicken coop were constantly interrupted by the Johns.

John With and John Without (hair) used to be my neighbors on my left, but after they made all of the repairs and improvements they could force onto, into, and under that house, they sold it to an investor from Houston for four times what they had put into it, then bought the house on the other side of me to start all over again.

And they had started renovations during my nap time.

I pulled the comforter up to the headboard and draped my arm over my eyes, pitching a little tent with my elbow. The hammering continued and the tent started drifting down around my mouth, making it difficult to breath.

"Not like that!" John Without said. It wasn't so much the yelling as the "you're such an idiot" tone of voice he used that pried my eyes open.

I have a harmless, but not-so-secret crush on John With. He's six-foot-two and solid without being muscle-bound. He has a crooked smile and lovely olive skin that gets too dark in the summer months, but looks just right in the winter. He's generous and sweet, and always in a good mood.

He didn't deserve to be talked to like that, and I deserved a peaceful afternoon. I threw off the covers and marched outside. John With stood near the top of a ladder, crouched under an eave nailing something to the house. John Without held onto the ladder with one hand and a Cosmopolitan with the other, looking like the dictionary definition of a poseur.

John Without is the opposite of his boyfriend in every way. Not only without hair, but without tact, charm, or height. He stands five-foot-eight with a close-cropped tonsure of dirt-brown fuzz surrounding his pale head like a bathtub ring, a scrupulously trimmed goatee, and beady blue eyes. He sounds like a castrato when he's ticked off, which is most of the time. He works out obsessively and loves to expose his triceps cuts and muscular quads. That afternoon, he had chosen to greet the neighborhood in red, white, and blue spandex. John With has a more reasonable style and usually dresses in hiking shorts and a polo shirt.

Together they own Four Corners, a small, successful art gallery in a strip center a couple of blocks from Markham's. I never understood how those two got together in the first place, but like every romantic relationship I'm not involved in, it's none of my business.

I walked over to the trendy buffalo fencing they had installed the week before. "Hey Johns," I called.

They both turned at the sound of my voice. John With smiled. "Hey Poppy Markham!"

John Without took in my pajamas and bare feet, then let go of the ladder to raise his wristwatch pointedly to eye level. "Are we interrupting something?"

I ignored him and looked up at John With. "Are y'all going to be hammering much longer?"

John With said, "No." John Without said, "Yes."

The sun had turned the crown of John Without's head a piggish shade of pink. He said, "What John means is, we just started and we've only got a few hours of daylight, so we'll be done when it's dark."

John With smiled his crooked smile. "You trying to sleep?"

"Of course she is," said John Without in the tone of voice that had propelled me out of bed. He waved his pink drink in my direction. "She's wearing sleepwear in the middle of the day." With a few choice words, he had managed to make me look like a no-job-holding loser and John With sound like a dunce. If John With refused to come over to my side, he could at least find a nice guy who respected him, and who didn't get his clothes at Spinal Tap swap meets.

Again I ignored John Without and addressed John With. "I just need to sleep for a couple of hours."

John Without rolled his eyes. He probably would have stalked off were it not for his instinct to protect his possession from jammie-clad sirens like me.

"No problem," John With said, descending the ladder. "We have a thousand things we can work on inside."

"John!" John Without whined, stomping his foot. Pink liquid sloshed out of his glass and down his hairy forearm. "We need to fix that today."

But John With had already turned toward the house. "See you later, Poppy Markham."

"I hope so," I said, making my tone purposely suggestive.

Inside, I crawled back under the covers, wondering why neither of them had asked about Évariste or Ursula. Either they didn't know what happened, which was likely why John With hadn't asked, or they didn't care, which was why John Without hadn't. Regardless, I was glad not to talk about the murder.

I woke up to a ringing phone. I usually don't answer my land line because it's either a telemarketer or Olive trying to sneak past my radar because she knows I don't have caller ID, but I was groggy and momentarily confused. I brought the receiver to my ear. "Go."

"Poppy!" Nina said, "I've been calling you for hours!"

"What's wrong! Is Mitch okay?"

"Your father is fine," she said. "I heard from Ursula."

Nina seemed strangely calm as we discussed the new developments. Perhaps, like me, her emotions had been discharged by the initial urgency of our double-decker family calamity sandwich. Emotions are useless in emotional situations. Facts are important, and speculation can help. As I had done with Ursula, I assured Nina that the police had made a mistake and she would be released soon. "Probably tomorrow. We can throw a homecoming party for Mitch and Ursula," I said. Nina loves any excuse for attention and I wouldn't have been surprised if she called her caterer when we hung up.

"Is Mitch really okay?" I asked. I resented that I had to rely on her for information about my own father.

"He's been singing."

I couldn't have heard her right. "Mitch doesn't sing."

"He does now," she said, amused. "Rat Pack numbers. When I left his room to call you just now, he was entertaining his nurse with 'That's Amore.'"

"Frank Sinatra?"

"Dean Martin."

"Can I see him?"

"In the morning. He's resting."

"I thought you said he was singing."

She hesitated. "He told me he wanted to go to sleep."

My suspicious health inspector kicked in. "Is that what he told you, Nina, that he wanted to go to sleep?"

She sighed, exasperated. Or caught in a lie. About what, though? "I need to go," she said suddenly.

"What's wrong?" I demanded. "Is it Mitch?"

"Nature calls."

I hung up, then looked at the time on my cell phone—7:23 PM. Jamie must have turned off the ringer. I had missed several calls.

I went into the kitchen and saw that Jamie had prepared coffee for brewing. A note on the counter read, "Everyone knows Ursula is in jail, so don't worry about spilling the beans." He had trailed a few coffee beans over the paper.

I flipped the switch on the coffee maker, a sleek, burnished silver gizmo that I had never really gotten the hang of using. I didn't even know Porsche designed kitchen appliances until Jamie gave the thing to me as a birthday present.

While the coffee brewed I took the longest, hottest shower my water heater allowed. There's something deeply satisfying about washing off significant amounts of dirt and ickiness. Restaurant cooks experience this, as do, I imagine, coal miners, garbage collectors, and armed insurgents. In a few minutes, all the sweat, filth, and frustration washes down the drain, leaving your body and your outlook clean and renewed. Could the water in jail refresh anyone? Was Ursula even showering?

As I dressed, my stomach reminded me that I hadn't eaten since noon. I scooped up a handful of raw pecans and poured a cup of fresh coffee into a mug Jamie had set out, the one he bought for me when I started my new job. White ceramic with "Health inspectors do it with gloves on," in bold red letters. I added maple syrup to the brew then sat at my kitchen table and tried to see things from a detective's perspective.

Ursula's knife as the murder weapon couldn't be ignored, but it didn't mean anything in and of itself. Every cook brings their own personal knives with them to work. They're usually kept together

87

in a canvas roll that has slots for whatever knives the cook needs on a regular basis. Some cooks buy ready-made kits, and some cobble together their own sets from here and there as they have the funds. A respectable collection could take years to acquire and cost several thousand dollars.

I had forgotten to bring mine last night and borrowed from Trevor and Shannon, but not without cross-my-heart-stick-a-needle-in-my-eye promises to return them immediately after I was finished with them.

When their knives are not in use, cooks don't store their rolls out in the open. They find a place that's the safest and most convenient to access, like on a high shelf or inside a rarely used stock pot. Ursula stores her knives in different places depending on what she's working on, but I know she trusts her cooks and wouldn't have kept a close eye on them.

The killer could have been any of the hundreds of guests in and out of the restaurant that night, but it's unlikely any of them could have gotten their hands on Ursula's knife.

Unless …

Unless it was someone Évariste had brought back to tour the kitchen. But that seemed unlikely, too. Even if they had found someone's knife roll, the guests I saw would have been too drunk to open it, much less hit a bull's-eye.

Still, Ursula's attorneys could successfully argue that anyone with access to the kitchen that night had access to her knives. That argument might also get her out on bail, assuming that's how bail worked. I had managed to live my entire life without having to know how bail worked. Darn Ursula.

So how would the cops build a case against her? I began by making a list of pros and cons in my head.

On the pro list I put the arguments I had witnessed between Ursula and Évariste in the few hours I had been around both of them. In my mind, they blended together into one big verbal ultimate fighting match. Évariste didn't seem to take anything seriously, and he undermined Ursula's authority. He made the kitchen prepare an entire menu of dishes they had never cooked before, but he didn't stick around during service to help or answer questions. The night celebrated his Texas debut, but he didn't cook a single dish, leaving everything to Ursula and Trevor.

When I put myself in Ursula's shoes, Évariste became my rival. One who had a formal education from the best culinary school in the world, an instinctive cooking brilliance, an international reputation, a quick wit that easily charmed reporters and party guests, successful restaurants in Monte Carlo and Las Vegas, and a coveted Michelin star. As Ursula, I felt inferior and insignificant. I also wanted to do anything to get him out of my life.

On the con side, I put the logistics of the head chef killing the guest of honor at the busiest and most-watched restaurant in Austin that night. Ursula was consumed with preparing hundreds of complicated meals and simply didn't have time. She worked on the line the entire night, surrounded by witnesses. Even if she could have left the line, she wouldn't risk her life and her future for something so trivial in the grand scheme of things, would she? And to do it with her own knife and leave it at the scene? No, General Ursula York would never be that careless. She had already endured Évariste for two weeks; she could have gone four more days.

Plus, it would have scandalized Nina, and while that would have been a reason for me to do it, it would have deterred Ursula.

I stood and stretched, then stepped to the counter to refill my cup. I reread Jamie's note. Even his handwriting was beautiful. I should have stuffed it down the disposal and ground it into confetti. But I didn't. And I didn't want to think about why.

I turned off the coffee maker and considered the predicament of a chef in jail at dinnertime. During my tour, the guard had told me that inmates were served a lot of bologna sandwiches. I had already seen a truckload's worth of packages in the jail's walk-in, so it hadn't surprised me. At the time, I questioned whether an inspector's time couldn't be put to better use. The food was intended for a bunch of criminals, and if it was bad, so what? It would just add to the punishment they deserved. Now I felt like a jerk. Poor Ursula.

Who else? Trevor. He threatened Évariste with a meat cleaver, but he had been cooking all night too. He took a few smoke breaks out back, though. Can you kill someone in the time it takes to smoke a cigarette? Yes.

And then waltz back into the restaurant and resume plating rabbits and flirting with waitresses? Possibly.

I had seen Trevor go from simmering to sizzling within moments and then act as if nothing had been burned, but would he jeopardize the restaurant and his career? Unknown.

Belize, the waitress, had a strange reaction to Évariste yelling at her about bumping into him. I had expected her to cower, but she acted familiar with him. Did they have a personal relationship? An affair? Is that who BonBon was so bothered about? Love and money are the two biggest reasons for murder because they fuel the same kind of passion, and BonBon would be fueled by both. If Évariste left her, she would be the ex-wife of a rising culinary star. Definitely not as desirable as being the current wife. Or the widow.

So many other Markham's people had been in and out of the kitchen and could have taken Ursula's knife, including Mitch, Nina, and Will. Would any of them want Évariste dead? Mitch had a lot invested in the four days Évariste had been hired to cook at Markham's. Maybe more than I realized. But I couldn't begin to suspect my own father. And I would never be so lucky that Nina killed Évariste. She wouldn't have stepped her designer heels behind the restaurant, much less gotten close to a dumpster full of kitchen refuse. And Will. I had seen him handle Évariste with only words, so he probably had no need to involve blood and death.

Those were the only people who had access to Ursula's knives and had strong opinions about Évariste. At least the ones I knew about firsthand. Évariste had been at Markham's for two weeks and could have inspired the desire for his swift elimination in any one of the other wait or kitchen staff, or even a food supplier. Heck, that kind of thinking would add me to the list.

What did police detectives do when they felt overwhelmed by possibilities and needed to take a break? They probably ignored their feelings and kept thinking.

But I wasn't a detective. I had other options.

TEN

WHEN I NEED TO get out of my house and out of my head, I visit my cousin Daisy. She has a husband, kids, pets, a plant nursery business, and a calming presence a tranquilizer would envy. She's my best girlfriend, and being around her always brings balance to my life.

Daisy's daughter Logan answered when I called. "We just finished supper, TeePee," she said. When Logan was first learning to talk, Daisy tried to teach her to call me Auntie Poppy. Logan would miss some syllables and it always came out TeePee. Twelve years later, she still calls me that. "We'll save some pie for you."

The night turned out to be perfect for driving al fresco, but removing the top from my Jeep by myself would take too long, so I compromised and took off the doors. I drove west on Highway 290 toward Oak Hill. At the red light at the Y, where 290 splits off to go west, I watched as the driver of a black Volvo sedan with Arizona license plates threw a cigarette butt out the window.

I used to sit in my car and think vengeful thoughts when I saw something like that. Now I do something about it.

I shifted the Jeep into neutral, pulled the brake, flipped on the emergency flashers, then grabbed my badge and a pair of tweezers and approached the driver's side. The full-grown idiot held a cell phone in one hand and a cigarette lighter in the other. He probably lived in a new condo.

I tapped on his windshield with my badge and left it positioned where he could see it. He rolled his window halfway down. "Hold on, sweetheart," he said into the phone, then to me, "Yeah?"

"Travis County health official," I said. "Hang up the phone."

"What?"

"End your call now, sir."

He did as he was told.

I bent down and used my tweezers to pick up the butt near the tip, then passed the smoldering trash through the window. "Have you seen the red, white, and blue road signs that say 'Don't mess with Texas'?"

He shook his head.

"There's one right there," I said, pointing to a sign. "It's part of our anti-littering campaign. Perhaps you should do less talking on the phone and more paying attention to the road."

The traffic light turned green, and a refrain of car horns blared instantly. The man looked confused about what to do. I moved the butt farther inside his car and said, "Take this and put it in your ashtray." Again, he did as he was told. "When you get home, you can dispose of it properly."

The light turned red and the drivers behind us calmed down. "I won't report you to the Texas Department of Transportation." I glared at him. "This time."

"Thank you."

"Have a nice evening, sir."

Jamie and Daisy are both convinced that I'm going to bang on the wrong window one of these days, but so far everyone I've stopped has been too shocked to do anything but comply.

I pulled up to Daisy's front gate around 8:30 PM and honked. Logan and Othello, a Dalmatian/Lab mix they rescued a few years ago, ran out to let me in. Logan hopped into the passenger seat to ride the few hundred feet to the house, hanging out the side to laugh at our spastic yapping escort.

We left Othello whining on the porch and entered the kitchen that smelled like fried eggplant and apple pie. I felt better already. Daisy greeted me with a long hug. My cousin is two years older, and except for the braid down to her waist, we look exactly alike and are often mistaken for each other.

Daisy prepared a pitcher of fresh lemonade, then poured three tall glasses. Logan sliced the pie and we ate as she caught me up on the new boy from Phoenix all the neighborhood girls had a crush on, club volleyball championships, and the trouble she was having with math.

"Speaking of math," Daisy said. "You have word problems due tomorrow." Daisy home-schooled her kids. She eased up during the summer when their nursery business picked up, but she didn't take a break from schooling entirely.

"Yes ma'am," Logan said. She took our plates to the sink and washed them, refilled her lemonade, then scooped up their blue point Siamese cat, Desdemona, who had settled on my lap. Logan gave me a kiss on the cheek and said, "Good to see ya, TeePee," before bouncing down the hall to her room.

"Cute boys and hard math," I said. "I wouldn't be fourteen again for anything."

Daisy and I sat in silence, which was unusual, and it dawned on me what was missing: men. "Where's Jacob?" I asked.

"Erik took him down to the valley to fetch some palm trees and do a little fishing. That's why we didn't come to the party last night."

"I forgot. Sorry."

Daisy arranged the salt and pepper shakers in the center of the table. "You've had a lot going on lately."

"That's a Zen way of putting it."

"How in the world did our little Ursula get mixed up in a murder?"

I hit the highlights of the evening, revealing that Évariste had been killed with Ursula's knife. My job and some recent personal events have made me jaded and I tend to suspect everyone and everything until I'm proved wrong, which doesn't happen very often. But Daisy has always been more generous and accepting, and she has a sixth sense about people. "Do you think Ursula could do something like this?" I asked.

With no hesitation, she said, "Absolutely not. Ursula is territorial and self-absorbed, but to plunge a knife into someone's heart? Could you imagine?" She sipped her lemonade. "On the other hand, I don't know her all that well. Surly cooks may be the secret ingredient in her wonderful soups."

"We won't be calling you as a character witness at the trial."

She laughed, then said, "How is Uncle Mitch?"

I told her about Mitch's accident. "Somehow Nina is trying to make me responsible for his condition. Like one tasty beverage and a few harsh words could take Mitch Markham out."

"If Mitch is still there tomorrow, I'll take Logan to visit him."

"He'd love that," I said, tracing swirl patterns in the sweat on my glass with my pinkie.

I felt Daisy's eyes on me. "What else is bothering you?"

I picked at a crumb on the table. "Jamie stopped by my house today."

Daisy stared at me as if I told her I had eaten a hamburger. "And?"

I brought my glass to my lips and looked at my cousin over the rim. "He looks good."

In the aftermath of my breakup with Jamie, she had dried a million tears and murmured a thousand comforts. I waited for a reminder that he looked good the night he cheated on me and that he looked good the next day when I discovered his treachery. I wanted her to tell me those things. Instead she said, "That's like saying the sky looks blue. What did he want?"

"He wants to do a story on the murder."

"I don't like the direction this story is going," she said.

"With Mitch and Ursula out of commission, I have to take care of Markham's."

"Isn't that the GM's job?"

"Will isn't family. I'll let him do most of the work, but I promised Mitch I'd oversee things. I have to make sure Markham's comes out of this okay."

96

"Yes, I suppose you do. So tell me how keeping an eye on Markham's requires you to get involved with Jamie again."

"I'm not getting involved with him. I'm just going to make sure he puts the right spin on the truth."

"Uh-huh."

"I also want to do some poking around into the murder, and he can help."

"Of course he can." Raising two kids had helped Daisy refine her skeptical tone.

"Really, Daze. He put me through too much. You know that. I don't want him back."

"That's good, because it's up to you. Jamie won't beg you."

She was right. Jamie's confidence and maturity is what attracted me to him in the first place. He knew himself, knew what he wanted, and never manipulated me. Almost never. It would be my choice to take him back, and as far as that went, it wasn't a choice at all. "Now that I work all the time on these special projects, I don't have time for Jamie."

"That's a chicken-or-egg statement," Daisy said. "You took that position so you would be too busy to think about him."

I finished my lemonade. "It's working."

"Too well. Yoga class isn't the same without you, and Erik misses you on poker night."

"He misses my money."

"That too." She upended her glass sending ice sloshing toward her mouth. "Have you heard from Luke?"

Luke, my aimless, globetrotting little brother. "He sent an email from Madrid a couple of months ago. The usual stuff: 'eating great food, seeing great sites, you should take some time off and

97

meet me.' I sent him an email about Mitch and Ursula, but haven't heard back."

"When you do, tell him the brood and I say howdy," She took our empty glasses to the sink then wrapped the remaining apple pie in foil while I put the pitcher of lemonade in the refrigerator.

Daisy walked me out to my Jeep. "How about you come back Sunday night?" she said. "It'll just be me and Logan and some homemade spinach lasagna."

I hugged her tightly. "Extra garlic, I hope."

She handed me the pie, careful to keep it away from Othello's drooling chops. "How are you going to watch Markham's *and* save the city from mad cow disease?"

"I'm babysitting Gavin's restaurants for a couple of weeks, so I can take the weekend off if I need to. Ursula or Mitch should be back by Monday."

"You better hope so," Daisy said, "otherwise, you'll get sucked back in and be making schedules and doing checkouts when you're seventy."

"No way," I insisted as I started the engine. "I'm out and I intend to stay out."

The next morning I checked Jamie's website, relieved but not surprised that he had kept his promise not to publish anything scandalous about the murder. He hadn't written a word, actually. It was one of his hallmark moves to use silence to build suspense about what he would eventually say. Even I was curious.

Jamie worked for newspapers for years, both as a freelancer and an on-staff investigative reporter, then started a website called

Amooze-Boosh. He says it's the Texas spelling of the French *amuse-bouche*, a sort of pre-*hors d'œuvre*, that translates to "mouth amuser."

He covers all aspects of the Austin food scene, from food and wine reviews to industry gossip to murders of famous chefs, and believes that if you give enough time and attention to something even mildly interesting, it will eventually pay off. He broke a money-laundering scandal six months earlier when he chanced upon a story about dishwashers quitting their jobs at several chain restaurants. Four restaurant managers, two county judges, and a city councilman had been indicted.

I checked the *Statesman's* website and read, "Chef Jailed, Owner Hospitalized" on the home page. As if one caused the other. A better story about Mitch would have been headlined, "Hippie Hits Head, Sings Show Songs."

I prepared coffee to brew, then checked in with Nina. Mitch still had low blood pressure and the doctors wanted to run some tests, so he might be hospitalized for another day or two. She told me that Mitch approved of re-opening the restaurant early. "He feels better that you're out there managing the restaurant for us and taking care of Ursula."

I wanted to correct her, tell her that I was doing neither, but she wouldn't have listened.

It was late morning when I pulled into Markham's front parking lot and noticed something odd by the front door. A big something. As I drove closer, I couldn't believe my eyes. I had only ever seen one on television, but the size and swiftness of its appearance would have made a flash flood proud.

ELEVEN

BRIGHTLY COLORED CARDS LEANED against bouquets of fresh roses and daffodils. Photographs cut from magazines rested in heart-shaped frames decorated with glitter. Interspersed were crystal crosses, tongs, spatulas, and old and new stuffed animals, teddy bears mostly, but a few true foodies had hunted down foxes to honor the memory of Évariste Bontecou, the French Fox.

I parked and approached the slapdash memorial. It blocked the front doors, so it couldn't stay there, but a lot of it could be recycled. We could shorten the stems of the flowers and put one or two in small vases on each dining table. We could also take the new stuffed animals to a women's shelter or children's hospital. I bent down and picked up a few of the cards. "We'll miss you, Éva-riste!!!!!!" "U R the BEST chef in the world." "Cook one for the Gipper." Those could be bundled up and sent to BonBon.

I heard rumbling along the blacktop and saw Amado rolling a large garbage can around the side of the building toward the front. He had started washing dishes for us when he was fifteen years old, and is now in his late twenties with two kids and another on the way. He has seen Markham's through four chefs, including Ursula, which makes him not only loyal, but tolerant.

"*Buenas días, amigo*," I said.

He smiled. "Your accent needs work, *gringita*."

I laughed. "So does yours."

He looked at the mess in front of us. "Why these people doing this?"

We watched a silver pillow balloon bob in the breeze. It had a picture of a black tombstone with R.I.P. on one side and "Look Who's 40!" on the other. These people couldn't be bothered with fresh balloons? "It's a tradition made popular when Princess Diana died a few years ago."

He began winding clean white aprons around each arm to act as protective sleeves, then stooped and wrapped his arms around a section of flowers and dumped them into the garbage can. So much for recycling.

"How do they know this man?" he asked.

"They don't know him. I'd like to believe they want to acknowledge that a life was lost, but more likely they're just following the crowd, doing what everyone else is doing without thinking about whether they need to spend time and money to honor the memory of someone they didn't even know." I scanned the empty parking lot. When had Évariste's fans been here? "They probably hope a television crew will catch them in the act and interview them. There are lots of aspiring actors in this city."

He pointed to one of the cards. "What is this word, 'admirer'?" He used the Spanish pronunciation, ad-mee-rer, emphasizing the last syllable.

"Admirer," I said. "It means that someone likes and respects him."

Amado spat into the trash. "What is there to like? He is mean and bad. To everybody. If I didn't herry with a derty pot, he scream at me. He was especial mean to Belize. *Gordo cabrón.*" He spat again.

"How was he mean to Belize?"

Amado stepped on a pink envelope addressed to Chief Bontikoo. "Always she was crying after he talk to her."

"Did she tell you what they talked about?"

"I ask her, but she tell me 'Nada, nada, Amado.' Nothing." He picked up a stuffed teddy bear and tweaked its nose before throwing it into the trash. "*Gordo cabrón.*"

A horn beeped and I turned around to see Trevor pull up on his motorcycle. Will's better idea. Of course—that's what sous chefs are for, to take over for the head chef when she's been jailed.

I usually saw Trevor working in the kitchen, his body covered by a baggy uniform, his hair secured under a hat. That day he was dressed in a wrinkled Metallica t-shirt, colorful tattoos illustrating his biceps and sinewy forearms. He pulled off his helmet, releasing dark blond hair that had grown past his shoulders since the last time I had seen it down. He looked hung over, but the dark circles under his eyes gave him a rakish look.

"Hey Popstar," he said, revving the engine, "want to go for a ride?"

I didn't want Trevor to end up being the murderer, but knew I would have to keep my personal feelings in check, both positive and negative, if I wanted to get to the truth. "Next time I feel like risking my life."

"That a promise?" he asked, revving the engine once more before cutting it.

I said *adios* to Amado, then followed Trevor through the front door and into the dining room. The dirty dishes and linens had been cleared, and several waiters and waitresses busied themselves relocating all the tables and chairs into the second dining room so they could mop the main one.

"Your hair is getting long," I said.

"Chicks dig it." He dropped a white paper bag on the table closest to the door, then sat and pushed out a chair for me with his foot. "Want one? Potato, egg, bacon, and cheese."

"You know I don't eat chicken embryos," I said.

"More for me." He opened the tortilla of one of the tacos, poured a plastic container of hot sauce along the length of it, then pinched the sides together and ate it in three bites. He did the same with another taco.

"What happened to your hand?" I asked, pointing to a small cut.

He rolled his wrist. "Huh. No idea. War wound in the line of duty." He opened another taco. "Have you seen Ursula? How is she?"

While Trevor ate, I told him about speaking to her in jail. I didn't mention that Évariste had been killed with her knife. It was always best to let the other player show his cards first.

"Tell her we're all thinkin' about her," Trevor said as he stuffed the last bite of his fourth taco into his mouth. He wadded up the foil and tossed it at a passing waitress.

"Hey!" she said, playfully hitting his arm on her way to the wait station.

Flirting came so naturally to Trevor and I wondered if he'd had a hard time turning it off when he dated Ursula. She demanded absolute allegiance in the kitchen, and I suspected she demanded the same in a relationship.

Trevor leaned back in his chair and interlaced his fingers behind his head, revealing more ink on his elbows and triceps. Those had to have hurt going on. "Did you see the reservations for tonight?" he asked. "We're booked solid. No one can resist a scandal, huh?"

His attitude fell a long way short of regret. Shouldn't he be more concerned about his boss and sometimes girlfriend than his paycheck? He had always been like that, I realized. Always looking out for himself. If Trevor killed Évariste, he did it for his own selfish reasons, not for anything noble. And what better reason than to take over as executive chef of Markham's? I decided to fish a little.

"Lady Luck is smiling on you," I said.

He balanced on the hind legs of his chair, his feet hooked around the table legs to keep himself steady. "Yeah, but can she get a mess of French cheeses delivered to me at the last minute?" He lost his balance and almost fell backward, but grabbed the edge of the table and recovered quickly. "I can't make everything Évariste had on his menu, but we'll cook our regular menu and use his dishes as specials."

"And when those run out?" I asked.

"I'll make my own."

It sounded like Trevor had already put a lot of thought into this. Had he worked it all out since Will told him Markham's would reopen, or had he been planning this for a while? Regardless, Ursula would be out of jail soon and Markham's would be serving her specials, not Trevor's or Évariste's. "Sounds like a lot of expensive ingredients will go to waste," I said.

In one smooth move, Trevor pushed back his chair and stood up. "Will knows that. He said to do the best I can." He pulled a rubber band from his pants pocket and tied his hair into a long ponytail. "Better get busy before my luck runs out," he said, then headed for the kitchen.

As soon as Trevor left, Belize approached me. "Excuse me," she said, pulling out Trevor's vacated chair. "We need to move the table."

"Are you okay, Belize?"

"Why?"

"It must have been quite a shock finding Évariste like that."

"Oh, that. Yeah, I'm okay,"

"What is everyone saying about last night?"

"I don't know," she said, looking down at her hands resting on the back of the chair. "Some people think it sucks and others think he got what he's been asking for since he got here."

"What do you think?"

"A little of both, I guess. Évi could be a jerk, but he could also be sweet."

"You're the first person I've heard say anything nice about him."

Belize laughed and pushed a strand of black hair behind her ear.

"You also called him Évi."

A wall went up around her. "So."

She snatched up the chair, but I stopped her before she could walk into the other dining room with it. "Was something going on between you and Évariste?"

"Like what?" she asked, staring at me.

"Like a crush of some sort?"

"A crush?" she asked. "Are we twelve?"

"Okay, a flirtation, then. Or an affair. Why did you come back to the restaurant after your shift ended? Were you meeting him?"

"He's married," she said quickly. "Was married. And he was short."

"Mickey Rooney is short and he's been married eight times."

"That guy on *Sixty Minutes*?" she asked, hoisting the chair. "Never mind. I don't really care." She turned to leave.

"Amado said Évariste made you cry."

She stopped. "Amado is just a stupid dishwasher." And then she walked away.

After talking to Trevor and Belize, I had even more questions. Trevor had just become the most important person at Markham's. And although I couldn't picture Belize having an affair with Évariste, I got the feeling they had some sort of connection. I needed to talk to Will. A good general manager knows everything.

I found him in his office. It felt strange knocking on the door to a room I had been raised in, but it no longer looked like the office of my youth. It too had been renovated with cherry wood furniture, soft carpet, and brown leather club chairs.

Will sat on his executive chair like a king on his throne. But that was far from reality. A restaurant manager's life is more like a peasant's. Working every day, even on days the restaurant is closed, making schedules or catching up on paperwork. Late nights reviewing waiters' checkouts. Never enjoying a relaxing evening at home or a night at the movies. Gaining weight from eating dinner most nights at 10:00 PM or later.

Will looked up and motioned for me to come in. "How are you holding up, Poppy?"

"Tired, frustrated, wanting to know who really killed Évariste."

He started to speak, then stopped himself, choosing his words carefully. "You don't think Ursula killed him?"

"I know she didn't! Don't you?"

"Yes," he said. "It's just that the police—"

"The police are wrong," I said, immediately sorry I had interrupted him. If I was going to play detective, I needed to get better at letting people talk.

Will leaned back in his chair. "Of course they're wrong, but it doesn't look good for her."

"From what I saw that night, Évariste made an effort to tick off as many people as he could."

"Évariste did try the patience of much of the staff," Will said. "He eventually had words with everyone from Mitch to Amado. But he and Ursula fought from day one."

"He had words with Mitch?" I asked.

Will waved off my question. "Just Évariste being his usual self-serving self. My point is that he managed to push a button on just about everyone."

"Which of your buttons did he push?"

Will smiled, displaying perfectly straight, perfectly white teeth. "I had to counsel him about food costs, but I've dealt with enough chefs to know that when reasoning with them doesn't work, pulling rank does."

107

"You just described what I do every day during an inspection."

Will picked up a sheet of paper from the top of a neat stack on his desk. "Our food costs are reasonable, even with the bunny order." He tapped the page. "We did very well Wednesday night. In spite of closing earlier than expected."

I reached out for the paper, but Will's eyes stayed focused on the numbers and he didn't see me. I let my hand drop back to my lap. "Was something going on between Evariste and Belize?"

The smirk on his face told me he thought the idea absurd. "Not that I know of."

"So Evariste never made her cry?"

He replaced the paperwork on the stack. "She seems to cry a lot, whether because of Evariste, I couldn't say."

Maybe Amado had lied to me. But why? "Thanks for getting her and everyone else in here to open."

"I've done what I can." He rolled his chair back from the desk. "Several employees were unreachable or they're spooked. A couple have quit. We'll be running a skeleton crew, but I think we can handle it."

"Trevor is pretty sure of himself."

"Isn't he always?" We both laughed, then he said, "We could use your help cleaning up today."

"Oh, Will, I know it was my idea to open, and I know you're doing all the work—which I really appreciate—but I need to be somewhere else."

"Of course," he said, nodding toward the door.

I headed out to do the only thing that brings me true joy in life.

TWELVE

WHILE IT'S MUCH EASIER to inspect a block of restaurants in the same geographical area, it's far less effective. After presenting myself at one restaurant, cooks and managers are burning up the phone lines warning each other that I'm in the area, which significantly reduces the most crucial element of a successful inspection: surprise. If they have time to clean up and be on their best behavior, I won't see how they operate day-to-day. But since I didn't want to be away from Markham's for very long, I decided to make things easy on myself and inspect the string of restaurants along Barton Springs Road.

I had two things that would work in my favor. Showing up in the middle of the Friday lunch rush meant that some of these restaurants would be too busy to stage very much for an inspection, even with advanced warning. And if I hopscotched between the restaurants rather than go from address to address like an evil postman delivering bad news, I might catch one or two off guard.

I parked near the Shady Grove RV Park and found a spot under a canopy of gnarled Live Oak trees. The temperature had reached the upper-nineties by noon when I arrived at the back door of Mostaccioli's Italian Grill. I took a moment to inhale the yeasty fragrance of pizza dough mingled with onions and garlic while I pulled out my badge and switched my phone to vibrate.

I rang the doorbell and looked around the parking lot and dumpster area while I waited for someone to open the door. A cook pushed his arm through the door with his finger already pointed in the direction of the sign on the outside wall that read "No Deliveries Between 11 AM–2 PM."

I held up my badge. "Surprise."

"Oh, sorry ma'am," he said.

I don't like being called ma'am. People call women of a certain age ma'am. And they had been calling me that a lot lately, "Can we do anything else for you ma'am?" "I'd like to ask you a few questions about the murder ma'am." "I'm sorry to tell you this, ma'am, but you need a new transmission." I tried to view it as a sign of respect, but knew it was a sign of age.

"Thirty-eight isn't that old," I said.

"Huh?"

"Who is the M-O-D?"

"The what?"

"The manager on duty." He must be new. I would watch him closely.

"Oh," he said, tapping his chin with a bare index finger. "Vito, I think."

110

"His name is Vidal," I said, stepping through the threshold which forced him to move back to let me in. "And you can tell him I'm here after you wash your hands."

I had every right to begin the inspection without notifying anyone, and a lot of inspectors did that. But if a restaurant was going to fail a surprise inspection, they failed before I even walked in the door. Plus, I liked Vidal, and he had enough stress managing the lunch rush without happening upon the health inspector examining expiration dates in the walk-in.

In a restaurant, which is where most people are concerned about contracting food poisoning—if they're concerned about it at all—patrons are satisfied with making a visual inspection of their waiter and determining whether he's fit to serve their meals. But that's a false reading.

Who they should worry about is the kitchen staff preparing the food. The dishwasher who hasn't had a proper bath for a week, but thinks it's okay because he works with soap and water at work. Or the prep cook who was up all night partying with her Goth friends, but has to clock in at 7:00 AM, so she sweats out all of the tequila she drank while she bags pasta and slices mushrooms. And when she nicks her finger and starts to bleed, she wraps a napkin around it because she doesn't have time to bandage it. The sooner she finishes, the sooner she can take a break before she passes out. And besides, a little blood never hurt anybody. She and her friends drink each other's blood all the time. Or the line cook with the new flaming skull tattoo on his forearm that's finally starting to scab over. It's also starting to flake off into the chipped beef.

"That kind of thing doesn't happen in my restaurant," the owners and managers say. "My people know better." Yeah, and their people also know about food costs, docked pay, and lost jobs.

Basically, I'm the food police, keeping the dining public relatively safe from gross and careless people.

"Poppy!" Vidal said, approaching me with his quick, small steps. "So good to see you."

I know Vidal from the Austin Bar and Restaurant Alliance meetings and socials I used to attend when I worked at Markham's. As the children of restaurant owners, we always had something to commiserate about. Like me, Vidal had worked in the family business through high school and college, but moved to air-conditioned offices after he graduated with a degree in architecture. When his father was diagnosed with cancer, Vidal came back to help out. Ten years later, he's still helping.

He took my extended hand in both of his. "Where is Mister Kawasaki?"

"Vacation."

"I believe I've heard of that," he said. "It's when you take time off work, isn't it?"

"I hear there's something called 'relaxation' involved."

"I'll leave you to your work." He patted my hand before letting it go. "Please find me if you need anything."

I clipped my badge to my waistband, found a clean apron in the linen room, washed my hands with soap and warm water for the regulation twenty seconds, then stretched on a pair of gloves. Over the next thirty minutes, I sidestepped sweaty cooks and harried waiters as I shined a flashlight under ice machines and stoves, and took temperature readings of refrigerators and cold food tables, ovens, and steam tables, working my way full-circle to the walk-in.

While I scanned the shelves for unmarked containers, cooks came in and out, pulling tubs of marinara sauce, bagged calamari rings, stuffed mushrooms, butter, and veal cutlets. As they moved one item out of the way to get to another, they were careful not to put any items on the floor, or place raw meat above anything, even temporarily. They knew the rules, but whether they adhered to them because I was there or because they cared about food safety I would never know for sure.

I felt heavyhearted as I stood in the refrigerated room. The kitchen and the cooks reminded me that Evariste Bontecou had been just another one of them. Not a nice one of them, but an alive one.

Vidal opened the door. "Is everything okay? You've been in here a long time."

"I'm making notes on a couple of minor infractions." We stepped into his office and went over the score sheet. I had seen the busboy sneaking a smoke in the linen room and a cook not wearing a hair restraint. "Ninety-six isn't bad," I said.

"No, not bad," Vidal said lightly, but I caught a flash of anger in his brown eyes. Mostaccioli's would have received a perfect score otherwise. Then he pressed his lips together, a look of concern crossing his thin face. "I'm so sorry to hear about that terrible business at Markham's. And Mitch. How is he?"

"Thank you, Vidal. He's still in the hospital, but should be out today or tomorrow."

"Very good," he said, placing the inspection sheet on his desk. "I hope to see him at a ABRA meeting soon. The Markham's presence is sorely missed."

"Will Denton should be attending the meetings."

We were interrupted by the busboy, the one I had caught smoking. "Oh, sorry," he mumbled then disappeared.

"You're going to fire that kid, aren't you?" I asked.

Vidal sighed and shook his head. "That is my son, and you know as well as I that you cannot fire family."

And Vidal knew as well as I that the life you felt entitled to could be eclipsed by the life you were obligated to. He would be doing that boy a favor to fire him. I remembered Daisy's warning that I could get sucked back into Markham's. It made me even more determined to find Évariste's killer.

My phone vibrated. "Nina?"

"Nope, Jamie."

So, he still had my number. "What's up?"

"Want to meet me at the University of Java?"

"I'm in the middle of inspections."

"I need some info for my piece. Can you take a quick break?"

If I left the area for a little while, I might regain the element of surprise with another restaurant. "If you're buying."

I found Jamie at a two-top on the patio, making notes in a reporter's notepad, oblivious to a foursome of college girls openly ogling him. Regardless of who he is with or how he is dressed, Jamie's smooth pale skin, curly brown hair, brown eyes that looked copper in a certain light, and high cheekbones invite ogling wherever he goes. That day he wore a maroon t-shirt and dark blue cargo shorts that showed off his adorable knees.

He looked up as I approached the table, then grinned as he stood and pulled out a chair for me. Gorgeous and chivalrous. "You're looking much better today, Poppycakes." And sweet.

"Thanks," I said, trembling at the deluge of feelings coming too fast to process. Elation at being with the man I thought I would one day marry gave way to gratitude for taking care of me the day before, which turned into anger and then sadness at what he had done to me, to us. And underpinning all of that lay an attraction so suddenly powerful that I didn't so much sit as collapse into the chair. I wanted to kick him and kiss him. But I stayed put. "What do you want to know?"

He clicked his pen. "Everything."

After making him promise that he wouldn't publish anything without my prior approval, I went over what I remembered. I told the story slowly, answering his questions as they came up, mining my memory banks for the littlest detail. "Are you sure it was a meat cleaver Trevor put against his neck?" Yes. "How many people heard Ursula threaten him?" About ten. "What did the body look like before the medical examiner pronounced him?" Dead.

Jamie looks affable and kind, so people tend to underestimate him. He asks more questions than most strangers do, so anyone who has his attention assumes that he's interested in them as individuals. Which is true, but only to get what he needs from them, whether it's information for a current story or a lead on a new one. One earnest look and a "Please go on" in his serious voice and people answer every question he asks, plus some he doesn't.

"Do you want another espresso?" I asked. He nodded, still writing notes. I picked up his empty cup and walked indoors. In the main dining room, college kids studying for exams crowded the tables, and young couples who probably had thousand-dollar multi-cup espresso makers sitting on imported Italian marble countertops at home sat across from each other tapping on their PDAs. I like quieter places, like the Green Muse, but Jamie is an espresso snob and U of J puts a perfect head of foam on theirs. I placed his cup and saucer in the overflowing bus tub, which sat too close to a plate of fresh brownies.

I stood in line behind two long-haired sweaty dudes holding skateboards who fidgeted behind a Black lesbian couple cooing their Asian baby. The manager, Rex, stepped behind the counter to help. He blanched when he saw me. I get that reaction a lot. In the time it took toast to burn, every restaurant in Austin knew that I had left Markham's to become a health inspector.

"Relax," I said. "I'm here as a customer today. An espresso and a coffee please." He turned to make them. "But you need to empty that bus tub and relocate the brownies. I'd hate to see what the kitchen looks like right now."

He turned back and pushed my order toward me on the counter. "On the house," he said. "For the long wait."

"I didn't wait that long," I said, handing him a ten-dollar bill. Accepting anything but tap water from a restaurant is grounds for dismissal, and his gift of free coffee was insulting. As if six dollars worth of hot brown caffeinated water could make me ignore the fact that he was endangering the public's health.

By the time I returned to the table, Jamie had made more scribbles in his notepad, circling some words, joining others with arrows. The college girls grumbled when I blocked their view of him. He didn't look up until I set his cup down. "What do I owe you?" he asked.

"Help me prove Ursula didn't kill Évariste."

"The police will do that," he said, gazing lovingly at the foam on his espresso before tossing it back in one gulp. "Ambrosia."

"I know, but it might take time. And if the police are happy with Ursula in jail and her knife dripping with Évariste's blood as Exhibit A, they're not going to look too closely at anyone else."

"Aren't we pleased with the idea of Ursula sitting in jail for a while?"

Ursula thinks that because Jamie gives her food glowing five-star reviews, he likes her personally, but she has no idea of his true feelings. He can't stand her, mostly because she made me so miserable for the seven months I worked under her, but also because she's just not that likable.

"Look," I said, "I'm going to put aside my personal feelings for you, and I'd like you to put aside your feelings for Ursula. You know she didn't do it."

"You have personal feelings for me?"

Thousands of them, all safely tucked away in a box on a shelf in a locked room I never go into. "Don't be fatuous, Jamie."

He leaned back in his chair, into a stream of sunlight that lit his curls and brought out deep auburn highlights. The girls behind me gasped. He hadn't shaved and I remembered how his scratchy chin felt on my face.

And then I remembered *her*.

Like just about everyone in the Live Music Capital of the World, Jamie is also a musician. A drummer who plays in a few local bands. He was playing a gig one night. Crown Royal was on special. He was drunk. She was drunk. It just happened.

From the beginning, I suspected that she hadn't been some random girl at the club, that he knew her, which meant that I probably knew her. But he refused to tell me even that much. Not that it mattered, really. He was the one who had betrayed me, not her. Still, I wanted to know what the chances were that this girl could show up again and tempt him. When he stayed mum, I simply eliminated the possibility of him cheating on me again by ending our relationship.

He must have interpreted the look on my face. "Are you ever going to forgive me?" He sounded exasperated rather than contrite.

"Are you ever going to tell me her name?"

He tapped his pen against his notepad. We had arrived at a familiar impasse.

"I'm sure you've been working on a story about Évariste since before he arrived in Austin," I said. "Find out anything that could help us?"

He flipped through his notes without reading them. "I did some digging into his background. He's in Dutch with a lot of people."

I slid my coffee toward him. "Like who?"

"Like investors, the Internal Revenue Service, casinos." He sipped "He owes money to all of them."

"Are you thinking it's a hit?"

"I don't think the IRS would kill him because he owes back taxes. And it's unlikely that an investor or casino would kill him; otherwise, they wouldn't get their money."

"Casinos have been known to break a leg or two," I said defensively.

"You've seen too many movies."

"Ralph Fiennes and Nick Nolte," I said, playing one of our favorite games. One of us names two actors and the other has to name the movie they starred in together.

I had caught him off guard, but he didn't miss a beat. *"The Good Thief.* It would have been a better movie if Nolte didn't sound like he had wasps in his throat."

"What if the investors have an insurance policy on Évariste?" I asked. "It would be like setting fire to a restaurant and collecting the payoff."

"Can you insure a chef?"

"Dang, Jamie, if you're going to shoot down all of my ideas, maybe I should do this on my own."

"I want to help you," he said. "I just don't think casinos or investors got hold of Ursula's knife and stabbed Évariste on his smoke break. If they wanted him dead to collect the insurance money, they'd make it look like an accident. They'd run him off the road in Las Vegas or set his restaurant on fire with him in it."

"I guess you're right," I said. "I just thought it could be significant somehow that he owed a lot of money. People murder for money every day."

"It is something. It'll just take some time to see how it fits in with the picture so far."

I sipped the coffee I had offered him. "What do you know about Évariste's wife, BonBon?"

"She's also his business partner."

119

"So if Évariste owes money to investors, she owes money to investors."

"Correct."

"That might explain her outburst the night he died." During my information dump, I had told him about the excellent smack down BonBon gave Évariste.

"I thought you couldn't understand what they were talking about."

"I couldn't. They did most of their yelling in French. The only word I understood sounded like 'imbecile.'"

"Probably a term of endearment," he said. "The French do things differently."

"I assumed they were arguing about something personal, but maybe it was business."

"I know it happens all the time, but I really don't get how someone who is so successful can get himself in so deep," Jamie said. "A Michelin star and two restaurants packed every night with an average check of at least three hundred per person. Surely he has enough money by now that he doesn't need investors. He could have bought them out."

"Maybe Évariste lost all of his money at the craps table," I said. "It's probably no coincidence that his restaurants are located in the two gambling capitals of the world. You said he has gambling debts, too."

"Nothing significant, though, when you think about it. A couple hundred thousand. Between his restaurants, television appearances, and product endorsements, he probably makes that in a few months."

"I'm still betting it was a crime of passion," I said.

120

"You said you never got an answer from Belize about why she came back to the restaurant after her shift ended. Do you think she was meeting Évariste?"

"Maybe. And she acted strange when she dropped the lemons on him." I took another sip of coffee. "She seems to have more looks than brains, though, and she's not that pretty."

"You don't have to be a criminal mastermind to take advantage of a quiet moment behind a busy restaurant."

"Even BonBon could have done it, then," I said.

"That would fit in with your crime of passion theory. But how did she come to possess Ursula's knife?"

I had already considered that, but then something else came to me. "I've been assuming someone took Ursula's knife from her knife roll, but maybe it was lying around the kitchen somewhere. BonBon could have picked it up when she argued with Évariste."

"If she swiped the knife ahead of time, it was premeditated."

"Unless she hadn't meant to kill him. Either way, that's a wicked thing to do to your own husband."

Jamie leaned forward, put his elbows on the table, and fixed his dark eyes on me. I missed him so much.

"Okay," he said finally. "Before I say this, I want you to know that it has nothing to do with how I feel about Ursula."

I nodded.

"It's entirely possible that the police have the right person in custody."

I had seen that coming.

"And there's a chance that what we find out, if we find out anything, could help them prove their case against her."

That, I hadn't seen coming.

121

"This is Ursula York we're talking about. She skewers beef, not celebrity chefs."

Jamie drained the last of the coffee and shot me a serious look.

"I want the truth," I said. "If she killed him, then I'll have to accept that."

"Okay," Jamie said. "Who's minding the store while Mitch is in the hospital and you're going for your detective's shield?"

"The new GM, Will Denton. I'm surprised you don't know about that. Your grapevine is usually well-tended."

"That's right," he said, nodding. "I heard something about that, but Markham's hasn't been on my radar lately. Is there a good reason why Mitch hired a GM?"

"You mean is there a good story? Not really. He wants to spend more time with Nina, traveling, country clubbing, and playing golf, so he hired Will to run things about a month ago."

"Golf?"

"He bogeyed the eighth hole at Silver Niche last week."

"It's about time he took some time off." Jamie flipped the cover on his notepad. "Is there anything you haven't told me about that night?"

"Nope," I lied. I hadn't told anyone I found Évariste before Belize did.

THIRTEEN

JAMIE WALKED ME TO my car. A few months ago, he would have kissed me goodbye, but we stood there awkwardly, on the verge, until I held out my hand. He took it, then pulled me close to him. He felt so solid, smelled so comfortable.

"I miss you," he whispered.

I thought I was finished shedding tears over Jamie, but they had just gone dormant for a while. They were back now, stinging my eyes, reminding me of my broken heart. "I've got to go," I said, pulling away from him and climbing into my Jeep. With one stupid, selfish act, Jamie had dumped more pain into my life than I ever thought I could handle. I didn't know if I could forgive him, much less give him another chance.

Nina called as I pulled out of the U of J parking lot. "Your father is in surgery," she said, her voice scratchy.

"For what?"

"I'll tell you when you get here."

"I'll be there in ten minutes."

I stepped off the elevator and saw Nina on the couch where I had left her the day before.

"Is it his head?" I asked.

She closed her eyes, willing the tears to stay back. I sat next to her and took her hand. It felt cold, the skin as thin as tissue silk. She took a deep breath. "He had a mild heart attack the other night. That's probably why he fell."

"He's having heart surgery?"

"They're putting a stent in an artery." She wrapped a cold, bony arm around my shoulders. "He's going to be okay. He has to be."

I closed my eyes and slowed down my breath, and understood for the first time in my life, that my father wouldn't be around forever. Hot tears dripped onto my lap. How could that be? Mitch was Superman. There wasn't enough kryptonite in our galaxy to take him out.

I let Nina soothe me, which seemed to soothe her, and we sat huddled together for a little while, probably looking like mother and daughter to the people getting off the elevator.

"This waiting is killing me," Nina said. She stood up and adjusted her cardigan. She wore yellow capri pants and a white cotton twin set that showed off her tan. Her clothes looked fresh, but deep lines etched her face. "Can I get you some coffee?" she asked. "The stuff in the machine is undrinkable, but I could go to the lounge."

Tragedy seemed to bring out the best in Nina. "I'm okay right now."

"Have you heard from Ursula?" she asked.

"Not since yesterday. I've been thinking about the murder, though, and have some ideas about who might have done it."

"Really?" she said, sitting down again. "How soon will Ursula be out of jail?"

124

Maybe Nina had a real hearing problem. She could get checked out while she was here at the hospital. "I said I had ideas. I don't have any proof. But Jamie's helping me."

"Jamie!" she said, clapping her hands. "Are you two getting back together?" Nina likes Jamie, but not because he's a good guy. She likes the reviews he gives Ursula and Markham's, and especially that he mentions her name as Mitch's wife.

"No, we're not getting back together. He has access to information I need, and he believes me that Ursula didn't do it."

"Well, of course Ursula didn't do it." She busied herself settling back onto the couch, slipping off her kitten heels and tucking her pedicured feet under her. I made a mental note to pumice my heels.

After she arranged a *Vogue* magazine on her lap, I asked, "Who do you think killed him?"

"How should I know?" she said, her peevish tone returning. "He was a horrid, classless little man. He had no business in Ursula's kitchen in the first place. Your father knew how Ursula felt about him, but he did nothing. He deserved what he got."

Did she mean that Évariste deserved to be killed or that Mitch deserved to have a heart attack? "I'm surprised to hear you say that."

"Well," she said, already backing away from her strong statement, "I'm not glad he's *dead*. I'm glad he's out of Ursula's hair. She doesn't need anyone's help. She can handle Markham's just fine on her own."

"Why would you think Évariste was there to help Ursula?"

"Because he *was*."

We were in dirt-clod territory again. "Nina, Évariste was there to help boost sales."

"Then why was your father talking to him about a partnership?"

"Partnership? Like an investment?"

"Ira Gross is in Monte Carlo doing due diligence on Évariste right now. Ari went with him and they took their wives. That's why they couldn't make opening night."

Ari and Ira Gross, of Grimm, Grimes, and Gross, LLC. "So that's why Ari isn't here to represent Ursula."

"They're coming back as soon as they can get a flight."

"Does Ursula know about this partnership?" I asked.

Nina ran a manicured finger along the razor-sharp crease in her pant leg. I took it as confirmation that she did know. Great, another reason for her to kill Évariste.

"Who else knows?" I asked.

She counted on her long fingers. "Me, Ari and Ira, Trevor—"

"Trevor knows!"

"Ursula told him," she said. "Your father didn't want anyone to know who didn't have to. You know how rumors fly about." She waved her hand in the air to illustrate rumors in flight. "But Ursula said that Trevor was becoming hostile toward Évariste, and she had concerns that if Trevor continued, he would be putting his future at Markham's at risk if the deal went through."

Trevor's future was already at risk. So was Ursula's. If Évariste invested in Markham's, everything she worked for would be gone in the time it took her to say "Oui, Chef." Évariste would become executive chef, which would demote Ursula to sous—if Évariste would even allow it—which would put Trevor under her, near the bottom.

I stood and paced in front of the couch trying to get a handle on what this meant. Not much money would be involved, but certainly prestige, and I had never known Trevor to be satisfied with what he had. I even suspected that he had started romancing Ursula so she would promote him to sous chef over me. And now, not only had Évariste been taken out of the game, a conviction for Ursula would take Trevor off the bench and move him to first string. Trevor was good, but too young and inexperienced to run a kitchen. It's a high-level management job that requires many more skills than just braising beef tips and mashing potatoes.

Yet in spite of all that, Markham's was opening that night with Trevor as quarterback.

Jamie had told me that I may not be happy with the way things turned out if we investigated the murder, and he was right. While the impending partnership would have immediate effects on Trevor's career, Ursula and her attitude toward Évariste would be as welcome in Markham's kitchen as a cannibal at a daycare. Mitch had appointed Ursula to executive chef because he was married to her mother, but she kept the job because she knew what she was doing. And then some culinary school canid had sneaked into her kitchen, threatening everything she had worked for. Had Ursula taken matters into her own hands?

I sat on the low table across from Nina. "Why didn't Mitch tell me about the partnership?"

"You know too many food people," she said. "He couldn't take the chance of this leaking out."

I stared at her. My own father didn't trust me?

A man in blue scrubs and a sweat-soaked surgeon's cap walked into the waiting room, followed by another man carrying a clipboard. "Ms. Markham?" the surgeon said.

"Yes," Nina and I said at the same time.

"Wife, daughter," Nina said, giggling like a geisha, pointing first to herself then to me. "How is he?" She cast an expert glance at his left hand, ever alert to any man of means she could set up with Ursula. He wore a shiny gold band, but I amused myself thinking about how Nina would have handled his request to meet this wonderful daughter of hers. *Well, you can't meet her just yet. She's indisposed at the moment.*

Nina held onto my arm as he told us details of the stent operation and that Mitch came through it all quite well. We could see him in a few hours, and barring any unforeseen circumstances, he would be able to go home in a day or two. "Just keep him away from stressful situations," he said.

Had he seen a newscast recently?

"There's no reason for both of us to stay here," Nina said. She put a hand on my back and guided me toward the elevator, pressing the down arrow. "You go on. I'll call as soon as your father wakes up."

That wasn't the first time I had been hustled toward an exit. Managers and cooks did it all the time when it looked like I had finished my inspection and hadn't seen whatever it was they were hiding. Nina hadn't stored rat poison on top of canned tomatoes or come to work with a cold. I stepped into the elevator wondering what my stepmother could be hiding?

I didn't feel like doing any more inspections, which left me free to speak with the only person who could give me real answers about the partnership between Mitch and Évariste.

FOURTEEN

Évariste had been staying at the one of the oldest and most expensive hotels in Austin, the Driskill on 6th Street, and I hoped BonBon hadn't checked out. I knew that the front desk wouldn't tell me her room number, so I went around the back of the hotel to the service entrance, flashed my badge at the guard, then turned into the room service hallway. The café's assistant manager fluttered his hand over his heart when he saw me.

"Relax Luis," I said. "I'm not here for an inspection. But from your reaction, maybe I should be."

"Not at all," he said. "We're above ninety-five for sure."

Everyone is always above ninety-five before an inspection. And I always hope they are when I walk in the door, but then I'll see a cook observe the three-second rule. This rule isn't written down anywhere, but it is universally accepted that any food that falls from a grill, stove, plate, countertop, or tray can be picked up off the floor with tongs, fork, or fingers and served to customers if the time spent on the floor is no longer than three seconds. Timekeeping, of course, is left to the person who dropped the food, and can vary depending on how many people witnessed the drop and the dropper's rank in the kitchen. I had never seen that happen at the Driskill.

"I'm here for a favor," I said.

"If I can."

"I need the room number for a guest."

He knitted his bushy brows.

"I wouldn't ask if it weren't important," I said.

He walked to the computer and placed his fingers on the keyboard. "What is the name?"

"BonBon Bontecou," I said. Her name sounded ridiculous when I said it out loud and I expected Luis to laugh.

He dropped his hands. "Four eighteen."

"I'm impressed, Luis. You know it off the top of your head."

"Everyone knows her room number."

"Because she's such a good tipper?" I ventured, but I already knew the answer. Waiters keep big tippers to themselves, but could spend months telling and retelling the story of being unfairly stiffed.

"Yech!" he said. "What a nasty woman!" Two passing waiters looked at him and he lowered his voice. "So demanding, so rude."

To his employees, Luis would downplay any guest's behavior, but I could tell he was dying to unload about BonBon to someone, so I pulled the trigger. "She can't be that bad."

"The Helmsley Palace had an easy time with the Queen of Mean," he said. "Calling room service at all hours, insisting we bring her items not on our menu. Asking for champagne we don't stock. Calling down every five minutes after she orders to ask what's taking so long. She's like a spoiled child making prank phone calls while the babysitter is off kissing her boyfriend."

The phone rang and he sighed extravagantly before answering it. "Yes Mrs. Bontecou? It is on the way."

"You're sending something up to her room?" I asked, giddy at my luck.

"A duck breast sandwich we had to get from the Intercontinental," he said, lifting his chin toward a tray with a silver dome on it.

"Don't y'all have duck on your menu?"

He pinched the bridge of his nose. "She said she wouldn't feed ours to her cat."

"Can I take it up to her?" I expected him to demur, to say hotel policy forbade it, to ask why I wanted to deliver food to the shrew.

"Be my guest," he said.

Fetching and delivering a sandwich from outside would be a bellman's job because technically, room service is not supposed to serve food that they didn't make in their own kitchen. By letting me deliver it, he relieved one member of the hotel staff from having to deal with her and made me very happy.

Luis placed the plate on a silver cart covered with a white tablecloth. "*Vaya con Dios*," he said, making the sign of the cross in front of his thick torso. "Go with God."

Luis must be exaggerating, I thought, as I wheeled the cart into the service elevator. I rode up to the fourth floor, then followed the hallway signs to 418. The Driskill is one of many haunted places in Austin, and probably the most famous. The story goes that a woman who had been jilted by her fiancé checked into a room on the fourth floor. She went shopping all day with his credit cards, then came back to her room, sat in the bathtub, and shot herself in the stomach. Every so often, someone swears they see a ghostly figure, laden with shopping bags, entering the room where it happened.

I knocked on BonBon's door. "Room service."

The door cracked open, then nothing happened. I waited for it to open wider, but still nothing. Was this the haunted room? I turned the cart around and started to back in, but the door wouldn't open wide enough to allow the cart inside. I turned to see what blocked it.

It looked like thieves had tossed her room. Shopping bags and magazines, dry cleaning plastic and lingerie, clothes and high heels littered the dresser and king-sized bed. On the desk lay un-opened packages of stockings, a jewelry box, a laptop computer, two Prada shoe boxes, and a melted bucket of ice with the butt end of a champagne bottle sticking up. Apparently, gambling wasn't the only reason Évariste teetered in the red. Wedged behind the door lay a jumbled pile of Évariste's dirty white chef's coats em-broidered with his name and *Chef du Cuisine*. They were large and billowy enough to be used as hot air balloons, which in a way they had been.

Ursula does not permit colorful uniforms in her kitchen. Her reasoning is that everyone cooks as a team and she insists that ev-eryone wear the same traditional uniform of white coats and black-and-white checked pants. Évariste had plenty of white coats and could easily have met the dress code, so had he special-ordered a red one just to provoke Ursula the night of the party? If Évariste was that shrewd, those two weeks he spent in her kitchen must have been more hellish than I imagined.

I saw the back of BonBon's head in the bathroom. She sat at the vanity applying color to her thin lips, a lit cigarette within easy reach on the side of the sink. I always sneeze at my first whiff of cigarette smoke in an enclosed space. She looked up at the tiny sound that escaped.

I saw no place to leave the domed plate, so I slid a pile of clothes away from the corner of the bed to make room. "Your duck sandwich, Mrs. Bontecou."

"Bring me my purse," she said as she blotted her scarlet lips on a tissue.

No wonder everyone from room service despised her. It was one thing to be cheap and nice, but cheap and dismissive was unforgivable. The entire hotel staff was probably counting down the days to her departure. Maybe one of them killed Évariste just to get them out of the hotel.

I located her purse on the dresser under a lavender silk scarf. It was unzipped, so I made a show of continuing to look for it while I inspected the contents. I wasn't looking for anything in particular, but it wouldn't hurt to see what the wife of a famous chef, now famously dead, carried around with her. Wallet, makeup bag, plane tickets, two bottles of prescription meds with labels written in French, a half-full bottle of aspirin. Nothing to alert the authorities about.

I picked my way back to the bathroom and checked for water splashes on the vanity before I placed her purse next to her. She put her hand inside and came out with a tube of lip gloss and applied it carefully over the lipstick, stroking first the right side of her upper lip, then the left.

I stood by the bathroom door. "BonBon?"

She looked at my reflection in the mirror, registered my street clothes, and sneered. "Where is your uniform?"

"I don't work for the Driskill. I work for the restaurant where Évariste was killed." I expected some reaction to the mention of her husband's death, a downcast of the eyes or a sad sigh, but she continued to stare. "My name is Poppy Markham. My father is Mitch Markham."

"What do you want?"

"You speak English very well," I said, trying to soften her with a compliment.

"What do you expect? I learned English as a child in school. And I live half my life in Las Vegas."

I remembered the cards and letters from Évariste's impromptu memorial that Amado had thrown into the trash. No doubt the widow Bontecou was capable of reading them, but she wouldn't.

"Can I ask you some questions about the night Évariste died?"

She shrugged in that noncommittal, infuriating way Évariste had. French shorthand for, "You can ask, but I probably won't answer."

I started with what Jamie had told me. "Is it true that Évariste owed money to investors?" She shrugged again and I kept going. "Were they the investors in Monte Carlo or Las Vegas?"

She pulled the wand away from her lips and said, "They are the same people."

"Are they the kind of people who kill people who owe money but don't pay?"

She took a deep drag on her cigarette, then blew the smoke out one side of her mouth. "Why are you asking me these questions? Your sister killed him."

"She's my stepsister, and I don't think she did it."

"Her knife was poking from his heart," she said matter-of-factly. "If it was not her, it was the girl, Belliss."

"Belliss?"

"The waitress. With the ugly hair."

"Belize."

"Yes, that one. My husband was having an affair with her."

So I was right! Euw. "You knew?"

"Pft," she said, waving her hand. "He always has someone." She still spoke about him in the present tense. "What is an affair? It is nothing."

"How do you know he was involved with her?"

"A wife knows," she said. "When I came to the restaurant, I saw her. I have seen that surprised look many times before. He never tells them about me. Anyone who reads the magazines knows he is married, but he always takes up with the ones who cannot read."

"Is that what you argued about in the kitchen?"

She shrugged again then picked up her cigarette.

"Why were you in debt?" I asked. "The restaurants are doing well from what I see."

"What do you expect? Évariste Bontecou is the best chef in the world. He has a Michelin star. But why we owed money is not any of your business."

"Would your investors kill Évariste?"

"For what purpose?" She stood up and I exited the bathroom ahead of her. She walked to the tray on the bed and lifted the silver

135

dome. "*Merde!*" she cried and threw the dome across the room. It clanged against the wall, then thudded on the carpeted floor. She snatched up the phone and pushed a button. "Where are my bloody fries!" she screamed. She listened for a moment, then slammed down the phone. "Idiots! I hate this one-horse town!"

She fixed me with an icy stare. "Why are you still here? Are you waiting for a tip?"

Weren't we just having a conversation about Évariste's death? "Sorry to disturb you, ma'am," I said, and backed out of the room as she picked up the phone again.

I left the delivery cart in the hallway and took the guest elevator instead of the service elevator to ground level. I would have to walk around the hotel to get to my car, but I didn't want Luis to ask me to deliver her bloody fries.

On the walk around the block, I had time to process this revelation that Belize and Évariste had been engaged in an affair. Or at least BonBon thought so. She said it was nothing, but no woman is entirely okay with her man knocking boots with another woman, unless she despises her husband or she herself is having an affair. Was BonBon involved with someone? The investor perhaps? Maybe the investor wasn't the type of man to kill someone who owed him money, but he was the type of man to kill the husband of the woman he loved.

I was making this too complicated. The killer used Ursula's knife, so he or she had to be someone close to home. I wouldn't take BonBon off the list of suspects, especially after that Madame Hyde tantrum. She had a short fuse and obviously liked to use it to incinerate other people.

I had a good parking spot on 7th Street, so I left my car where it was, walked up Congress toward the capitol building, and hung a left on 11th Street.

Time to see Ursula.

FIFTEEN

On my first visit to police headquarters, the cop had told me that Friday visiting hours started at 6:00 PM, but he didn't tell me that I would have to sign in and wait until actual visitation began at 7:00 PM. He also didn't tell me I should get there early. By the time I arrived at the jail, the waiting room already overflowed with the worried parents, crying babies, and disappointed friends of loved ones whose last name began with T through Z.

They say that every choice you have ever made in your life brings you to the exact moment you are currently living. If that is true in general, then it would have to be true about Ursula. Although I couldn't imagine what choices she had made that led up to being arrested for murder. Arguing with Évariste? Becoming the chef at Markham's? Taking her first job in a restaurant?

I was finally led into a private room and Ursula came through a door on the other side. She smiled at me through the Plexiglas and we both picked up a receiver at the same time. "I'm so glad to see you, Poppy."

"I'm glad to see you, too. I think I'm making progress."

"First tell me how Mitch is doing."

I told her about speaking with the surgeon, then said, "Nina told me about the partnership."

"Oh, my mother cannot keep a secret!"

"Why did y'all keep this from me?"

Ursula shook her head. "You know too many people in the industry and Mitch didn't want it to leak out." Same reason Nina had given me.

"I can keep a secret! First," I said, counting on my fingers, "I never told anyone about your mammary enhancement, did I?"

She scowled at me.

"Second," I went on, "why would a restaurant partnership need to be a secret? It happens all the time."

"Mitch told me he didn't want anyone to think Markham's was in trouble."

"Is it?"

"Not that I can tell," she sad. "We've been busier than ever, and not just because of the fat fox. But Mitch and Mom spent a lot of money on the renovations."

"Ursula, this partnership would have made Évariste your boss, which gives you a major motive for killing him." I couldn't keep the stress out of my voice. "Another one."

"I didn't do it! I didn't do it! I didn't do it!" she screamed, punctuating each statement with her open hand on the counter. The door on Ursula's side opened. A large black female guard with close-cropped hair revealing a shiny scalp looked in. Ursula held up the offending hand. "Sorry."

139

"No more of that, young lady," the guard said. She spoke as if she'd had the authority of a gun behind her voice her entire life. "No ma'am. No more." Ursula nodded meekly at the guard, then turned back to me. The door closed with a soft click.

"Great," Ursula said, "that probably got me half rations of bologna sandwiches." She looked into my eyes. "Poppy, I swear. I did not kill Évariste. I know it looks like I did, and I know I had a lot of reasons for doing it, but I didn't do it."

As my resentment withered, I took in Ursula's black-and-white jumpsuit, her defeated slouch, her limp hair, the circles forming under her eyes. I felt bad about coming at her so strongly. It was her future dangling by a filament, not mine. She had her own feelings of betrayal and desperation to deal with. I tried to sound soothing. "I believe you. It's just that if someone doesn't come up with another suspect soon, the police are going to be more determined to pin this on you."

"Where's Ari Gross? You're the first person I've seen since I've been in here." She plucked at the front of her jumpsuit. "Besides a bunch of jerk detectives who keep saying that things will go easier on me if I just confess."

"Ari and Ira have been in Monte Carlo. They're already on their way home."

"How nice," she scoffed. "My lawyers are gallivanting around Europe while my career is going down the toilet."

"No one is flushing just yet," I said. "In fact, the phone hasn't stopped ringing for reservations."

"Are you serious?" she asked, her smile returning briefly.

"Looks like everyone wants to eat food prepared by an accused murderess."

140

"Do you think I should get a press agent?"

I couldn't tell if she was joking, but I laughed. "Let's wait until you're not referred to as an inmate, okay?"

"Oh, no," she said, blubbering suddenly. "I'm going to spend the rest of my life in prison for killing Évariste Bontecou-hoo-hoo."

"No you're not," I said, putting the palm of my hand against the Plexiglas. "We're going to figure this out. Or at least divert suspicion from you onto someone else to give the police reasonable doubt."

Ursula leaned forward, her blue and red eyes hopeful. "Who?"

"Trevor had a good reason for killing him."

"Trevor?"

"Nina said you told him about the partnership to protect his job. He had a lot to lose if Évariste took over."

"Trevor is such a hot—" Ursula tried to slump back in her chair, but the short connector cord snapped the receiver away from her mouth. She sat back up. "—a hothead. And he ran hot and cold with Évariste. Sometimes he'd be kneeling at that greasy gourmet's feet, asking questions and making suggestions, in complete awe of his greatness." She made a face like she had slammed a dram of vinegar. "Then something would happen. Évariste would do something that rubbed Trevor the wrong way and Trevor would sulk and throw things around."

"What did Évariste do to him?"

"Trevor would never say. I thought maybe he insulted Trevor's cooking. Or he found out something about Trevor and teased him about it. You saw how mean Évariste could be." She glanced around the tiny room as if weighing her situation then against her situation now. "Anyway, I told Trevor about the partnership to

141

calm him down and make him play nice. It mostly worked. Until the night of the party."

"Do you know why Trevor attacked him that night?"

"I asked Trevor about it later, but he wouldn't tell me. He said it was a guy thing."

"That could mean anything from one owed the other money over a pool game to they had the hots for each other."

"That's more creative than what I came up with. I assumed it had something to do with a woman." .

I sat up straighter. "Who?"

Ursula hesitated. "Belize Medina."

First BonBon and now Ursula had dropped Belize's name in connection with Évariste. Ursula didn't have anything more than a suspicion about Belize, but at least it gave me an angle to work. I promised her I would visit again the next morning, and left her with genuine hope that she would be out soon.

As I walked through the streets of downtown Austin, it struck me that I was the only person in my family who could do that. With Mitch confined to a hospital bed, Nina tied to the waiting room, and Ursula stuck in jail, I felt a little guilty about my freedom. I needed to do whatever I could to return the status quo.

At home I took a quick rinse-off shower, then dressed in black capri pants, an aqua t-shirt, and black sandals. I had just shut my front door when Jamie called my cell phone. "How's your dad?" he asked.

I updated him quickly on Mitch's surgery, Nina's disclosure, Ursula's confirmation, and my new suspicions about Belize. "She's working tonight, so I'm going to try to talk to her."

At 8:00 on a Friday night, everyone at Markham's would be too busy to keep iced tea glasses filled much less answer questions about their involvement with a murder victim. But even if my investigation didn't progress, I could slip into the role of the good daughter who kept promises to her sick father.

"Care for some company?" he asked casually.

"Not really. I've gotten rather used to doing things on my own the past few months."

"You've always been independent," he said, ignoring my snark.

"We'll stay for dinner. I can review Trevor's debut."

"Oh, Jamie, you're terrible!" Formally reviewing Trevor on his first night under those circumstances was just plain mean.

"You're right." He chuckled and I knew that the left side of his mouth had turned up. "Okay, not a real review, a sort of pre-flight check. We'll make—"

I couldn't hear Jamie over the high-pitched whine that started in the next yard over. "Hang on," I said. "The Johns just started drilling." I went back inside my house. "What did you say?"

"I'll meet you there in fifteen," he said, then hung up before I could respond.

I brushed out my hair and ran a flat iron over it to smooth out the ponytail kink, then applied mascara and a bit of pink lip color. Then I changed into a black skirt.

The marquis at Markham's read, "Open — Call for Reservations," which everyone in Austin had done. The valet service Mitch had hired for the duration of Évariste's visit had a line ten cars long. I was glad Will had had the foresight not to cancel them, even if they were expensive. I didn't want to wait, so I pulled around to the employee parking lot.

143

I opened the back door to a rumble of chopping, banging, stirring, and sizzling. Amado moved like a cheetah from sink to line, carrying double stacks of steaming plates. Trevor ripped a blizzard of chits off the printer and yelled, "Orderin'! Two nachos, five salmons, three primaveras, eight filets, two well, four medium, two rare, makin' twenty-two all day."

Restaurants have a reputation for hiring from the dregs of society. Over the years, Markham's has employed people just out of prison, kicking a drug habit, in the early stages of Alzheimer's, and two steps away from homelessness. But the great thing about working in a restaurant, whether in the front or the back of the house, is that it doesn't matter who you are or where you come from. What matters is that you can get the food out and keep tables turning. Even if Trevor was a murderer, he could do the job.

"Where's that cheese?" Trevor called. He looked at Shannon who thwacked the butt end off a head of romaine lettuce with a knife.

"Coming," Shannon said. He dropped the lettuce and hurried to the walk-in.

Trevor saw me and took in my outfit. "Me like," he said. "Stayin' for dinner?"

"Absolutely. I wouldn't miss your debut." I left out the part about dining with a food critic.

I followed Shannon through the kitchen, stepping over the rubber mats on my tiptoes, side-stepping splatters of sauce and grease, and a mound of carrot greens that had fallen to the floor. I didn't look as elegant as BonBon had when she chased Évariste into the kitchen, but it didn't matter. Unless I could be grilled, garnished, and arranged beautifully on a plate, no one had time to pay attention to me.

Shannon stood in the middle of the walk-in with his hands on his hips, scanning the shelves.

"It's right in front of you," I said.

He turned quickly, surprise making him look like a teenager. He wasn't much older than one. "What?"

"The parm," I said, pointing to a middle shelf. "Right there."

He blinked. "Man, I'm so off tonight."

"Has it been like this all night?"

"Since the doors opened."

"You guys seem to be keeping up okay."

He grabbed the wheel of parmesan cheese and held it under his arm like a football. "Trevor's just barely keeping it together."

I didn't know how much time I would have with Shannon, so I ignored that comment and asked him what I had followed him in there to find out. "You remember when Évariste ran into Belize and all the guys pointed at you and said 'you called it.'"

"Yeah," he said warily, looking past me to the door.

"What was that all about?"

"It's dumb, really." He drummed his heel on the concrete floor. "A couple of days after Évariste got here, the kitchen started betting on how long it would take him to call someone an idiot. We called it the Idiot Pot. That night, most of the guys thought it would be some time during service, but I bet it would be before service even started. I didn't think I'd win, but he said it when he ran into Belize."

"How much did you win?"

145

His face brightened. "Fifty. We had another Slacker Pot going for when he would skate out without helping to clean up, but then..." His voice trailed off and he looked at the floor.

"Évariste seemed to like that word, 'idiot.'"

"Yeah, it was one of his favorites. He also liked 'stupid American' and 'ignoramus.' Someone taught him 'chowderhead,' and he called me that for an entire day." Shannon clenched his teeth. Anger made his face look more mature.

I waited, letting him work through his thoughts, hoping he would feel chatty. He didn't disappoint me.

"Man, all of us were so sick of him by opening night. It's like degrading us was his idea of fun. If you hadn't gone through cooking school, you may as well be a porter in his eyes. Intuition didn't count unless you had a degree to back it up." He shifted the parmesan to his other arm and stopped tapping his heel. "After a while, everyone quit talking to him and just did what he said. But even when we followed orders, no one could do anything right." He snorted. "Except Trevor."

We had been in the walk-in for a few minutes and the cold seeped through my thin clothing. My words came out stammered. "Why was T-trevor special?"

"Look, I need to get back out there," Shannon said, turning toward the door.

I stepped in front of him, which wasn't such a great idea. He would have no problem getting past me if he had a mind to. I put my hand on his arm. "P-please, Sh-shannon, this is important. T-tell me how T-trevor was special." I sounded pitiful.

146

He switched the wheel of cheese in his arms again. "He just was. Évariste got on him too, and at first Trevor hated him as much as the rest of us, but then one day, everything was different."

"D-different how?"

"Évariste wasn't as harsh with Trevor. He seemed to . . . I wouldn't say *like* Trevor more. It was more like respect, like Trevor had finally passed some sort of test. Which is ironic because Trevor didn't even graduate from high school."

"If they were so ch-chummy, why did T-trevor threaten Évariste with a m-meat cleaver?"

"No idea. But I can tell you that it happened right after Évariste said something to Belize."

The walk-in door flew open with such force, the backdraft parted the plastic strips of the octopus. Trevor yelled, "Where is that cheese!" He stopped when he saw us, confusion turning to suspicion as he looked from Shannon to me. Then he smiled. "Aw, Popstar," he said, "here I thought I was your favorite cook."

———

Jamie hadn't arrived yet, so I decided to wait in Will's office, maybe peruse any financial statements left lying around or look for a file labeled "Secret Deals I'm Keeping from Poppy."

He had locked his door, but I had a master key. I hesitated to use it though. I wouldn't appreciate someone letting themselves into my office, but if I milled about the restaurant, I would either get in everyone's way or be put to work. I inserted the key and turned the door handle. Nothing.

Daisy says that the amount of fun a person has is inversely proportional to the number of keys on their keychain, so the more

SIXTEEN

I JUMPED AT THE sound of Jamie's voice, my heart taking off at a gallop before I realized that I wasn't in any danger. At least not in danger of being caught snooping. Jamie was dangerous in other ways.

I turned around too quickly. "Nothing," I said, also too quickly.

He crossed his arms and raised one dark eyebrow, amusement in his eyes.

"I, uh, was just admiring this boating scene on Will's door."

"Really," he said.

"What took you so long?" I asked, changing the subject to wipe that knowing look off his face.

"Valet guys are slammed." The look stayed put.

We sat ourselves at a two-top near the bathrooms, a table that Markham's never seats no matter how busy we are. A constant stream of people flow past the table, the audible flush of toilets is loud and unromantic, and the occasional foul odor wafts out when the bathroom door opens. No waiter is ever assigned to the table, so I stopped the first black apron I saw whizzing by, which, to my delight, happened to be Belize.

"This isn't my section," she said.

I had already excused her for dismissing me the morning after the murder, but she didn't get to do it twice. I needed information. And I was the owner's daughter. "It is now," I said. "Please bring over some menus."

She looked like a hungry cat that had been fed an organic kiwi, and stopped short of hissing at me. When she stalked off, Jamie said, "Ease up, babe. We're here to get information from her."

"We'll get it. And I'm not your babe."

"I didn't mean *my* babe, I meant *a* babe."

"I know what you meant."

Belize brought glasses of ice water and menus to the table, and as she recited the dinner specials, I examined this waitress who seemed to have everyone tied in knots. I saw nothing special about her looks—straight black hair in need of a trim, wary brown eyes, heavy makeup. Her voice had a flintiness that made her sound older and harsher than her years. She told us that Chef Trevor offered Ginger Salmon en Papillote with cumin carrot coins, Tournedos Bontecou with white truffle sauce and steamed asparagus, and one other dish I didn't need to listen to. I knew exactly what I would get with the Saddle of Roasted Hare á la Évariste.

Jamie ordered his favorite crabmeat nachos, half without crab for me, and a bottle of pinot noir. The look of disgust on Belize's face told me her thought process: *I'm in the weeds so bad I can't even think straight, you're forcing me wait on you, and now you're ordering a bottle of wine? I better get a really good tip.* Her attitude already had her tip on a downslide.

When Belize left, I leaned across the table and Jamie automatically leaned into me, our faces inches apart. He smelled like cinnamon. "Pretty sure the salmon is Trevor's," I said.

"Because it doesn't have one of Évariste's names attached to it?"

"I'd make a pretty good detective, huh?"

I sat back and watched Will, poised as a prince, standing at a four-top near the bar. He held menus in one hand while pulling out chairs for three well-dressed men with the other. He whispered something to Belize as she passed by, then picked up dirty cups from the next table and took them to the wait station. On busy nights, the general manager's job could morph from host to expeditor to busboy to waiter within five minutes. I didn't miss that job, and I didn't want it back, in spite of the cushy office.

I turned back to Jamie, who had been watching me watch Will. "Do you still attend ABRA meetings?" I asked.

"I never miss them. That's where I hear all the good gossip."

"What's the dirt on Will?"

Another waiter delivered our appetizer. Jamie placed his napkin in his lap. "Nothing. This is the first time I've seen him."

A large man with a black moustache hummed softly as he passed us on his return from the bathroom. Jamie wrinkled his nose. "This is the worst table. Why didn't they get rid of it during the renovation?"

"Beats me. But if they had, you'd have to stop boasting on your website that you have a permanent table at Markham's."

We sipped our water as I looked around the dining room again, feeling a twinge of sadness. Even with all matching place settings arranged on pearl-white tablecloths, the rich leather chairs against a background of heavy blue drapes, and professional lighting recommended by expensive consultants, nothing could make up for Mitch's absence. Was I the only one who noticed that no Markhams were running Markham's?

"Does it feel strange knowing that Ursula isn't in the kitchen?" I asked.

"Not really," he said serving each of us a nacho.

After two years of nearly constant companionship, Jamie and I had lost our facility for small talk with each other, but I wasn't ready for the Big Talk. Not yet. "How come you never complain that I like to drink red wine with everything?" I asked. "Nina says I'm uncouth."

"Nina doesn't love you."

You still love me? He wanted me to say that. But he didn't get to just sprinkle a little Jamie Sherwood charm here and there and make my heart thump with longing. I put him on notice. "True, but at least she backs up her sentiment with appropriate actions,"

He shot me a hard look, which turned into a charming smile when Belize showed up with the wine. She remained stone-faced as she presented the label to Jamie, who nodded a confirmation.

As she removed her wine key and prepared to open the bottle, I said, "I need to ask you some questions about the other night." She looked up at me, but didn't say anything. I looked at Jamie who had taken an interest in the bricks on the wall.

"Well?" she said, using her forefinger to guide the corkscrew into the center of the cork.

"BonBon thinks you were having an affair with Évariste, and Ursula and Shannon both told me Trevor and Évariste had words over you."

"And?" She pulled out the cork, removed it from the screw, and handed it to Jamie.

This girl made Oliver North seem gabby under oath. "And I want to know why you lied to me about you and Évariste having a relationship."

"I didn't," she said, plunking down the bottle of wine on the table, hard enough to punctuate her answer, but light enough to call it an accident.

"I think she was about to crack," Jamie said as she walked off.

"Shut up."

While the wine breathed, I told Jamie about Mitch's negotiations with Évariste. "According to Nina and Ursula, Mitch thinks I can't be trusted with restaurant secrets."

"That's odd," he said, pouring half a glass of wine into my goblet and the exact same amount into his.

"I know," I said. "I can't believe he thinks I would blab! I never blab. I'm like a bank vault with information."

"No, it's odd that Mitch would want to partner with Évariste. His name is curdling in Las Vegas."

"What's wrong with Évariste's name? Aside from the fact that it sounds like a blood disease."

"I told you he owes a lot of money to investors, right?" he said, sipping the wine and holding it in his mouth, chewing before swallowing. "Nice."

I sipped mine, but swallowed without chewing. "Very. Tell me about Las Vegas."

"I have some restaurant friends up there and checked around. Nothing's official, but there are rumors that Évariste's investors were so unhappy with him that they demanded early repayment."

"Mitch's lawyers have been in Monte Carlo checking him out. They probably already figured out he's bad news."

"There's even more bad news," he said. "There are also rumors that he was about to lose his Michelin star."

"What!" I said, choking on a mouthful of wine.

"That's the rumor." He sat back in his chair and popped the rest of a nacho into his mouth.

"Didn't a chef kill himself a few years ago because he lost a star?" I asked.

"Bernard Loiseau at *La Côte d'Or*. He had three stars, and rumors floated about that Michelin would be dropping him down to two. But it turned out not to be true. The last thing he ate was his hunting rifle."

The Michelin star is the most coveted culinary honor in Europe. It got its start in 1900 when touring the countryside in an automobile became all the rage. To help travelers wear out their tire treads faster, the Michelin family—yes, the tire people—published a rated guide to hotels and rooming houses. The guide has evolved into the single most powerful arbiter of European restaurant worthiness, and the opinions of the anonymous reviewers, in the form of stars, are accepted as gospel. Careers are built or broken within its pages, but most chefs handle the loss of a star less definitively than Bernard Loiseau.

"Losing his only star would be a big deal to Évariste," I said, "but I don't think he'd kill himself over it. He was more surly libertine than Samurai warrior. Although if you listen to Ursula, Évariste hated her enough to frame her for his death."

To Jamie's confused look, I said, "Don't try to make sense of that."

"Rather than someone framing her," he said, "it could be dumb luck that Ursula is in jail and the killer is free."

"That would send things in another direction entirely if this had nothing to do with Ursula."

"Indeed."

"Amado told me he didn't like the way Évariste talked to him or Belize. He said Évariste was fat and mean. Maybe Amado was protecting her honor."

"Even if he didn't frame Ursula, would he let her take the rap for him?"

"Possibly so, but probably not. Amado worships Ursula."

"What if this wasn't a crime of passion?" he suggested. "What if his death is related to his Michelin status or his financial situation?"

"And I quote, 'I don't think casinos or investors got hold of Ursula's knife and stabbed Évariste on his smoke break.' Isn't that what you said a few hours ago at U of J?"

"Darn your memory."

Belize materialized to take our order. She had just delivered food to a four-top and held a large oval tray smeared with grease in her hand when she approached our table. She dropped the short end of the tray on the floor and caught it between her legs. "Have you decided on entrées?" she asked.

Even before the renovation, when Markham's served T-bone steaks and bread pudding, waiters knew better than to approach a table with a dirty tray in their hand. Tipsy from the glass of wine I'd had on an empty stomach, I became annoyed at Belize's attitude toward me and Jamie. "We'll be ready to order as soon as you get back from returning that tray to the wait station."

155

Belize looked at me as if to ask if I was serious, but when she saw my face, she knew the answer. She pulled the tray up and walked off without saying a word.

"What is with you tonight?" Jamie asked.

"I don't know," I said, but then changed my answer as my reasoning formed in my head. "No, I do know. Ursula is in jail and Mitch is in the hospital, and everyone around here is acting like neither of them exist. Will is striding through the dining room like he's lord of the manor, and Trevor has everyone in the kitchen saluting with both hands. And now Belize is acting like I'm a pain in her side. Me! My last name is on the sign in front of the building she works in, the guest check she drops at every table, the menu we're ordering from, and even the apron she's wearing. I'll be signing everyone's paycheck until my dad gets out of the hospital, and I think I deserve more than a crappy table by the bathroom and an ornery waitress."

I flung myself back in my chair, then heard what I had said. It happened so rarely that Mitch needed me in an official capacity, I had forgotten that I was a backup signature on paychecks. Monday was the fifteenth, which meant I would have to sign checks.

Jamie poured more wine into my glass. "We'll get this figured out, Poppycakes."

Belize returned without the tray. "May I take your order, ma'am?"

Jamie ordered for both of us, Pasta Primavera for me and the Salmon en Papillote for himself. Trevor could handle everyday menu items with or without Ursula, but Jamie wanted to see what he could do on his own. So did I.

As we waited for our food, Jamie and I drank our wine and talked about people we knew and happenings in the Austin restaurant world. After the months I had spent trying to expunge all traces of Jamie from my life, I could hardly believe we were sitting in a restaurant, talking and laughing like old friends with no secrets between them. We were within striking distance of being on a date, and I needed to be careful.

A few minutes later, Belize arrived at our table. She placed two fresh appetizer plates in front of us, then presented three jumbo shrimp prepared scampi-style with butter, garlic, and parsley. As big as Shaquille O'Neal's fingers and the perfect shade of pink. "The kitchen apologizes for the wait," she said.

By "the kitchen" she meant Trevor. So, he knew that my waitress was Belize, my table number was eleven, and my dinner companion was Jamie Sherwood. Trevor would make sure that everything brought to our table was perfection on a plate. "Oy," I said.

Jamie knew exactly what I meant. "I *am* the most influential food writer in the city. And this is what amounts to Trevor's debut."

"Only because Ursula is in jail," I said. "This seems too convenient, doesn't it? That two heavyweight chefs are out of the way, and Trevor is cooking for a hundred people two days later."

Jamie placed a shrimp on his plate and said, "If you're right, Trevor has pulled off the caper of the year."

"If I'm right, and I can prove it, Ursula can get out of jail and I can get on with my life."

Jamie cut into the shrimp and I watched as he chewed his first bite, closing his eyes to give more attention to his senses of taste and smell. By the time he opened his eyes, I knew the verdict. "Heavens to Murgatroyd," he said.

After dropping off our entrées, Belize spent as little time as possible at our table, making it difficult for me to question her again, so I listened to Jamie rave about the salmon. He used words like "velvety blend," "flakey texture," and "delightful treat," already writing the review in his head. Trevor passed the pre-flight check and had been cleared to fly solo.

Guests still occupied every table at 8:30 when Jamie and I finished our espressos. I needed to talk to Will about employee paychecks and get a master key, but I knew he would be busy for at least another hour, so Jamie and I went to a movie at the Alamo Drafthouse downtown. "We'll make it dinner and a movie," is what I had missed hearing him say on the phone earlier. In spite of my best efforts, this had turned into a real date.

SEVENTEEN

JAMIE DROPPED ME IN front of the restaurant a little after 10:30 PM. A few guests still lingered in the dining room. Two or three couples in for a late-night supper, one drunk guy trying to feed his drunk girlfriend crème brûlée with predictable results, and the three men I had seen Will seat a few hours earlier, two half-full bottles of red wine on their table. Belize cleared their dessert plates, ignoring heavy-lidded appraisals of her body. One tried to slap her bottom, but missed and cuffed the back of her leg. Money never can buy class.

I found Will in his office counting cash from the waiters' check-outs. Customer checks, credit card slips, and bundles of paper money covered the desktop, and a long paper chit curled from the adding machine to the floor.

"Hello Poppy," he said. "Sixty … eighty … nine hundred. I thought I saw you leave a couple of hours ago."

I eased into a chair across from him. "I'm just keeping an eye on things until my dad and Ursula get back." As if they had taken a Caribbean cruise leaving me to fetch the mail and feed the dogs until they returned. "Are you doing a check run on Monday?"

He glanced at the calendar on his desk. "I believe so."

"I can come in later in the afternoon to sign them," I said.

"That won't be necessary."

"I don't think Mitch will be out of the hospital by then, and even if he is, he'll be recovering at home."

Will wrapped a rubber band around a thick stack of twenties. "Let's hope they let him out sooner, but Mitch doesn't sign checks anymore. I'll be in Sunday morning to do the paperwork."

It was unlike Mitch to trust anyone so completely so quickly, especially a restaurant manager. But okay, I conceded, maybe as the general manager, Will did need check-signing privileges. I should have felt relieved that I didn't have to perform that duty. I was another step removed from Markham's, which was what I wanted. So why did it feel like being left out?

I stood up and walked slowly to the door. "This etched glass is beautiful, Will," I said, running my finger along the curved hull of a sailboat.

"I'll give your compliments to my wife."

"She's an artist?"

"She dabbles."

I had attended enough openings at the Johns' gallery and personally knew enough artists to have a more-than-amateur eye for professional art. "If this is dabbling, I'd like to see what she can do when she gets serious."

He glanced at a photograph on his desk. Will at the beach, his arms around identical twin girls, blond curls blown into angelic

160

faces. His wife must have been the photographer. She had talent there, too.

"While I'm here," I said, "do you know what Évariste and Trevor were in a glitch about?"

A look of annoyance crossed his face when I sat down again. "Was there a glitch?"

"You didn't hear about Trevor threatening Évariste with a meat cleaver a few hours before I . . . " I coughed to cover my almost admission. "Before Évariste was found murdered. Everyone saw it."

"I heard nothing. Of course, something like that would get lost in the aftermath."

"What about BonBon?"

"What about her?"

This was like deboning Coho salmon. "Do you know why she slapped Évariste?"

"I don't know her well enough to even venture a guess, but I will say they seemed to have a tumultuous relationship," he said. "Really, Poppy, I don't want to seem unhelpful here, but I'm exhausted and I just want to finish these checkouts and go home. I haven't seen my girls in days."

"Sure," I said, and stood.

Between the red wine at dinner and a couple of hours in a warm, dark movie theater, I felt sleepy, but I still had work to do. Real work. Covering for Kawasaki didn't mean I could put all of my SPI investigations on hold. A weekends-only bar in the warehouse district had been operating without public toilet facilities. I gave the owner a week to fix it or risk being shut down. By me. That night.

In the wait station, I pulled a half-full coffeepot from the burner and sniffed it. Decaf. It was the only thing Markham's brewed after 9:00 PM. Blech. Coffee is decaffeinated with the same chemical they use to preserve frogs, pigs, and starfish for dissection in high school science classes. I headed for the bar.

I sat on one of the barstools and watched Andy pour hot water into the ice bin. "How's the mighty Mitch?" he asked, placing a bevnap in front of me. "We've been thinking about visiting him."

It reminded me that I hadn't heard from Nina. I took that as good news. "Nina tells me he's been singing."

"Mitch? Singing?"

"Brush up on your Sinatra and you can harmonize with him."

"That's way before my time," he said. "You look like you need an espresso."

"Double."

Andy ground the espresso beans, tamped them into the filter basket, then pulled the strong coffee into a heated demitasse cup. He handed me the cup brimming with a perfect head of foam, a twist of lemon on the tiny saucer.

I heard a yelp and turned to see the three men laughing as Belize stormed back to the wait station. The men pushed back from the table, scraping their chairs against the tiles, standing and hitching up their waistbands. They looked to be in their mid-fifties. All three had graying hair and ruddy complexions. Two had goatees, and one a bristly moustache. They wore expensive-looking suits and conservative ties that had been loosened at the neck. Except for undertakers, TV anchormen, and politicians, no one in Austin wears a suit. They had to be from out of town.

I turned back to Andy. "If only all our customers were like them."

"Hardly."

"But they have two bottles of Diamond Creek on their table."

"After they sent back a bottle of Atlas Peak, a bottle of Gun-Bun, and a bottle of Treana. Said they tasted corked." He shook his head. "In four years here, I've never served a bottle of wine that's turned. And three in one night to the same table? No way."

I felt lightheaded. "We ate six hundred dollars of wine for those guys?"

"Probably more like eight for wine and brandy and another two for food. Unless they ordered the specials, in which case add another bill to the food comp."

"Their food is comped!" I knew my rage wasn't fueled by the jolt of espresso because I hadn't touched it yet.

Andy drew back and raised his hands in confused surrender.

"I'm just assuming. Will usually comps them."

"Who are they?"

"Not sure," he said, restocking wine glasses in the overhead rack. "They come in two or three times a week and always sit in Belize's section. I'm surprised you don't know them. I think they're friends with Mitch."

I thought they looked familiar. They were the Easter Island guys I had seen Mitch talking to at the party. I abandoned my espresso on the bar and marched back to Will's office. I stopped when I heard voices behind the door. Will and Belize. I couldn't understand their words, but there was enough emotion in their voices to fuel a Broadway production of *The Taming of the Shrew.*

Belize yelling and Will calming, which only seemed to provoke her. I tried the door handle. Locked. I still needed to ask Will for a key.

I rapped hard on the wooden frame of the door and the voices stopped, then Belize flung open the door. "What the devil do you want?" Then, "Oh, I didn't know it was you." She wiped her runny nose on her sleeve.

"Everything okay in here?" I asked.

"Tell her," Belize said to Will as she tramped past me out of the office.

"Tell me what?" I asked.

Perspiration dotted his upper lip and wet stains had formed under his arms. "Just restaurant business."

"I assumed so since we're in a restaurant, Belize is a waitress, and you're the general manager."

Will sat, his body relaxing into the squeaky leather of his executive chair. "She got stiffed on a big check."

"So she came into your office, locked the door, and yelled at you?"

"Storm in a teacup." He rubbed his eyes, then leaned forward. "Now, what brings you in here?"

My anger simmered up again as I remembered why I wanted to talk to him. "Who are those three men she was waiting on when I came in tonight?"

"Those would be the stiffers."

"Andy tells me they come in once a week, Belize always waits on them, and you always comp their check. He thinks they're friends of Mitch."

"In a way." Will stood, signaling the end of the conversation.

164

He needed a reminder about who he was talking to. "Will," I said evenly, "I'm very tired, and not getting straight answers from you is making me a lot cranky. Until Mitch comes back, *I'm* Mitch. Comping three thousand dollars worth of food and wine every week is going to stop." He looked up at me, surprised at the decisiveness in my voice. "Tell me who those men are."

"Very well." Will's smile told me I wasn't going to like the answer. "Those three men are my business partners. Together we own forty-nine percent of Markham's."

"You're lying."

"Mitch and Nina own forty-nine percent."

"And the other two percent?" I asked, my voice almost a whisper.

"Évariste Bontecou."

EIGHTEEN

A TSUNAMI OF QUESTIONS, speculations, and accusations converged in my mind. I couldn't grasp onto any thought long enough to form a coherent string of words. I left before I became the second woman to spill tears in front of Will that night.

I didn't realize where I was going until I turned onto my street. The frat boys on the corner had engineered an especially grand weekend party and I ran a gauntlet between cars, trucks, motorcycles, and even a golf cart, lining both sides of the street. I couldn't get inside my house fast enough and shut the door on all of the chaos threatening my mental balance.

I knew I should wait to talk to Mitch in the morning and get real answers instead of make assumptions and jump to conclusions, but my brain wouldn't turn off. I called Jamie, hoping he could help me make sense of everything. No answer. Where could he be at midnight?

When I'm feeling lost, I crave the comfort of cold-weather rituals. But since I live in south Texas where a morning temperature in the high-eighties in May is often referred to as "a bit cool," I had to fake winter conditions. I set the air conditioner to fifty degrees, slipped on my favorite pair of hand-knit cabled socks, then prepared a mug of vegan hot cocoa, sprinkling in a little cayenne pepper for some bite.

On the couch, I snuggled under my mom's afghan, then turned on my little television and played a *Cracklin' Fire* DVD, video footage of a large stone fireplace, complete with crackling and popping sound effects. I pretended to be safely ensconced in a warm Swiss chalet high atop a picturesque mountain instead of trapped under a dark, suffocating avalanche of deceit.

But I couldn't relax. The socks felt scratchy and my butt sank into the break in the couch cushions giving the zipper an opportunity to scrape my back. I had put too much cayenne in the cocoa, and my house would never be cold enough to make me forget that my family no longer had controlling interest in Markham's.

I flung the blanket to the floor and sat up, my mind scanning fact after fact. Évariste wasn't negotiating with Mitch as Ursula told me, he was already a partner. If Will owned part of Markham's, it should have been his idea to re-open the restaurant early. And no waitress gets that upset about a bad tip. Will had tried to calm Belize, but he didn't really have to listen to her complaints in the first place.

The video had played through to my favorite part. I sipped my cooling cocoa and watched the flames start to die out. My puddle of suspects had grown into a pool. Now splashing around were Trevor, Belize, BonBon, Will, and three obnoxious men in suits. And to be completely objective, I had to include Amado, Mitch,

Nina, and Ursula, regardless of what I thought I knew about them. The only person I was sure didn't kill Évariste was me.

I started to feel drowsy from the fake fire and late hour, so I re-started the video with the volume turned up as I fought to stay fo-cused. I needed to get my mind around some conscious thoughts about this situation so I could figure out what to do next.

Mitch bringing investors into the restaurant—especially strang-ers, and most especially out-of-town strangers—confounded me. He loved Markham's. He knew everything about it and still loved it, like a father loves his child. When I was little, he used to joke that he had made a deal with a man on a farm to trade me for a yellow puppy. At my wide eyes, he would laugh and pull me to him, saying he was kidding; he wouldn't trade me for the world. He never even joked about trading Markham's. And he had turned down generous offers over the years to buy the restaurant.

And Ursula. Évariste's two-percent ownership trumped her lowly stepdaughter status. His vested interest gave her the same two choices she had given him that night: help or leave. But within a much bigger context. Had she taken a stab at a third option?

I was exhausted, and frankly, tired of major news being re-vealed to me by-the-by. I laid down on the couch, fuming. If Mitch and his new family wanted to keep secrets from me, why should I bother to help any of them? If Ursula really didn't do it, the po-lice would figure it out, and she could ferment in jail until they did. Why should I risk my job, which I had been neglecting, and spend my precious free time trying to find the real killer when none of them valued me enough to tell me about all the significant changes at Markham's?

Sleep chased me down like a hawk after a hare. I set my mug of cocoa on the table, then pulled the blanket up to my chin and closed my eyes. I had finally figured out what I would do next: absolutely nothing.

I awoke with a start to someone banging on my front door. "Poppy! Poppy! Wake up! Poppy!"

I recognized John Without's voice and jumped off the couch, tripping over my blanket, slipping on the floor in my socks. I flung open the front door.

He grabbed my arm and jerked me into the front yard. "Your house is on fire!" he screamed.

I pulled back, twisting my arm to wrench free of him. "No, John, it's just a video," I said, still groggy. "A Swish chalet. With the volume loud."

He tightened his grasp and yanked me into the street. I heard sirens and saw John With at the top of a step-ladder in their back yard aiming a hose at my house, the puny stream of water doing no good against the blaze.

Firemen arrived, and within moments confirmed that I had neither spouse, nor child, nor pet to be saved inside. "Just save my house!" I yelled at their backs. I felt helpless as I watched them battle a force of nature intent on complete consumption. Within a few minutes, the firemen had won, but not before the fire had snacked on my bedroom.

A thin, soot-streaked fireman approached me and asked if I knew what may have caused the fire. Had I left a cigarette burning or a gas stove on? I hesitated, but after a stern look, I broke down. "Just a *Cracklin' Fire* DVD." He didn't see the humor.

I didn't notice that John Without had been holding onto me until he let go of my arm and shot me a "how embarrassing" look. He had no room to scoff, dressed in shiny pink shorts and a white tank top.

John With jumped off the ladder and ran toward us, flushed and panting. "You'll stay with us tonight," he said, putting a sweaty arm around my shoulder. "Let's go make up your bed while these guys finish up."

"I need my phone," I said, turning toward my house.

John With stopped me. "John will get it. Where is it?"

I started to direct him to my night table, but remembered I had fallen asleep on the couch. "I don't know where I left it," I said.

"Wonderful," John Without said testily. "Go with John. I'll find it."

John With walked me to their house and into their guest bedroom, which doubled as a temporary lumber yard during the renovations. We worked together in silence putting fresh sheets on the bed.

"Thank you," I said as we cased a pillow together.

"Are you okay?" he asked.

I felt better when I looked into his sweet brown eyes, but not okay. How could I be okay after almost being burned alive? "Not sure yet."

"Come on," he said, hugging me from the side. "Tea makes everything better."

170

I sat at the kitchen table and watched him pour water into a kettle and turn on the stove. He opened a cabinet and moved a fiery red cup out of the way to get to a tranquil green mug, I smiled at the sweetness of that gesture. I disliked John Without all the more for not appreciating him.

"Chamomile okay?" he asked.

"Perfect."

The kettle whistled, rousing me out of my moment of amiable domesticity with John. Then John Without banged open the back door and trudged into the kitchen, jarring me out of the moment completely. "The charger was in your room, but I had to call your cell phone to find it." He threw two backpacks onto the table. "They were in your Jeep." He held up a third one, the one I had left in the living room the day after the murder. "This one stinks." He let it fall at his feet. "So it must be important to you."

"Thanks J," John With said.

John Without ran a hand over his shiny head. "I need a shower."

"Don't mind him," John With said after he had left. "The only thing he likes less than getting out of bed in the middle of the night is having dirt on him."

"I won't envy you when he's old and has to get up every half hour to pee."

John sat down and looked into my eyes. "I want you to stay with us as long as you need to."

"Thank you," I said. Being doted on by John With for a few days was a nice fiction, but the fact of John Without couldn't be ignored. I could endure him in small doses, but spending a significant amount of time around him would chip away at my sanity. I

171

prayed the damage to my house would be minor, but if it needed major work, I would probably move in with, Heaven help me, Ursula or Mitch and Nina.

John With patted my hand. "You don't need to decide anything tonight, Poppy Markham."

My phone rang and I fished it out of my inspector's backpack.

"I'm standing in front of your house," Jamie said. "Where are you?"

Moments later he knocked on the Johns' back door. John With handed him the cup of tea he had prepared for himself, then busied himself at the sink.

"What are you doing here at this hour?" I asked as Jamie pulled out one of the high-backed chairs and took a seat at the table.

"Police scanner." I had forgotten that he often fell asleep with the scanner as background noise. "When I heard the name of your street, I woke up, then I heard the address."

"Don't you run a food website?" John Without asked, pulling on a fresh tank top as he walked into the kitchen.

"You know I do." Jamie dislikes John Without as much as I do, but often found himself united with him in their silly mission to keep me and John With apart.

"Why would you be listening to a police scanner?" John Without asked. "Think you're going to get a big story when someone expires in their spinach?"

"John!" John With said, and we all turned to John Without.

"Oh, brother!" he said. "That French guy was stabbed. I'm talking about food poisoning."

We stared at him and he walked down the hallway in a huff.

"Sorry," John With said. "He's—"

"Just being himself," I said. "Don't worry about it."

John With stood up and stretched. "Morpheus beckons," he said. "You should have everything you need for tonight, but if not, tap on the wall and I'll come running."

"Sure," I said, then, "John?" He turned to me. "Thanks for hosing down my house until the fire department came. You're my hero."

He blushed, deepening the hue of his suntanned face. "Don't mention it."

When he had gone, Jamie said, "I can't leave you alone for a second. How did the fire start?"

I hadn't cooked anything when I got home, and I had made the cocoa by heating water in my coffee maker, which turned off automatically if I forgot to do it manually. Even my kitchen appliances were more nurturing than John Without. "I know I didn't set it, so insurance should cover it."

The look on Jamie's face told me he was about to say something I would rather he didn't. "What if it wasn't an accident?"

I blew on my cup of tea that had already cooled. "You think John Without decided he wanted a new neighbor?"

"Be serious, babe. You've been asking a lot of questions about Évariste's murder. What if someone doesn't want you to ask any more?"

"That's ridiculous."

"No, it's not. I know I'm only a food writer," he glanced down the hallway where John Without had gone, "but things are starting to add up in the wrong way."

"It's probably just faulty wiring," I said, trying to convince Jamie as much as myself. "That house is like eighty years old."

"Mitch had the wiring redone before he sold it to you."

If someone had set fire to my house, that would mean I was onto something, even if I didn't know what that something was. But if it was an accident, life would go on. I needed to know for sure how the fire started. I pushed back my chair and stood up. "Come on."

Warmed by adrenaline and confusion earlier, I hadn't noticed how cool the night had become. Light from the waning moon cast long shadows throughout the neighborhood. I closed my eyes and inhaled deeply, enjoying the comforting fragrance of wood smoke—until I remembered it was coming from my own house.

I removed my socks, then Jamie and I picked our way across ankle-high grass made wet and sloppy by the firemen's water, and stopped in the driveway. The firemen had stripped off their heavy protective gear and worked in their shirt sleeves. A couple of them rolled up the big fire hose while another talked into a hand radio.

Jamie offered to speak with the arson investigators and I let him because I felt guilty about rousing these guys in the middle of the night to risk their lives to save mine. I stood on the sidewalk and watched the enormous light green truck drive off, taking with it the noise and color of the sirens and lights, the shouts and efficiency of the firemen. Neighbors went back inside, perhaps a little nervous about the safety of their own homes, and probably a lot upset with me for getting them out of bed so early on a Saturday morning.

Jamie ran back over to me. "They're pretty sure it was deliberate. The burn pattern in the grass outside your bedroom window indicates an accelerant. It's not gasoline, but they need to run tests to determine exactly what it is."

Jamie was right. Someone had tried to kill me. Panic began an excruciating climb up my chest and into my throat. I didn't even have a chance to stop the tears.

He pulled me to him and I laid my head on his chest. "You're safe with the Johns tonight," he said, stroking my back. "And a policeman is going to patrol the area."

I focused my eyes on an overturned potted pencil cactus on my porch to take my mind off of Jamie's familiar sleepy scent. I pulled back from him. "I called you around midnight. You didn't answer."

I sounded a little jealous, and maybe I was.

"Brian called at the last minute. He sprained his elbow kickboxing and needed me to sit in for him. He raised an eyebrow. "What did you want me for at midnight?"

"Come back to the Johns' and I'll tell you."

We sat at the kitchen table, keeping our voices low while I told Jamie about Will and the investors. He whistled softly, as surprised as I that Mitch would relinquish control of Markham's.

"See what you can find out about those three men," I said. "They could be mafia or something."

"Investing in an old restaurant in Austin, Texas? I doubt it. Besides, I think Mitch would have better sense than to get mixed up with *la familia*."

"My father has better sense than to do a lot of things, but that hasn't stopped him lately."

"Some of us would like to sleep!" John Without shouted from the bedroom.

175

Jamie got up and took his cup to the sink. "George Clooney and Jeff Daniels."

I laughed. "*Good Night, and Good Luck.*"

NINETEEN

I DON'T LIKE SLEEPING in someone else's house, especially one I've never stayed in before. Like most adults who have lived alone for many years, I like things just so. I like it quiet—no fans, radios, televisions, or police scanners in the background. I like the heft, protection, and warmth of a comforter when I sleep, so in the summer I turn down the air conditioner temperature, and in the winter, I crack open my windows. I also like to sleep with my bedroom door shut and locked. Jamie likes lots of background noise, a thin sheet, and a warm room. Thank goodness I didn't have to make those sorts of compromises any more.

I changed into the white men's t-shirt laid out on my bed, then slid between the cool sheets. I assumed that my mind would keep me up all night as it played and replayed the night's greatest hits, so I was surprised to wake up in the Johns' guest room with sunlight streaming through the window. Perhaps the sweet smell of two-by-fours curing in the room, or the fluffy down comforter, or the crisp white sheets that smelled of bleach and lavender had lulled me to sleep.

I smelled coffee and heard whistling—two sure signals that it's time to start the day. I abhor whistlers, all fake cheery, filling a silence that doesn't need to be filled. After a quick trip to the hall bathroom and a glance in the mirror to see if I looked as refreshed as I felt (I didn't), I walked into the kitchen. The Johns each had a cup of half-full coffee in front of them on the kitchen table. A plate of cranberry bagels sat between them, next to the bulk of the Saturday paper.

When I appeared in the kitchen, John Without raised the sports section in front of his face and stopped whistling. I knew it was him. John With looked up and smiled. His hair, untamed by styling gel, spiked out in all directions, and he hadn't shaved. He looked adorable. "Hey, Sleeping Beauty," he said, standing to give me a brotherly hug. "John just made a fresh pot."

"Smells like hazelnut," I said, waving him back into his chair. I looked for my green cup from the night before, but all the dishes in the sink had already been washed, dried, and put away. I pulled a fresh cup from the cabinet and filled it, then refilled their cups before joining them at the table.

After assuring John With that I had slept like a butterfly in her chrysalis, I told him I didn't want to overstay my welcome, but he again assured me that I could stay as long as I needed to. John Without didn't say anything either way. Maybe coffee and ball scores made him docile.

"I don't know how to thank you," I started.

178

"Please," John Without said from behind the newspaper. "You're giving John something to do. He's been clucking like a mother hen all morning."

"I have not!" John With said.

John Without dropped his paper to the table. "Oh, you have so!" he said playfully.

His glimmer of affection blinked out, and I noticed a strange look pass between them. John With cleared his throat. "We need to ask you for a favor, Poppy Markham."

I hate favors. I hate doing them and I hate asking for them. They always sound so quick and innocent at first. A favor. Like a sneeze. But favors replicate, taking on a life of their own. Lending a hand in the kitchen for a few hours turns into a murder investigation, and then one night your house is set on fire. But how could I refuse after what they had done for me?

John Without crossed his arms and looked out the back window. What on earth could this favor be? Did they want me to mow their grass? Clean their house? Lend them money? I should just say no. Have John With's baby? "Depends," I said.

John With nudged a wavy lock of hair off his forehead. It immediately dropped back into place. "I'm not sure how to ask this," he said. He seemed nervous.

I helped him along. "What would you say if you were asking John for this favor?"

John Without grunted, his face so tight, he looked like he had just come from the taxidermist.

I turned back to John With and he said, "Will you be my wife?"

John Without catapulted out of his chair, sending it banging onto the hardwood floor. "You don't have to ask her like that!" he cried, his voice as high as Dora the Explorer's.

Was this a joke? I looked at John With hoping to share a secret moment of silliness at the outburst, but he dropped his eyes to his lap, suddenly intrigued by the frayed hem of his shorts.

John Without said, "He needs you to *pretend* to be his wife, don't you, John? You left out that word. *Pretend*."

The Johns explained that they were in danger of losing their most promising artistic discovery, an artist named Rodrigo Luna, whose gallery opening was scheduled for that night. His mother, Carmen, with whom the forty-two-year-old Rodrigo still lived, and who had been instrumental in getting her son's work into the gallery, had a strong Catholic faith and disapproved of gay relationships. She had tried to play matchmaker between the Johns and Rodrigo's six single sisters until John With told her they were both happily married. Carmen, apparently, couldn't wait to meet their wives at the gallery opening.

"It seems absurd, but this is becoming a major issue," John With said. "We've agreed to all sorts of changes to our standard contract which basically gives her the authority to pull the plug on this whole deal for any reason." He swiped again at the obstinate curl. "We can't let that happen. Rodrigo is too important. We need at least one wife to show up tonight."

John Without had calmed down, still not happy, but resigned to the situation. He could be John's partner, but not his wife. I felt sorry for him, but not sorry enough to stop myself from throwing my arms around John With's neck and saying, "I do!"

"Thanks Poppy Markham," said my new pretend husband.

I pulled back and tick-tocked my finger at him. "Uh, uh, uh. It's Poppy Jones now."

John Without stomped down the hallway and slammed their bedroom door. John With sighed and dropped his shoulders, then went after him. I didn't want to make matters worse for my new mate, so I vamoosed to my house for a change of clothes.

I walked slowly up the flagstone path to my front door, which was mostly missing. As a reflex, I had shut the door behind me when John Without pulled me into the street. The firemen had banged through the door, fire hose in hand, ready for anything. Not that I faulted them for that. But they could have at least tried the knob.

I stood in the doorway and surveyed my small living room. Except for the smell, the water, and the dirty footprints, everything looked as if I had gotten up to answer the door to let in a friend. But I had not invited this. Someone had violated my space. They walked into my yard, stood outside my bedroom, poured an accelerant on the grass beneath my window, and set a match to it. Whoever did this possessed some admirable arson skills, but also a heap of dumb luck. Had someone not tried to fry me, I probably would have followed through on my vow to mind my own business and let Mitch, Nina, and Ursula extract themselves from their own secretive mess. That couldn't happen now. I would get to the bottom of whatever it was that had a bottom, and *then* I would leave my family to their own predicaments.

But first I needed fresh underwear.

I gathered a change of clothes and a few essentials, then returned to the Johns' house to shower. In the twenty minutes I had been gone, my bed had been made and all of the lumber removed from my room. Toiletries materialized in the bathroom, along with two fluffy white towels. Maybe I would take them up on their offer to stay awhile. After all, I had just become the lady of the house. Well, one of them.

I had forgotten to grab my toothbrush at home, then remembered I had an extra one in the smelly backpack that had so offended John Without. Also in that bag were my unused party clothes that had been marinating with my dirty chef's coat for two days. Everything reeked of old grease and old food, an odor only slightly less offensive than the stench of smoke embedded in the clothes in my closet. A few hours in the sunshine might refresh them.

I hung them on hangers, then took them into the back yard and hooked them on a clothesline left over from the previous owners, my former neighbors. I never did like the sight of the man's tattered boxers waving in the wind like jumbo flags of surrender. The Johns would eventually either take the line down or drape it with outdoor lights for a kitschy ambiance.

As I hung my chef's coat on the line, my eyes lingered on the embroidered logo. My mind tingled with an idea that wouldn't quite solidify. A memory of something. The old logo was a simple graphic of a spatula crossed with a spoon set inside a circle. My mother had designed it, and Mitch had printed it on everything from menus to guest checks. What would Iris Markham think of her restaurant now?

I went back inside and spent a long hour on the phone with my insurance company who told me they had already been notified of "the fire situation" and an adjuster would be out to my house by the end of the day. The rep told me I didn't need to be there unless I wanted to. I didn't. I had a killer to catch.

By 9:00 AM, I had showered, dressed, and fed myself. Saturday's visiting hours at the jail for T through Z didn't start for another two hours, so I decided to go straight to the source and demand some answers.

TWENTY

I HAD A SHOCK when the elevator doors opened. Nina had been replaced on the couch by two multi-pierced, multi-colored black-clad teens intertwined in an embrace better suited for a no-tell motel. They both looked like boys. Or girls. It was hard to tell with Austin's youth.

Not much else had changed, though. The television in the corner still broadcast the news, and Évariste's death still made the headlines. They ran the same packaged story they had been running for days: a full-screen picture of Évariste's face followed by footage of his body being swallowed by the ambulance. Seeing it felt routine, until they flashed a new element—Ursula's face. Not a good indication that the police were considering other suspects.

I walked to the couch and tapped out the kid on top. He, or she, jumped up as if poked with a cattle prod. "Suck face somewhere else," I said. "You're making people sick."

They boarded the open elevator without so much as an "Aw, man."

184

Seeing Nina first thing had also become routine, so I felt obliged to find her and check in. But why do that when I could finally circumvent the gatekeeper? At the nurse's station, I discovered that Nina had arranged for my father to have a private room. It was what she wanted for him, not what my father would have wanted.

Mitch does not like to be alone. It's one of the reasons he spends so much time at the restaurant, and probably one of the reasons he remarried only a year after my mother died. Unlike me, he actually enjoys the surprises and complexities of other people, and I know he would have preferred a roommate. But in Nina's mind, prosperous people recuperate without an audience.

A nurse stood outside my father's room making notes in his chart. I nodded hello, then reached for the door. She moved her hand to the door handle. "Family only," she said.

"I'm his daughter."

"Which one?"

"Poppy," Nina called from down the hall.

I looked at the nurse. "Markham. Only daughter of Mitch Markham."

The nurse looked at Nina, waiting to be told what to do.

"It's okay," Nina said to her. "I'll take care of it."

The nurse walked away and Nina held onto my upper arms as she maneuvered me around so that her back was to Mitch's door, blocking my entrance. "What are you doing here?" she asked, a strange mix of frustration and defiance in her voice.

I plucked her hands off me. "Visiting my sick father." I hoped she heard the warning in mine. "Where have you been?"

"Checking on Dolce and Gabbana."

Nina is certainly the type of person who would make a special trip home to cuddle her haute couture, but Dolce and Gabbana are her dogs, two copper-colored hairless Chinese Cresteds. She claims to have them because of an allergy to pet dander, but they also conveniently meet her three requirements for just about everything: they're unusual, rare, and expensive.

"How is the gruesome twosome?" I asked.

"Fine." She smoothed her hair. "They miss your father."

Only because he hadn't been home to sneak them table scraps the past few days. "I miss him too. Why are you trying to keep me away from him?"

The look on her face confirmed what had, until then, been only a suspicion. It explained her strange behavior—ushering me out of the waiting room after his surgery, neglecting to call me with updates, being nice to me.

"I'm doing no such thing," she said.

I crossed my arms and glowered at her.

She turned briefly to look at Mitch's door. "I don't think it's good for you to see your father in this condition."

"I'd believe a prediction from the mythical Cassandra before I believed you cared about my feelings." I stepped toward her and lowered my voice. "What are you hiding, Nina?"

"Nothing." She looked toward the nurse's station. "There's nothing to hide."

"Tell me, Nina, or I drop everything right now and we'll wait and see what happens to Ursula." I didn't mean it, but it was the only hand I had with her.

Her face fell like a soufflé with too many eggs in it. "Every time you see your father, you upset him."

As usual, she was exaggerating. Or was she? "I'll take the blame for the argument at the restaurant, but how was I supposed to know he didn't know about Ursula's arrest?"

"Because if you'd thought about your father, you'd know that telling him something like that is not in his best interest at the moment."

"I think about him all the time."

"Then think about him in this condition." She looked defeated, but I took no pleasure in it. "If you want what's best for him, you'll let him rest."

Darn. Nina was right. I had gone there with my mind loaded and my mouth cocked, ready to fire questions and accusations at him. "Fine," I said, stomping off.

Mitch wasn't the only one involved in this partnership. There were plenty of other people I could get information from. I drove to the restaurant hoping Will would be there and that he would be in a mood to talk.

I didn't see his car when I passed by the front or when I parked in the back, but I knew he would arrive soon to finish up the night's paperwork and make the bank deposit. I inserted my key into the back door and slowly turned it in the lock. If these locks had been rekeyed too, I wanted to delay my disappointment as long as possible. The key turned as it always had. Finally, something that hadn't changed.

I looked around the kitchen, assessing how Trevor had left things. The pots hung on their hooks, by size. The pans, also stacked by size, sat on the lower shelves. Trays of clean glasses and coffee cups waited neatly by the door for the waiters to trade out for empty trays in the wait station. The silver work tables gleamed.

The rubber mats stood on end near the back door. Rolled up and secured with bungee cords, they looked like sushi for a T-rex. Everything looked as if Ursula had been in charge.

I had eaten a banana for breakfast at the Johns' house, but felt hungry again, so I opened the door to the walk-in and entered food Nirvana, taking care that the door didn't click shut behind me and I got stuck in there until the cooks showed up. I gathered a couple of pears and a few sprigs of fresh mint, then backed through the door.

In the kitchen, I put a cutting board and knife on top of the prep table, then went into the dry storage room for the honey I had stashed there. When I cooked at Markham's, I hid a lot of things in the kitchen so I would have them when I needed them—slotted spoons, bread knives, grill towels, and quart-sized metal tins that became as valuable as rubies at the end of the night when it came time to switch prepped ingredients to clean containers for overnight storage. These were items every cook coveted and sometimes, when my treasures were discovered, they would either be taken outright or replaced by something completely useless, like potato peelings or chicken bones or a note with nothing but a smiley face. I eventually became more creative with my hiding places and loved the envious look on a cook's face when he saw me wiping down countertops with fresh white towels at the end of the night.

I had just found my jar of honey on a top shelf behind some ancient sacks of dried peas when I heard voices. A man's and a woman's. The man had to be Will. Had he brought his artist wife to work? I really wanted to see what she looked like.

Their voices got louder as they walked toward the kitchen. The man's voice definitely belonged to Will, but the woman wasn't his wife. It sounded like Belize Medina had come to the restaurant to continue her harangue from the night before. Will spoke calmly, but not as softly as he had spoken to her the previous night when people were around. They had come in through the front door, so they didn't see my Jeep. They were, as far as they knew, in an empty restaurant.

My instincts told me to stay hidden. Truths are told when people are emotional. But if they saw my snack on the prep table, they would know they had company. I decided to let them find me, but I wouldn't show myself.

"This sucks!" Belize screamed as they walked through the swinging doors into the kitchen. "This restaurant sucks. Your partners suck. And you can go to hell!"

Unbelievable. Even Belize knew about the partnership.

"Belize," Will said, "get control of yourself."

"Or what?" she said. "The puppet master will start pulling strings?"

I heard Will's voice followed by something that sounded a lot like when BonBon slapped Évariste across the face. Then Belize said something I couldn't make out and the word "strike" or maybe "spite." It took every milligram of self-control not to sneak a peek at them, but I didn't know exactly where they stood in the kitchen or if they would see me as soon as I poked my nose out of the dry storage room. I stayed put and stood as close to the doorway as I could so I wouldn't miss anything else.

"I'm not waiting on them anymore," Belize said

"You will if you want to keep your job," Will said, unruffled by her violence. "I have work to do. I'll see you tonight."

"Maybe," she said. Then I heard the kitchen doors swing open.

My brain has always needed a logical answer to every question. Even if the answer was as simple as they were having an affair, I had to know. Will seemed too self-contained to blabber about anything, so I had a better chance with Belize. I looked around the doorway to make sure Will had left, then snuck out the back door.

I sprinted around to the front of the restaurant and saw Belize sitting in her car, talking on the phone, waving her free hand around, then slamming it onto the dashboard. As I approached, I saw tears slipping down her cheeks. When she looked up at me, I motioned for her to let me in the passenger door. She rolled her eyes, but leaned over and pulled up the lock. She hung up the phone before I closed the door.

"What do you want?" she asked, wiping her eyes on a linen napkin embroidered with the new Markham's logo, an extravagant script M enclosed in a circle.

There was something about Belize. The way she carried herself, a certain confidence. It wasn't Trevor's kind of confidence that came from being a twenty-five-year-old talented Adonis in a position of power. It came from either being something no one else was, like a Michelin-rated chef, or knowing something nobody else knew, like a well-guarded secret.

"What's going on with you and Will?" I asked. "I heard you just now, arguing in the kitchen."

She squinted into the distance and I could almost see her brain shuffling through the timeline, trying to remember what she had said and when, and what I could figure out from what I had over-

190

heard. She must have assumed that I had heard everything because she dropped her forehead to the steering wheel and started bawling. "I can't do this anymore," she said, punctuating each word with a head bang against the steering wheel.

I had two options. I could ask her what she meant, but that might shut her up and I would lose this relatively weak moment with her. Or I could pretend I knew what was going on, using what I did know to make her think I knew more. The tactic had served me well during health inspections. "It'll be over soon," I said. "Will's partners will go back to where they came from."

"Hell won't take them back," she said, regaining an air of composed anger at the mention of them. This was good. I sat still, waiting for her to say more. With the doors and windows shut, the heat index in her car rose at least ten degrees. Perspiration pasted my shirt to the plastic seat. She craned her neck to look at her face in the rearview mirror, then adjusted the mirror down and began wiping the mascara from under her eyes with the napkin.

"Belize," I said. She turned toward me and looked ready to shove me out of her car. Instead, she reached behind her to the back seat for her purse. She pulled out a tube of mascara, pumped the wand a few times, then began applying it to her swollen eyes.

She was so young, not even in her mid-twenties. It didn't seem possible that she could be involved with Will, his partners, Évariste's death, and Ursula's frame-up. But not everyone lived the sheltered life I had. Belize seemed like she had more street smarts than most homeless people and would see any manipulation coming. She had probably already figured out that I bluffed her. "You'll feel better if you tell me what's going on."

She started her car and I had a disturbing thought that she was going to take us down Loop 360 and drive us both off the Lake Austin Bridge. I wrapped my fingers around the door handle, ready to dive out if she touched the gear shift, but relaxed when she turned on the air conditioner and moved her sweaty face closer to the vent.

"That night, he was sitting right where you are," she said. "Looking so smug."

I tensed, but said nothing. Most people would just blurt it out to get it over with, but she was taking her time, setting it up, making me wait. I don't like waiting.

"You and Évariste were sitting in your car, and . . ."

"Not Évariste," she said, looking into my eyes. "Trevor."

TWENTY-ONE

BANGING ON THE DRIVER'S side window startled both of us out of our game of truth or dare. Belize turned quickly to push down the lock on her door, but wasn't fast enough. Will flung it open and bent down to look at both of us. "Hello ladies," he said. How did he even know to find us out here? He must have been who Belize was talking to on the phone.

"Shouldn't you be getting along, Belize?" he said. "You're first on tonight."

"Not any more." Belize looked at Will. "You and those jerk partners of yours can kiss my apron." Will looked as stunned as I felt. "You," she said to me. "Out! You." She pointed at Will. "Off." I got out of her car and she slammed her door as soon as Will let go of it, then she threw the car into reverse and roared out of the parking lot.

"What did you say to her?" Will asked, watching the dust settle.

"What did *I* say to her? When I came out here, I found her crying because of *you*."

He turned to me. "So, you were the little mouse who left food on the counter. Kawasaki might show up and cite us for improper storage of fresh produce."

"I might cite you myself," I said.

Will turned and went back inside the restaurant. Darn it! He did it again. He changed the subject, got me off track, and left without answering me. No wonder he made such a good general manager.

I sat on a marble bench beneath the shade of a new cobalt awning. Somehow all of these bits and pieces of information added up to the real murderer, but the more I learned, it seemed, the further away I moved from the truth. At least during an inspection, the food can't hide what's wrong with it. If it's spoiled, it smells bad. If the temperature is too low, the numbers on the thermometer don't go high enough. And it doesn't try to give me excuses about why it's been allowed to reach room temperature. How did police detectives stop themselves from going mad as a March hare from all the dead ends and answers to questions that only seemed to generate more questions?

I went back inside the restaurant, but couldn't find Will anywhere. I even checked the men's room and called the restaurant's number, but got no answer. The pears and mint were where I had left them on the counter, but I had lost interest in making the effort, so I took them back to the walk-in and returned the honey to its hiding place.

I had killed the two hours I needed to and took off for the jail. At least Ursula couldn't run away.

On the weekends, the jail split the alphabet in half, so instead of waiting with one fifth of Austin's criminal's loved ones as I had done the night before, I waited with half of them. A nice woman traded time slots with me, and thirty minutes later, I sat across from Ursula. The last time I had seen her, she looked tired and scared. Now she looked tired and ticked off.

"I am so sick of this place," she said when she picked up the receiver. "Someone's always crying or screaming or banging on the bars. I never sleep. I think I have fleas. And have I mentioned that the food is unconscionable?"

"Sorry," I said.

During my wait, I had decided to test her. All of the information I had uncovered clearly showed that there was as good a chance that she had killed Évariste as that she hadn't. At this point, her only defense had been that she didn't have time. I didn't like it, but I had to know if I was wasting my time trying to prove her innocence. I decided to fire facts at her and gauge her reaction. I didn't know what I was looking for, but knew I would find something.

"Will opened the restaurant last night," I said.

"Yeah? How'd it go?"

"They were slammed. Trevor took over the kitchen."

Ursula sat up and looked at me. I could tell she hadn't gotten that far in her thought process. "Chef Trevor." She grimaced. "I'll bet he just loves that."

"Maybe not."

"Now he knows what it's like," she said. "He used to tell me he could run that kitchen with his face, that he didn't need words, just the look on his face that told everyone he meant business."

"Well, he *is* twenty-five," I said. "He's chronologically predisposed to bravado."

She laughed and I had the feeling she had recalled a memory of him in some other context. Whatever it was, it released her from jail for a moment.

"The guys must have been reacting to the scowl on his face," I said. "They stayed in the weeds most of the night. But they got through it."

"We always get through it," she said. "The clock ticks, time passes, customers have to go home whether they're satisfied or not."

"Did you know that Will Denton is an investor in Markham's?" I asked.

"Will Denton? No, I already told you. Mitch wanted to partner with Évariste."

"That's not what's happening."

"What are you talking about?"

"Did you know that Évariste already owned two percent of Markham's?"

The look in her eyes told me she was hearing that for the first time. I took a childish satisfaction in finally knowing something she didn't. I waited while Évariste's behavior started to make sense for her as it had for me—acting as if he owned the kitchen and treating Ursula and her staff as if they existed to be commanded by him. Finally she said, "Why would Mitch tell me he was in negotiations with Évariste?"

"Maybe to get you used to the idea before he told you the real story." That was something Mitch would do to ease the pain. "Why would Mitch need investors?"

196

"How should I know?" she asked. "I'm obviously not esteemed enough for him to confide in me."

"I know exactly how you feel." Betrayed and unimportant. Exponentially compounded by the fact that she was behind bars, isolated from any familiarity or stability. "I know you're hurt, but I need you to help me help you. Why would Mitch need investors?"

"Any of the usual reasons, I guess. He wants to buy another restaurant or he's in debt from this renovation and needs a way out."

"My father has never been in debt," I said. "What about Nina?"

Ursula's glare could have melted the Plexiglas between us.

"You'll try to blame my mother for everything, won't you?"

"What are you talking about?"

"I know you refuse to believe this, but my mother loves Mitch."

"Along with the status of being married to a successful restaurateur."

"My mother isn't perfect, but she's not the monster you make her out to be, Poppy. Who's been with Mitch at the hospital around the clock? Who got him to finally see a doctor about his dizzy spells? You think Mitch playing golf is amusing, but he's finally exercising, and he's having fun. And it's because of my mother."

"What I see is your mother bending my father to her will. She wasn't satisfied after cutting off Mitch's ponytail and gutting their house. Oh, no. She had to ram her schnoz into the restaurant. Make Mitch spend thousands on fine Corinthian leather chairs and fancy white tablecloths. She hired a lighting consultant, for Pete's sake!"

"Mitch agreed to all of that."

197

"What needed a makeover was the kitchen. That stove is older than me. But no one sees the kitchen, so Nina ignored it." I snorted. "Except for all the new uniforms Mitch had to buy because she changed the logo, too."

I felt my heart rate speed up, but not from anger. I had finally jogged loose what had been bothering me about the crime scene. "The new Markham's logo. Évariste had it on his chef's coat that night."

"So?"

"It wasn't on any of his other coats. I saw them in BonBon's room. And they were white."

She looked at me impatiently. Or was it guiltly?

"He wore his red coat special that night," I said. "To send you a message."

"What? That he needed a lot of attention? I got that message the minute he waddled through the door."

"That he was now in charge of your kitchen." I didn't want to ask her, but I had to. "Did you kill Évariste?"

Ursula's face crumbled into a mixture of fury and disbelief before she hung up. And then she stood up and, without a glance back at me, walked through the door that led back to her cell.

I had heard of prisoners preferring incarceration to the outside world, but Ursula hadn't been inside long enough to associate bars with hard time rather than happy hour. Her bizarre behavior left me with two assumptions. Either she couldn't believe I thought such a thing or the police had arrested the right person. And how could I *not* think such a thing when faced with such overwhelming evidence?

But I couldn't stop now. I had to know without a doubt whether Ursula killed Évariste. My murder investigation was on hold, however, until I could track down Belize or talk to Trevor later when he arrived for work.

Even if I couldn't solve this murder, the mystery of the partnership with Évariste needed to be resolved. I could have waited for Mitch to get out of the hospital, but I don't like not having all the answers, and it's not in my nature to wait around for them.

I parked in the public lot next to the Driskill and called BonBon's room from my car. My sneakiness last time may have made me as welcome to her as a run in her stocking, so I asked the hotel operator to connect me with her room. When she answered, I told her my name and asked if she would meet me.

"For what?" she asked, sounding bored.

"I want to talk to you about Évariste." I heard her exhale and imagined smoke swirling around her lipsticked lips. I almost sneezed. "Please?" I said before she could say no. "We can meet in the bar."

"I will give you ten meenoots."

The bar at the Driskill is the kind of place that encourages a native Texan to indulge her fantasy of being the favored daughter of a wealthy cattle baron. The drinks are pricey, but I love the rough-hewn elegance of the cowhide chairs, leather sofas, and wooden tables. Take out the furnishings and remove the interior walls, and you could exercise a few stud horses around the perimeter.

I entered the bar from the street and waved to the bartender, Brian, who was speaking with two sunburned tourists. Brian is a drummer in the band The Tenders, and sometimes Jamie sits in for him.

I found BonBon tucked away in the alcove near the elevators and restrooms. It looked like she had tripped off the elevator and plopped into the first chair she came to.

As soon as I sat down, Brian arrived to take our order. It was much too early for cocktails, but people who drink take notice of people who don't, so when BonBon ordered a vodka martini, I ordered a gin and tonic. I loathe gin, which is why I order it when I am expected to drink but don't want to.

In her red suit tailored to make the most of every curve, Bon-Bon looked more like a party girl ready for a night of gambling at the casinos in Monte Carlo than a young widow grieving her murdered husband. She couldn't be older than thirty.

"BonBon," I said. "I want to tell you how sorry I am about Évariste. All of us are. Mitch and Nina are very troubled by all of this." She looked at her watch and then at me. "And your sister? Is she also very troubled?"

"Stepsister. She's sorry that he died, of course, but Ursula did not kill your husband." Probably.

Brian arrived with our drinks and BonBon recited her room number in French, then shook her head at her error and repeated the number in English. She motioned for him to bring her another drink before she had even touched the first. She appeared calmer than she had been the first two times I had seen her. Perhaps serenity was her natural state and I had caught her in some bad moments right before and right after Évariste's death.

200

She took a deep swallow of her drink that would have given Dean Martin pause, but she didn't even blink. "Then who killed him?"

"I don't know yet," I said, squeezing lime into my drink. "That's why I wanted to talk to you."

She took another swallow of her martini and my eyes fixed on the olives in her glass. I should have eaten those pears.

"Okay, talk," she said.

"You know that Évariste was in a partnership at Markham's with Mitch and Nina, Will Denton, and three other men."

"*Oui*. Yes. Of course," she said.

Yes, of course, everybody knew. "Were he and Will in any other ventures together?"

"Ventures?" she asked, taking an olive into her mouth. I was glad it wouldn't go to waste. "What does this mean, 'ventures'?"

I suffered a sip of gin. "Were Will and Évariste partners in anything else?"

BonBon pulled a pack of cigarettes and an ebony cigarette holder from her purse. I thought only Cruella de Vil and Batman's nemesis, the Penguin, used those things any more. She inserted a cigarette into the holder, then ignited the tip with a lighter. I tried to stifle a sneeze and sounded like a baby gurgling her first word, *kee*.

Brian returned with her martini and told BonBon that the Driskill bar was nonsmoking. BonBon took another drag of her cigarette and blew the smoke toward him. "*Comment?*" she asked innocently, then took another greedy drag.

He winked at me, then produced a small glass ashtray from his pocket and held it out to her. "*Défense de fumer,*" he said, smiling graciously. "*S'il vous plaît.*"

BonBon shrugged, then plucked her cigarette from its holder and tamped it out in the ashtray. She had gotten her nicotine fix. I suspected she knew there was no smoking in the bar. In fact, a city ordinance forbids smoking in all public places in Austin.

She sipped her fresh martini, recrossed her legs, then said, "What is your question?"

"Did Will and Évariste invest in anything else besides Markham's?"

"We invested, yes, in a few restaurants."

"In Austin?"

"Certainly not," she said as if I had suggested Africa. "Las Vegas, Phoenix, Miami, some place in California."

"How are they doing?" I asked. "In light of . . . uh . . . Évariste's death."

She tapped her empty cigarette holder absently against her front teeth. "They are gone."

"Were they sold or did they go out of business?"

"What does it matter?" she said impatiently. "They are gone." I couldn't stand it any more. "Can I have an olive?" I asked. She shoved her glass toward me. "Take them."

I slid an olive off the plastic sword with my teeth. The vermouth tasted strong. "I want you to know that Markham's is honoring Évariste's memory by serving his food this weekend."

She pulled the ebony stick from her mouth and demanded, "Who is making his food?"

Her reaction startled me. I thought she might think Ursula had been sprung from jail. "The restaurant's sous chef, Trevor Shaw, is filling in."

"*Mon dieu!*" she cried, leaping to her feet and sweeping into the elevator that had opened as if it understood French.

"*Mon dieu,*" I repeated, leaning back on the couch. Trevor?

Brian returned to check on us. "Everything okay over here?" He picked up BonBon's empty martini glass and napkin in one expert move.

"Just dandy," I said. "I hear you've been kickboxing."

"Not very well." He winced as he extended his left arm. "Jamie may need to fill in for a couple more weeks."

"Do you know that woman I was with?"

"Not by name, until today when she gave me her room number. But she comes in here a lot. One of the other guys she's with usually buys the drinks." He laughed. "I had to learn how to say 'No smoking, please' in French because she always pretends not to understand when I say it in English."

"Three guys?" I asked. "Mid-fifties, dressed in suits?"

He nodded. "Usually three. Sometimes four."

Mon dieu.

TWENTY-TWO

I CONSIDERED FOLLOWING BonBon to her room, but she was upset, or maybe insane, and I didn't want a replay of the bloody fries incident. I might need her later, so I let her go and headed back to Markham's.

Trevor wasn't around, or rather, I didn't see his motorcycle in the parking lot, although at one o'clock it should have been there. He needed to check reservations, oversee the prep, and develop the specials for the evening. Surely he hadn't already become so full of himself he thought he could skip that part. Not even Mario Batali was that good.

As I sat in my car thinking about my next move, Trevor roared into the drive and skidded to a stop near the side of the building. I waited for him to park and remove his helmet so I could gauge his mood. He walked with his head down, hands shoved into his front pockets. He didn't look happy, but that wouldn't stop me. I met him halfway in the parking lot. He didn't see me until he stepped on my shadow.

"Hi Trevor," I said. "Everything okay?"

"Poppy, hey, what are you doin' here?" I'm used to cooks not being excited to see me, but this was a first for Trevor. Everything about him looked disappointed.

"My last name is on the sign out front," I joked. "What are you doing here?"

"I, uh, I'm cookin' tonight." He was way off his usual game of banter and flirtation. I had never seen him this serious. Even his cocky standing slouch looked a little meek around the edges.

"Can I ask you about something?"

He checked the time on his phone. "I'm way late," he said, walking past me toward the door. "Later, okay?"

"I'd prefer to talk now."

He stopped and walked back to me. "Yeah, okay."

"What were you doing around the time Évariste was killed?"

A nervous laugh caught in his throat. "What kind of question is that?" he asked. When I didn't answer, he said, "You were standin' right next to me and saw me gettin' slammed from all the orders, tryin' to stay out of the weeds."

Actually, I hadn't been in the kitchen when Évariste died, so I couldn't vouch for Trevor, or Ursula. But he didn't need to know that. "So, do you think you talked to Belize in her car before or after he was killed?"

Trevor exhaled hard and looked away. "Before or after?" I demanded. I was getting good at pretending I knew more than I did.

He squinted up at the sun. "I have no idea."

I have always disliked that answer. "No idea about what?"

Trevor and I roasted on the frying pan of the blacktop like two bratwursts. He turned his head to wipe his upper lip on his sleeve.

"Before, okay?" Then he told me he had been dating Belize for a couple of months. She insisted that he not tell anyone and said that if he did, she would deny it and stop seeing him.

Trevor and Belize? That was like finding out Justin Timberlake was dating Sandra Bernhard. "Do you know why she wanted your relationship to be a secret?"

"I figured she didn't want Ursula to find out, which was fine with me. It wasn't a big deal, except when Évariste put his hairy paws all over her and I had to pretend it didn't bother me."

So that's what had set him off. "You call threatening him with a meat cleaver pretending it didn't bother you?"

He hung his head. "Not one of my finer moments. Poor guy didn't even know what he did to tick me off."

"Belize told me you had a smug look on your face that night in her car. What were you two talking about?"

"Smug?" He looked surprised. "I wasn't smug, I was happy. Belize was early-on that night, so she got to leave early, right? Usually when we're workin' the same shift, we'd find a way to hook up. If I was already at the restaurant, she'd come to work a few minutes early and call me when she was in the parkin' lot. Well, not the parkin' lot. She'd wait down the street so no one would see us. You know how Ursula is about takin' personal phone calls, so I'd leave my phone on vibrate and feel it go off in my pocket. Then I'd take a quick break and we'd meet in her car."

"How did you get away that night?"

"I said I burned myself and needed to bandage it. Once I was off the line and in the dry storage, it was easy for me to sneak out the back door."

206

Tributaries of sweat sprang out on my neck and ran down my back and chest toward my waistband, but the heat wasn't just from the sun. Trevor's attitude burned me, too. He was the sous chef. He knew better. "I can't believe you left everyone hanging just so you could feel up some waitress in her car!"

"Look, normally, I wouldn't have done that on such a busy night, especially when we were so behind, but I wanted to tell her—" He stopped, then said, "I just wanted to see her."

"You wanted to tell her what?"

His cell phone rang. "It's Shannon," he said looking toward the back door, then held up a finger to me while he flipped it open. "I'm almost there," he said and closed it.

He started to walk away, but I hooked a finger around his belt loop and drew him back. "Tell me what you wanted to tell Belize."

"It doesn't matter now," he said, pulling away.

"It matters to me and it might matter to Ursula. What were you so smug about?"

"I told you, I wasn't smug, I was happy." His lips tightened then relaxed. "Okay, one night Évariste didn't want to go back to his hotel, so he asked if I'd go have a drink with him. I took him to the Ginger Man and he was drinkin' all of these German beers, gettin' really drunk, and he asked me what would I think about workin' for him. I told him it would be an honor and a privilege to work with one of the greatest chefs of this century."

"You actually said that?"

He laughed. "I was a little drunk too, plus he loved to hear stuff like that. Anyway, we drink a couple more beers and he offers me a job. He asks me to be his personal sous chef and travel around with him."

That explained the change in Évariste's behavior that Shannon had been so envious of: "Opportunity of a lifetime," I said.

He pulled a cigarette from behind his ear. "It would have been. The job would be me preparin' ingredients for him, then helpin' him as he worked. I'd be in from the beginnin' of every recipe. He already took some of my suggestions when he was here. I think that's why he offered me the job. He said I had a natural talent."

"You couldn't ask for a better compliment. What did Ursula think about her favorite sous chef being drafted by her arch-enemy?"

"She didn't know yet. Évariste didn't want me to tell anyone. That night at the Ginger Man, right after I accepted the job, he got serious for a minute. He said it would be best if no one at Markham's knew about his plans. He needed to finalize some other deal before my job was official." He lit his cigarette from a pack of matches. "I told him I had to tell Ursula so she could start thinkin' about a replacement for me. After another pint of Guinness, he finally said okay, I could tell her, but I should make sure she didn't tell anyone else. I was supposed to let her know the night of the party."

"You were okay with leaving Belize?"

"Yeah. We weren't datin' that long. It's not like I'm in love with her or anything."

"Just territorial."

"What can I say?"

"Évariste still wanted you to work for him even after you threatened him?" I have never understood how men could want to kill each other one day, then be best buddies the next.

208

"Business is business and Évariste recognized talent when he saw it." He smiled. He did look a little smug. "I thought I had blown it with him, but I apologized later, and he said everything was cool." He tapped ashes onto the blacktop. "To be honest, Belize is startin' to bug me. She's real secretive, and always makin' a big deal out of little things."

"What is she secretive about?"

He glanced at the back door. "Besides us datin'? Everything. She never told me where she lived, never talked about her family. And you know how the waiters always brag about how much money they make or if they get a really big tip? Belize never does that. That's part of what made me notice her in the first place. She seemed different."

"Is something going on with her and Will?"

He pulled up the bottom of his t-shirt and dried his forehead. "I thought the same thing. When I asked her about it, she said she was a waitress and he was her manager, and that was all there was."

"Do you think they're having an affair?"

"If I'm her type, then he's definitely not. But I get the feelin' he knows we're datin'. I don't know why Belize would have told him of all people, but I think she did."

"Do you think—"

His cell phone rang again but he didn't answer it. "I really have to get in there."

"Just one more question."

He looked up at the sky. "Pah-pee!"

"Why did Belize come back to the restaurant that night?"

"No idea." He started toward the back door. "She told me she was goin' home."

I followed him. "If Belize found Évariste on her way back inside, why didn't you see him?"

He stopped and his face turned serious. "I don't know. I was so wound up from everything—the busy night, the offer from Évariste, seein' Belize. I was runnin' to get back, so I wasn't payin' attention to anything except how mad Ursula would be at me for leavin' the line for so long. I wish I had found him. To spare Belize."

I had lied to Trevor. I had one more question. "Do you know why BonBon would be concerned that you're cooking Évariste's recipes?"

The back door banged open and Shannon stood in the doorway. "Dude, where have you been?"

Trevor looked relieved and vaulted past me into the kitchen. Shannon held the door open. "Are you coming or going?" he asked me.

"Going," I said.

I wanted to get home and sift through all I had learned in the past few hours, but since my home had been barbequed and I didn't have a key to the Johns' house, I called Jamie and asked if he needed to review any coffee houses while I bounced around ideas with him. We agreed on Mozart's.

It was too hot to sit outside, and I found Jamie waiting for me in the second room at a table near the front windows that overlooked Lake Austin. Two empty espresso cups sat next to his reporter's notepad. He watched a boat loaded with bikini models motor slowly toward the dam. A woman pretending to read a book watched him from two tables over.

I sat down across from him. "The last time I wore a bathing suit was when we went swimming in Barton Springs last summer."

"That was a great day," he said.

I hadn't meant to stir that particular memory and quickly changed the subject. "If the parking wasn't so horrendous, I'd come here more often."

"Parking will get a mention in my review." He pointed to a cup. "You want one?"

"Maybe later."

He clasped his hands together and laid them on the table. "So, what has Ursula's private dickette learned today?"

I told him about overhearing Will and Belize arguing in Markham's kitchen, then about talking to Belize in her car, then my visit with Ursula and my conversation with Trevor. I skipped over my meeting with BonBon for the time being because the murder was more important.

"You have been busy, haven't you?"

"And lucky."

"That gives us one less suspect, doesn't it? If Trevor was going to be apprentice to one of the hottest chefs in the world, he'd be a fool to kill him."

"You're right, but a lot of murders don't make sense, so I'm not ready to rule him out. You hit on a reason for Trevor *not* to kill Évariste, but he could have plenty of other reasons to do it. His jealousy over Belize could eclipse his career aspirations."

"From what you told me, he doesn't seem that into her."

"He could have been lying about his feelings for her."

211

"It does seem odd that Trevor didn't see a red blob lying in the grass on his way back inside. He could have killed Évariste on the way to or from Belize's car."

"Belize could have killed him, then, on her way back to the restaurant. She stabs him, then I come into the picture and she has to wait me out, then she runs inside screaming and says she found him."

"That's possible. And we still can't rule out Ursula," he said. "Especially since she knew Évariste owned two percent of Markham's and was going to be her boss."

"Ursula didn't know about that until I told her."

"I thought you said she did know."

"She thought Mitch was in the negotiation stage with Évariste, but didn't know he already owned two percent."

"Are you sure?" he asked. "That doesn't seem like something that should be kept from the chef."

"This is Mitch we're talking about. He plays a lot of things close to the vest. He didn't even tell his own daughter."

"Regardless, whether Ursula knew it was a done deal or thought it was pending, Évariste was a threat."

"I know it looks bad," I said, "and if things proceed against her, she's in it for the long haul. So I need to find the real killer toot sweet."

"I have no doubt you will." He stood and stretched, his t-shirt riding up, revealing a glimpse of his innie and a hint of a six pack. His biceps weren't the only things he had been toning. He looked down and caught me staring.

"I'll take that coffee now," I said. My face felt warm.

"Coming right up, babe."

When he returned, I asked him about Will's business partners.

"Still working on that. I haven't found out anything through my restaurant sources, so I'm widening the net. Knowing their names would help."

I sipped my black coffee, which didn't taste as good without a shot of maple syrup. "Will won't discuss anything with me and I can't bother Mitch right now."

"Nina?"

"If I have to, but I may have been successful in getting her to stop speaking to me altogether. In the meantime, try to get to them through Will."

I told him about my meeting with BonBon to get information about the partnership. "I didn't learn much from her, but Brian told me she comes in there with four men, three of them in suits, who I assume are Will's partners, so the fourth is probably Will."

Jamie looked out the window toward the marina. "Nothing odd about that." He turned back to me. "As Évariste's business partner, she owned, owns, two percent of Markham's."

I hadn't thought about that. "Okay, but listen to this." I put my elbows on the table and leaned in. "When I happened to mention that Trevor was cooking Évariste's dishes, she shot out of her chair like I'd told her where she could find fifteen Dalmatians."

"The more you dig, the deeper it gets, doesn't it?"

"And my shovel keeps hitting Trevor at the bottom of the hole."

TWENTY-THREE

I LEFT JAMIE TAKING notes for his review and went back to the restaurant. Belize was pulling out of the employee parking lot as I pulled in. I motioned for her to stop, but she kept her eyes forward, ignoring me. She had probably been begging Will for her job back. It happens all the time, waiters quitting in a huff only to slink back when their rent is due or their party buddies stop buying them drinks.

I parked next to Trevor's motorcycle and saw a message written in vivid red lipstick on the black vinyl seat: "CALL ME!!!" Why do people use multiple exclamation points? One is enough, and often one too many.

Belize must be desperate. But about what? And why drive all the way here when she could just call Trevor, or open the back door and see him face to face? Perhaps Trevor had turned off his phone or she didn't want to take the chance of seeing Will if she went inside. But the method of the note wasn't friendly. In fact, it seemed threatening. Did they break up? Or maybe they had gotten into an argument and stopped speaking. What was so urgent? Jamie was right—it kept getting deeper.

Regardless of why Belize needed to talk to him, she knew he would respond either kindly to her message or unkindly to her method. He couldn't ride his bike until he cleaned the seat, and lipstick didn't come off very easily.

Inside the kitchen, Shannon alternated between two cutting boards, chopping parsley on one and onions on another, wiping his watering eyes with a grill towel. Another prep cook wrapped bacon slices around stuffed artichokes and poked them with toothpicks. And Amado scrubbed hardened cheese off large baking pans, preparing to run them through the dishwasher. The atmosphere, though, seemed tense rather than pressured.

Shannon jerked his head to the side when he saw me. "If you're looking for Trevor, he's in the walk-in. Conceiving." He set down his knife to put air quotes around the last word.

I opened the door and almost ran into the blond Adonis on his way out. "Hello again, Poppy," he said, no welcome in his voice. "Here to lend a hand?" Pure swagger. He placed a carton of eggs on the counter. "We're gettin' more behind with every minute." He looked at Shannon, who answered him with his own accusing glare, then went back to work. Cooks never think they have enough time to prep.

"I need to talk to you," I said.

"Four Corners is hostin' a gallery opening tonight and I have no idea what to make for a special." The Johns usually served wine and finger food, but a lot of people would dine at Markham's before attending the opening.

Trevor at a loss? Not likely. More likely he didn't want to answer any more questions. I played along anyway. "Well, the show is for a Catholic Hispanic artist with six sisters and a matchmaking mother."

"So that means I should serve . . .?"

"Fish," I said. "With some sort of tomato-y sauce."

"Vera Cruz?"

Not very imaginative. "Perfect."

I followed him back into the walk-in. Once inside, he turned to me and said, "If people didn't know you had a job, they might mistake you for my intern." Whatever had been weighing on his mind in the parking lot earlier had been lifted.

"I thought of another question to ask you."

"Oh, goodie." He started gathering tomatoes, garlic, and jalapeños for the Vera Cruz sauce.

"Did you know that Évariste already owned two percent of Markham's?"

He stopped with his hand on a jar of capers and slowly turned to look at me. "Since when?"

"Oh, goodie. I finally had his full attention. "I don't know since when. I only just found out myself."

Trevor pulled the jar off the shelf and handed it to me. "That little Napoleon must have been buildin' an empire. He said he was goin' to be the next Emeril."

"Seriously?"

"Actually, he said Emeril would be callin' himself the next Évariste. That guy was trippy."

"How so?"

"Full of himself, but at the same time kind of . . . encouragin', even when he was yellin'. It's like you knew he really cared about the food. He knew his stuff."

"I'm really sorry this happened to him," I said. And I meant it.

"Me too, but now I need to make things happen for myself. Évariste made me see how much I already know. I have talent that I've been wastin'."

Wasting? I felt my throat constrict around the verbal thrashing I wanted to give him. But I swallowed and said, "Being second in command under one of the best chefs in Austin is a waste?"

He scanned the shelves for more ingredients. "It's not about Ursula. But, she didn't go to culinary school, you know?"

No, it was about the divide between the two kinds of chefs in this world. The first kind were chefs like me and Ursula who worked our way through the ranks, some of us starting as dish-washers, learning and earning our way into a respectable position, perfecting our craft on-the-job by expensive trial and error. The other kind were the formally trained chefs who attended culinary academies where mistakes were included in the price of admission. They sat in air-conditioned classrooms and took notes on the perfect temperature to cook a sea bass. They arrived in the kitchen wearing a pleated toque and a sense of entitlement.

One kind isn't better than the other, because regardless of how a chef comes to the job, at the end of the night, you either got it done or you didn't. How it gets done is a matter not of education, but of attitude.

"Her lack of a formal education never seemed to bother you before Évariste came on the scene," I said. "She taught herself everything she knows, and then she taught you. Your talent is her talent."

"Look, I'm grateful for everything she's done for me. It's just that Évariste went to the *Cordon Bleu*. He has a Michelin star. He knows food like Stevie Ray Vaughan knows the guitar."

"Stevie Ray was self-taught. And you think that Évariste's opinion of you—or your opinion of yourself because of what he said—is more valuable to you than Ursula's?" Even though I knew what he meant, he didn't have the right to discount Ursula as some sort of home cook.

"Come on, Poppy, that's not fair. You know I respect the heck out of Ursula. I know I wouldn't be where I am if it weren't for her."

I wanted to make him confirm his last statement in writing. I wanted him to take out a sheet of paper and make a list of every technique, every recipe, every skill he had learned from Ursula or in Ursula's kitchen, which he was working in only because of Ursula. Who taught him how to manage people? Who taught him diplomacy? Who showed him how to deal with suppliers and managers and owners you didn't agree with or get along with? Who showed him how to do the same thing day after day and make it look easy and fresh and fun? Who taught him how to do what he needed to do to get the food out, because all that ever matters is getting the food out? Arrogant little Narcissus.

"You'd still be prepping enchiladas at a school cafeteria if it weren't for her."

"Maybe yes, maybe no."

I couldn't tell if his tone was only slightly less cocky or slightly more contrite. I looked into his eyes and saw craftiness and ambition. And I knew right then that an idea I had only toyed with had become a true possibility: Trevor really could have killed Évariste and then taken advantage of subsequent events to further his career.

However, I hadn't gone to Markham's to argue with Trevor about his job. "Why is BonBon upset that you're cooking Évariste's recipes?"

"Where do you get this stuff?"

"You'd be surprised how often it just falls into my lap," I answered. "So?"

He pulled a white tub of something from a top shelf. "First of all, Will doesn't want to serve Évariste's recipes. He wants me to come up with my own dishes."

I looked around the walk-in, the shelves filled floor to ceiling with raw ingredients. "What about all of his food we have for the next two days?"

"I'll use up the vegetables, but Will said he'd take care of the wildlife."

"And second?"

He looked puzzled for a moment, then, "Believe it or not, BonBon doesn't confide in me."

"Fair enough," I said. It probably didn't matter what BonBon's problem was, especially in light of Trevor's first reason. "Why aren't you speaking to Belize?"

"What makes you think that?"

"Don't worry about that, Trevor. Just tell me what's up with you and Belize."

"Nothing's up." His voice had lost his sharp edge.

"When was the last time you talked to her?"

He thought for a moment. "A couple of hours ago, I guess. I came here straight from her place." He held up his hand. "No, wait, I talked to her about an hour ago. She called and said she needed to talk to me about somethin'. I was busy and said I'd call her later."

I looked at him, trying to gauge whether he was telling me the truth, assuming that he wasn't.

"Cripes, Poppy!" he yelled, taking his phone out of his pocket. He punched some buttons, then held the screen in front of my face so I could see proof of an incoming call from Belize that lasted two minutes. "What does the last time I talked to my girlfriend have to do with anything?"

Before I could answer, his phone vibrated in his hand and he almost dropped it. I had time to register the Austin area code and caught the last three digits: 911, and either a 4 or a 7 before it.

Trevor looked at the screen, hit the "End" button to stop the phone from vibrating, and dropped it into his pocket. "I can't mess around with this anymore," he said.

I couldn't keep him from his job any longer if I wanted there to be a restaurant for Ursula and Mitch to come back to. I gathered a few more green bell peppers for the sauce and followed him to the prep station where I left him issuing orders to Shannon.

In the parking lot, I stood next to my Jeep and looked again at the glossy red-lettered note on Trevor's seat. Now this really didn't make sense. Why did Belize write that note if he said he would call her later? Had Trevor lied to me about talking to her? I didn't get a look at the date and time, so he could have shown me an old call. He also could have lied about the subject of the call. Perhaps they just argued some more and he hung up on her, so she drove over and splattered that note on his seat.

I called Jamie and left a message asking him to see if he could look up the partial phone number I caught, then I took off for the Johns' gallery to get a house key.

I had a key when they lived to my right. They traveled often to visit artists they could turn into the hot new thing or to view estate sales, hoping to unearth a forgotten art collection. I used to take care of their yappy, high-strung Maltese named Judy. She had been run over in the driveway of the new house by the moving company the Johns hired to move them two doors down. John With poured acid on the concrete to remove the blood stain, which it did. But now the clean spot acted as a reminder of Judy's death.

The Johns hadn't traveled much since they moved to the new house, in part because of grief over Judy, in part because they stayed busy with home renovations, and in part because they didn't need to go hunting for artists anymore. Four Corners was becoming well-known as a gallery that could launch a career. Painters, sculptors, and photographers had started to call them.

When I walked into the gallery, I saw John With standing on a ladder, adjusting a spotlight according to John Without's directions. "Not like that!"

I stood behind John Without and mimicked his head bobs and hand motions, which made John With laugh, a sound as comforting and rich as a glass of merlot.

"What's so funny?" John Without asked.

He extended his hand toward me. "Say hello to Poppy Markham."

John Without whirled around and rolled his eyes. "Just what we need. Another distraction."

"I came to get a key to the house," I said, "then I'm gone."

221

"Hang on," John Without said, exasperated. "My keys are in back."

John With descended the ladder and stood next to me as we faced the glass picture. He embraced me in a one-armed hug and said, "How are you holding up?"

I relaxed into his safety. "I'm concerned for Ursula and worried about my house."

"She'll come out okay." He wrapped his other arm around me and squeezed me into the sweetest, most genuine embrace I'd had in a long time. "You'll both be okay."

"Thanks," I said, wanting so much to believe him. I looked at the piece they had been lighting, a stained-glass rendering of an Aztec calendar in jewel colors framed by what looked like driftwood. "This looks kind of amateur compared to what you usually represent."

"Isn't it great?" John said, releasing his hold on me. "This guy's an outsider artist."

"Outside of what?"

"Art schools, society, museums. He's self-taught."

"Like a folk artist?"

He shook his head. "A lot of folk artists have gone to art school. This style is called *art brut*, raw art that hasn't been cooked by formal training." He took a step back. "I love the energy of his pieces. And the fact that light can completely change the image. A lot of outsider artists are insane."

Maybe Nina and BonBon were outsider artists. I looked up at him. "Is Rodrigo insane?"

"Possibly," he said as he ascended the ladder to make another adjustment to the light. "But we've been waiting years for an artist like him. Rodrigo is going to put us on the international map."

"Stop!" John Without squawked from the back door, freezing both of us in place. "The light is perfect. Don't touch it."

He walked up to me with a key ring in his hand, then removed a key with a leopard print design on it. "Take mine and I'll have another one made."

"Thanks," I said, "you'll hardly know I'm there."

"Please," John With said from the ladder, "don't feel like you need to live small around us. Make yourself at home."

"What time should Mrs. Jones be back?" I asked.

"Around eight," John Without answered quickly. "You won't need to stay long."

"Because I need to rush home to our kids?" I asked.

"Actually, we told her you're the assistant manager on the late shift at Wendy's and need to supervise the cleaning of the Fryalator."

John With laughed. "We did not, J. We didn't tell her anything, Poppy Markham. Just come by around eight and you can make some excuse whenever you need to leave."

TWENTY-FOUR

MY BROKEN FRONT DOOR and jamb had been expertly repaired. The Johns must have fixed it for me before they left for the gallery that morning. Even with all they had to do to get ready for the party, John With couldn't have done it by himself, so I momentarily disliked John Without a little less because he helped.

My house smelled like the frat boys down the street had roasted a javelina inside. I picked my way around the pieces of drywall that had given up their hold on the ceiling here and there. The worse part of the house was my bedroom where the fire had started. My bed and favorite tapestry comforter had become a soggy, stinking black mess.

My closet sat opposite the wall that had caught fire, so my clothes hadn't burned, but they had been drenched and smelled of smoke. I gathered bras and underwear from my dresser, then went to my office closet where I kept my winter clothes and chose a few light pieces to keep me decent for the next couple of days until I could buy a new wardrobe. I don't like shopping for clothes, but if

I had to, why couldn't it be for a better reason, like I had dropped a size or two?

I stuffed my clothes into one of the canvas bags I use for grocery shopping, then walked next door to the Johns' house. I had been between and among their housewares many times when I checked on Judy during their trips, so I had no curiosity about their stuff. Still, I didn't want to be surprised by anything, like they had become fans of Thomas Kincaid, so I made a cursory review of the house.

They had the best of everything—Ralph Lauren this and Tommy Hilfiger that, teakwood tables, silk window coverings, and a washer and dryer set that looked like it should come with its own astronaut. John With used to be a freelance writer and has traveled the world. I knew that he had the more down-to-earth tastes, because every time I asked them about something funky or cool, it turned out to be part of his dowry. John Without was a professional photographer, a very good one in my unprofessional estimation, and the label hound.

I put some water on to boil, found a couple of crispy carrots in the fridge, then stowed my clothes in dresser drawers lined with rose-scented paper. The fabricated smell of roses makes me nauseous. Real roses I like, but no one ever gets rose essence right. I took out the scented sheets and placed them all in a single drawer.

The whistling kettle called me back to the kitchen. As I poured the boiling water over a rooibos tea bag, I dialed the hospital to check on Mitch. "Stable and resting," the nurse told me. I realized that this whole time, I should have been calling the hospital for information, bypassing Nina altogether.

225

I hung up and laughed at the absurd situation I found myself in: while sitting at my gay neighbors' kitchen table because a murderer had burned my house, I had to confer with a stranger about my father's medical condition because I couldn't be with him in person because my stepmother was keeping me away from him, and my stepsister, who I don't like and who was in jail, accused of murdering a Michelin-rated chef who had visited the restaurant at my father's invitation because he needed investors, was putting all her trust in me to prove that she didn't kill Évariste Bontecou, and doing so was keeping me from my job of saving Austin from botulism, typhoid, and hepatitis.

Jamie called a few minutes later. And oh, yeah, I had to ask for help from my ex-boyfriend whom I haven't spoken to in months because he cheated on me one night with someone I may or may not know.

"That phone number ending in nine-one-one belongs to a lot of interesting parties," he said. "A couple of private individuals, a Mexican restaurant, a Catholic church, Texas Parks & Wildlife, the Attorney General, an apartment complex, a wedding photographer."

"Great," I said. "Who's got time to chase down all of those leads?"

He waited a beat, then said, "It also belongs to the Driskill Hotel."

"No shinola!" I said, sloshing tea onto the table.

"No shinola."

"BonBon."

"Do she and Trevor know each other?"

"She could be giving him French lessons for all I know."

226

"That sounds like frustration talking."

"You think?" I said sharply. "Do you know where I can get some truth serum?"

"What's your next step?"

"Drinks at the Driskill?"

"Give me an hour," he said. "I'm doing a profile of Nigella Lawson and she's supposed to call me right about now."

I hung up, a plan already forming in my mind. To pull it off, I needed a nice camera. I could borrow John Without's Nikon and tripod without asking. He would never know. But the way my luck was running, I would probably trip and fall into a vat of old molasses and owe him $5,000 for damages and another $10,000 for mental anguish. The mental anguish part tempted me, but I did the smart thing and called the gallery to ask if I could use his equipment. He had helped fix my front door, so maybe he would help me again.

"Not even if I liked you," John Without said.

"I'm not going to turn it on," I promised.

"Then go buy one and return it when you're finished."

I didn't want to say what I was about to say, but he left me no choice. "That's going to take a really long time. I'll probably miss the gallery opening. Please give Mrs. Luna my regrets."

Fuming silence, then, "Fine."

I hung up, grinning at my dual victory of getting what I wanted *and* annoying John Without. So much else hadn't been going my way that I drank my tea, enjoying the feeling longer than I should have. I looked out the window and saw my clothes hanging limply in the sun. They looked different, so I walked outside to check on them. Someone had swapped out the hangers for clothespins.

Again I had a strange fleeting thought when I looked at my chef's coat. "What are you trying to tell me?" I asked it.

I couldn't find a parking space near the Driskill, so I parked in the alley by the service entrance and came through the back way, flashing my badge at the security guard, then past the service station, through the café kitchen, into the lobby, up the majestic staircase, and into the cool, dim cavern of the Driskill bar.

I saw Jamie standing at the bar talking to Brian. When he saw me, he picked up his beer and a glass of red wine and walked toward me. His navy-blue t-shirt and faded jeans had just the right amount of cling to his muscular silhouette, his stride just the right touch of saunter in his brown boots. He smiled, and even from a few yards away, it devastated me. My breath caught at the sight of this tall, confident, intelligent, beautiful man I once loved. Still loved, darn it.

We met in the center of the bar near the bronze statue depicting a man about to kill a runaway horse that was dragging his friend whose leg had caught in the stirrup. "Tough decision," Jamie said, handing me the glass of wine. "Shooting the horse to save his friend."

I ran my finger along the small, bronze rifle aimed at the frightened horse's head. "The horse is innocent, but we don't know if the men are. They could have just robbed a bank," I thought about Trevor and how I would have to sacrifice him for Ursula. And then I realized that it wasn't such a tough decision.

We still had a few minutes before our con game started, so I led Jamie to the loveseat near the tiny fake fireplace. He sat against the armrest, and I plopped down right next to him. My head had almost reached his shoulder when I jerked up. I couldn't believe how easily I had fallen into routine.

I shot to the other end of the couch. "How's Nigella?" I asked breezily.

Jamie grinned at my pratfall. "Too busy making canapés for a dear friend's wedding to talk to me. Her assistant promised that Nigella would call tomorrow morning."

I sipped the wine. "This is nice," I said. "What is it?

"Not sure." He looked chagrined. "It's their house wine."

"Big spender."

"You don't know the truth you speak," he said. "Someone earning minimum wage would have to work for an hour to afford it."

"Well, whatever it is, it gets my approval. And you get my thanks." I raised up my goblet and he clinked his glass against it.

"Have you figured out the BonBon/Trevor angle?" Jamie asked.

"Trevor is BonBon's son whom she gave birth to as a teenager and had to give up for adoption to spare her family embarrassment."

Jamie raised both arms, sliding his hands along a marquee headline. "Starring Orlando Bloom and Victoria Beckham."

I took a big sip of wine to wash that thought out of my brain. "Okay, then how about something mundane, like they're having an affair." Trevor has a dangerous but vulnerable quality about him, and appeals to older women. Not even Nina is immune to his allure, often complimenting his tattoos or hair when their paths crossed. She would need smelling salts if she found out that her precious Ursula had gotten a close look at his illustrations.

"That's more reasonable," Jamie said, leaning his head on the back of the couch to look at the hammered copper ceiling. I had an urge to kiss his neck. "How about this," he said. "If BonBon convinced herself that Évariste was sleeping with Belize, she attempted to even the indentations in the bed by sleeping with Trevor."

I was sure Jamie hadn't meant to make me think about his own infidelity, but I was glad he did. It snapped me out of the silly love fog I had been in for the past few minutes. "If Évariste knew about an affair, would he still have offered Trevor a job as his personal sous chef?"

He lolled his head to look at me. "Maybe Évariste offered him the job *because* he was sleeping with BonBon."

"That makes no sense to me."

"To keep an eye on his wife's lover."

"Ah, smart man." I said. "But it seems a bit paranoid. And creepy." I threw out another idea. "BonBon wants to recruit Trevor for one of their restaurants."

Jamie threw it back. "She has plenty of experienced, well-known chefs to choose from."

"Maybe we're looking at it from the wrong point of view. What if Trevor went to BonBon, wanting her to make good on Évariste's offer and she refused?"

Jamie sat up and looked at me. "I like that."

I did too, but then remembered what happened in the walk-in.

"No, that's no good. He got mad when he saw the number and didn't answer his phone."

Jamie returned his gaze to the ceiling and we sat in amiable silence for a few minutes, both of us thinking. One would start to say something, then work out a rebuttal and fall silent again.

"Okay," Jamie finally said, "what if Trevor knew, or suspected, that his girlfriend was having an affair with his new boss. He told BonBon and she asked him to keep an eye on them. Then Évariste is murdered and . . . what?"

"And nothing. That would be the end. No reason for them to speak any more because the affair is over." I felt warm from the wine, or was it Jamie? "They could have planned to murder Éva-riste together. Trevor could easily have stabbed him on his way in from seeing Belize in her car. If he has it in him to kill Évariste and frame Ursula, he would have no problem lying about it."

"Are you suggesting that BonBon master-minded the whole thing and used Trevor's jealousy of Belize to prod him to murder Évariste?"

I answered his question with a nod, then stopped. "What doesn't make sense is why she would want her husband dead."

"It doesn't make sense with the facts you have now."

I banged my fist against the couch. "The entire world has stopped making sense."

He covered my hand with his. "You've seen me through enough investigations to know that this is the storm before the calm."

He interlaced his fingers through mine. "A breakthrough is just around the corner."

His hand felt rough and safe. "It better be."

Jamie sat up and looked around. "I assume we're at the Driskill because of BonBon. Is she going to meet us down here?"

I pulled my hand from his. "BonBon thinks my stepsister killed her husband, and the last time we met she whisked herself into an

231

"elevator without so much as a glance back at me, so no, she's not going to meet us." I didn't mean to come across so condescending and apologized.

"So what's the plan? Or do you just enjoy drinking wage-slave wine while your butt rests comfortably on cow's hide?"

"I called BonBon on the way over here. I said I was your assistant, and made an appointment for you to interview her."

"She agreed to speak with a food journalist?"

I squinched my mouth sideways. Jamie cocked his head. I sipped my wine.

"Who does she think I am?" he asked.

"It's not that bad," I said. "She balked when I asked for an interview, saying that she didn't want to speak of her husband's death. So I appealed to the socialite and publicity hound in her and told her you were a lifestyle reporter who wanted to do a profile on her for the Sunday edition. Front page."

"Her husband was murdered three days ago."

"Yeah, and what does that say about her that she agreed to meet you?"

"She'll know I'm a fake as soon as I walk in the door without a photographer."

I held up John Without's tripod and patted the black canvas backpack that held his camera. "That would be me."

"She'll recognize you," he said, his protest tinged with approval. Jamie didn't become the city's most influential food writer without pulling a few fast ones, and this was a great fast one. I learned from the best.

I pulled out a baseball cap and a pair of tinted glasses and set them on the table. Jamie looked at them, then at me. "That's your disguise?"

"It always worked for Jim Rockford," I said. "Trust me, that woman is so self-absorbed, she won't give me a second glance."

I stood. "Come on, I told her you'd call when you arrived at the hotel."

TWENTY-FIVE

"WHAT'S THE PLAN EXACTLY?" Jamie asked when we boarded the elevator.

"You're interviewing BonBon," I said, untucking my shirt so I would look sloppy and uninteresting.

"I mean what do we really want to know? I can't just ask her if she killed her husband."

I pulled my hair forward to hide more of my face, then snugged the hat down. "Just do your Jamie Sherwood thing. Get her talking about Évariste and go where that leads."

"Right," he said dubiously as the doors opened. "You look like a boy."

"That's the idea." I put on my glasses as we walked down the hall. "Barbara Hershey and Debra Winger."

He knocked on her door. "*A Dangerous Woman*."

The widow Bontecou looked deadly in a black suit and black platform heels. She had twisted her dark hair into a glossy chignon, and wore makeup that would have taken me hours to apply, but had probably taken her only meenoots. I wanted to look up at Jamie's face to see his reaction to her, but didn't want to risk her seeing through my disguise so I kept my eyes on the floor.

She invited us in by leaving the door open and turning her back to us. I couldn't believe what I saw inside. The room looked as if she had just checked in. No piles of clothes, no magazines, no upended shoe boxes. A gleaming silver bucket filled with fresh ice and a bottle of champagne rested in the middle of the table next to two champagne flutes.

"Mrs. Bontecou," Jamie said, extending his hand. "I'm very sorry for your loss."

She turned to face him and I watched her eyes travel from his face to his feet, her contrived smile turning predatory as she discovered a very handsome man standing in her hotel room. "*Merci,*" she purred, placing her hand in his.

"Thank you for meeting with me." He released her hand and gestured toward me. "This is my photographer, Timmy. If it's okay with you, he'll be looking around the room, assessing the props and lighting while we begin the interview."

She looked quickly at Jamie's left hand. "Of course."

Her black stockings swished softly as she walked to the small table in the corner of the room. "*S'il vous plait,*" she said, extending her hand toward the other chair.

I pretended to poke around the room, keeping the two of them in my sights from under the brim of my hat. As predicted, BonBon paid no attention to me. She inserted a cigarette into her cigarette holder and Jamie took the lighter from her and lit it. She beamed at him, then pursed her lips and blew out a long stream of smoke.

I felt a sneeze coming on and pressed my forefinger hard against my upper lip. *Not now*, I pleaded with my sensitive nose. A small sneeze escaped that I managed to turn into a cough. BonBon glanced in my direction, then returned her attention to Jamie.

Jamie removed a small, black voice recorder from his pocket and placed it on her side of the table. He had once told me that people were usually more talkative before he started asking questions on the record, so he didn't turn on the recorder until he needed to.

"How are you holding up?" he asked.

"I am okay, but the children are feeling very low."

Children?

Jamie said, "I didn't know Évariste had children."

"They are my children, from another man. Évariste does not want it mentioned. He says he wants to protect them. From what, I do not know. I think he wants to protect his image."

"How would children hurt his image?" Jamie asked.

"Children always do damage to the image of a playboy, *Monsieur* Sherwood."

Playboy? More like portlyboy.

BonBon looked at the champagne bucket and Jamie took the hint. "Shall I pour?" he asked.

I didn't like the formal tone he had adopted to impress BonBon. She nodded and sucked on her cigarette as Jamie expertly popped the cork and poured. I also didn't like where her eyes lingered. After he sat, she raised her glass and tipped it toward him, then drank deeply.

Jamie sipped from his glass, a small smile on his face that was meant for me. Champagne makes him as silly as a five-year-old with a secret. "His activities must have been difficult for you," he said to BonBon.

"We do each other the favor of not discussing our personal lives. He plays when it is convenient. The more famous he is, the more convenient it is." Her voice sounded shaky. A look of sadness crossed her face, but no tears, then she quickly composed herself. "I thought you were interviewing me, *Monsieur* Sherwood, for the society page."

So much for small talk.

"Yes," he said, turning on the tape recorder and taking out his notepad. "Tell me about your background, Mrs. Bontecou. What would you like the people of Austin, Texas, to know about your life?"

She told him about growing up in Nice, the daughter of a banker and a ballet dancer. How she rebelled against her parents' desire for her to meet wealthy men through the proper social channels, instead preferring to be a cocktail waitress in the casinos in Monte Carlo, which was where she met Évariste. "Évariste tells everyone we met at a casino, yes, but he always forgets to mention that I was serving him cognac and he tipped me one thousand francs each time." She laughed coldly. "Those lies of his do not matter now," she said, taking another swig of champagne, "so I will tell you the truth. It is true that he proposed to me the night of our first meeting, but he was drunk and I said no. *That* he does not tell about."

Too bad Jamie wasn't interviewing her for a real article. This was good stuff.

"Évariste has a drink problem," she continued. "And a gambling problem. And a women problem. Which means we have a

237

money problem." She stubbed out her cigarette and prepared another one, which Jamie dutifully lit for her. This time, she cupped her hand around his and gazed at him through the veil of smoke curling between them.

I shut the bathroom door harder than I needed to. BonBon let out a yip and looked my way, then back to Jamie. "Are you married, *Monsieur Sherwood*?"

Why did she have to keep calling him *Monsieur* like that? Jamie refilled her champagne glass. "Divorced."

"So you know about…how do you say…compromise. About doing what must be done for the sake of the marriage, for the children."

The smoke reached my side of the room, tickling my nose again. I pressed on my upper lip so hard my gums receded. I should have walked into the bathroom to let the urge pass, but didn't want to miss anything. I pressed harder.

"Yes, I do understand," Jamie said. "Were there a lot of compromises in your marriage?"

BonBon wouldn't pay attention to what I did, but she might notice if I didn't do anything. I held out my cell phone as if it were a light meter, then lifted the camera I had slung around my neck and took a couple of photos just to keep her from getting suspicious. It had the opposite effect. I looked up to see her staring at me. I quickly looked away and moved to one of the curtained windows.

"You were speaking of compromises, Mrs. Bontecou," Jamie prompted.

"*Oui*. Yes. Like coming to this God-forsaken town. Ow-steen. With its stupid accents and car jams and rude sales girls with steel sticking out from their faces. I hate this place." She leaned back into her chair, recrossed her legs, and drank more champagne.

"Why did Évariste come to Austin? To Markham's?"

"It does not matter, now," she said, waving off the idea with her cigarette. But I knew it did, and Jamie knew it did. He wrote something in his notepad, waiting her out. She leaned forward in her chair. "Do you want to know something, *Monsieur* Sherwood?"

My heart pounded out exclamation points. This was it!

"I'd like to hear anything you'd like to tell me," Jamie said.

She looked at the tape recorder. "How do you say 'off with the record'?"

Jamie reached over and clicked a button. "Now it's just between us." He gave her a full smile, dimple and all.

She hesitated as if she had changed her mind, but her eyes looked liquid and dreamy. Was she still trying to entice him?

Jamie prodded her. "Évariste had gambling debts."

"*Oui*. Yes."

"Was he in trouble with the people he owed money to?"

"Évariste was to get another Michelin star and we had to increase the standards of the restaurant. Both of them. It took a lot of money."

"Did you borrow the money?"

"Investors came to *Le Château*. We did not want them. Évariste does not like to work for other people. But it was the fastest way. After the second star, we could charge three times the price to twice the people and would pay them off in one year's time."

BonBon stood up and pulled the champagne bottle out of the ice bucket. Ever so subtly, she grazed Jamie's knees with her leg. As she refilled her glass, he looked up at me and winked.

I glared at him. Harmless flirting, until he was drunk and she was drunk and it just happens.

BonBon continued. "Men came into the restaurants and did things their own ways. They cared only about money, and the food suffered. We could do nothing. Our contract stopped us. Las Vegas was busy every night. Americans know nothing about food. But in Monte Carlo, everything is noticed. We had to use the money from Las Vegas for *Le Château*."

"Which meant you couldn't pay off the investors within the year as you had planned," Jamie said. "It must have been a strain to your marriage."

"*Pft*," she said, stubbing out her cigarette. "Everything is a strain."

"Is that why you argued at Markham's the night he was killed?" Her head snapped up. "How do you know about this?"

"There are no secrets in a restaurant, Mrs. Bontecou."

"Of course there are, *Monsieur* Sherwood. Evariste has very many of his own secrets." She didn't wait for Jamie to light her cigarette. "He was smarter than you think." She took a long drag, then leaned back in her chair and blew out the smoke.

And then I started sneezing.

"*Mon dieu!*" BonBon cried. She sat forward in her chair, craning her neck around Jamie to look at me. I turned toward the window, and the sunlight made me sneeze again. *Kee.*

Jamie stood and tried to block her view of me. "Please, let's get back to our interview."

"No!" she said, standing. "I know this noise."

Before she could unmask me herself, I took off my hat and glasses.

240

"You!" Her nostrils flared. "Out from my room!" In an instant she realized that Jamie had been part of the deception. "Both of you. Out!"

Jamie grabbed the tape recorder as BonBon herded us toward the door, cigarette in one hand, champagne glass in the other.

"BonBon, please," I begged, backing away from her. "Ursula didn't kill Évariste. I need to know who did."

Jamie reached the door before I did and opened it, but I wasn't giving up. "Why did you call Trevor?" BonBon stopped at the mention of Trevor's name. I had nothing to lose. "Did you kill Évariste and Trevor helped you frame Ursula?"

She flung the glass against the wall, exploding it into shards and foam. "I did not kill my husband! If Trevor framed your sister, he is on his own."

Jamie twisted my sleeve and pulled me into the hallway just before BonBon slammed the door.

"Darn your sensitive nose," he said on our way to the elevator.

"This nose sniffs out a lot of things people want to hide." I had caught Jamie in his fling because I smelled the other woman's perfume in places that a friendly hug wouldn't reach. I will never forget that fragrance. "We almost had her."

Jamie interlaced his fingers and placed them on top of his head, an unconscious gesture he makes when he feels frustrated.

"Do you think she killed Évariste?" I asked as we stepped into the elevator.

He dropped his arms. "She certainly has a motive and the temper, but gut feeling? No."

BonBon hadn't actually said Trevor framed Ursula, and for all I knew, she doth protested too much about killing Évariste herself,

241

but her comment about Trevor was enough to double my interest in him. "I don't think so either, but I wish I knew why she called Trevor."

"Let's ask him," Jamie said. "I'll drive."

I tucked in my shirt, then took off my hat and ran fingers through my hair. Trevor. Again. I said, "On *Law and Order*, Briscoe and Green talk to someone once and move on."

"Those guys have very good scriptwriters."

We arrived at Markham's around 6:00 PM. Land Rovers, Suburbans, and BMWs idled in the valet line, discharging short skirts, glittery jewelry, and shined shoes. It could only be the Four Corners crowd that early. Jamie drove me around to the back door and said he would wait for me at the bar.

Trevor would say he didn't have time to talk, but a lot of cooks say that to me. I had just taken hold of the door handle, when the door flew open and Trevor stepped out, a lit cigarette dangling from his mouth. "Cripes, Poppy! Again?"

"I'll be done when your cigarette is," I promised, then got to the point. "I just saw BonBon."

His sharp drag on his cigarette let me know that I had his attention. "So?" He overplayed his nonchalance by blowing a perfect ring of smoke toward the sky.

"Why does she want to talk to you?"

"Didn't you ask her when you saw her?"

Yes, and she stopped short of accusing you of murder. "I'm not sure I believe what she told me and I want to hear your version."

"She got it into her head that I have Évariste's recipes."

Recipes? What darn recipes? "Do you?"

"No." He took off his white beanie and ran his hand over the part in his hair, then down his ponytail, pulling out a few loose hairs and dropping them to the ground.

"Then why does she think that?" I asked, trying not to look guilty as I realized the answer. She assumed it earlier when I mentioned that Trevor would be cooking Évariste's food the rest of the weekend. That was why she ran off in the middle of our talk.

"I guess because of the sous chef deal I had with him. He kept them on one of those little keychain things."

"A flash drive?" BonBon had probably trashed her room the day before looking for the drive.

He blew smoke out of his nose. "Yeah. She thinks he gave it to me, but he didn't. She's drivin' me crazy! Callin' me all the time leavin' messages. First threatenin' me, then bribin' me, then promisin' me stuff." He held his cigarette between his lips as he readjusted his hat. "And now Belize thinks I'm cheatin' on her because of a note BonBon left on my bike."

BonBon wrote the note in lipstick? Good thing I hadn't tried to put my wrong assumption into play.

His body jerked and he reached into his pocket. He pulled out his vibrating phone and looked at the screen. "BonBon again. I haven't heard from her for about an hour and thought she finally gave up."

No, she had just been busy giving a fake interview to Jamie Sherwood. "That can't be the only copy of his recipes," I said.

He dropped the phone back into his pocket. "It's not, but it had the latest updates. And BonBon thinks there's some other stuff on there. Something about a deal he was workin' with Mitch. I swear, if I had the thing I'd give it to her just so I'd never have to hear her voice again." He shuddered. "I used to think her accent was sexy."

He held up the cigarette butt to show me he was finished, then let it drop to the ground. "Break's over."

He walked toward the back door, then turned and looked at me. "I'll be glad when all of this is over and you stop thinkin' I eighty-sixed Évariste."

TWENTY-SIX

I'LL BE GLAD WHEN this is over, period, I thought as I walked around the building to the front door. Although I had to admit that, except for someone trying to burn me alive and being forced to share living quarters with John Without, I was enjoying myself. When I investigate health violations, I almost always know what I'm looking for—proof that an owner is serving catfish that his cousin Ed caught at Lake Buchanan or that one of our own has been trading a higher health score for a $4.99 lunch, including chips and a drink. The answer isn't always obvious, but it's always there. I just need to keep digging, keep thinking, keep puzzling, and be patient.

I saw Jamie at the end of the bar, his back against the red brick wall. We waved to each other, and I threaded my way through the well-upholstered crowd that buzzed with mirth and wine-drenched conversations. Instead of talk of investments, tax shelters, and golf handicaps, I heard, "Where was he killed?" "Did you see any blood?" "Do you think she really did it?"

I thought of Ursula walking out on me earlier in jail. I hoped she hadn't given up hope. *Hang on*, I told her, *I'm getting close.* When I reached Jamie, he stood and bent to kiss me on the cheek. "Hello, Timmy."

"*Bon soir, Monsieur Sherwood*," I said, trying to mimic Bon-Bon's accent and tone, which came off more silly than sultry.

I leaned over the bar to get Andy's attention. When he saw me, he held up an index finger and mouthed, "One minute," then went back to pouring pineapple juice into the only blender behind the bar.

Jamie helped me onto his barstool then stood next to me and cupped his hands around the top of a glass of Guinness. "So did you get Trevor to confess?"

I slid his glass out of his hands, then grimaced at my mouthful of bitter stout. "No, but he threw a wrinkle into all the details I've been ironing out." I told him about the flash drive that contained all of Évariste's recipes and other documents that BonBon wanted.

"Trevor insists he doesn't have it."

Jamie gave some thought to this new motive. "Someone could have killed Évariste to get his recipes, or BonBon killed him to get the documents."

"I saw a laptop in BonBon's room when I delivered her duck sandwich. She could have downloaded whatever was on the drive while Évariste was sleeping. No need to kill him just for that."

"Assuming he was coming back to the room at night."

"Good point," I said. "But assuming he was coming back to the room, and everything was being downloaded to the laptop, then BonBon just wants the flash drive to make sure no one else gets their hands on the files."

246

Andy appeared and placed a napkin in front of me. "Sorry for the wait, Poppy." He substituted a look around the bar for an explanation. "Will got his hands on a really nice red. Want to try it?"

"Does a crab crawl sideways?"

"Thought so," Andy said. "It's in Mitch's office. Give me a sec."

I took another sip of Jamie's beer. "I don't know how you can drink that bitter stuff."

"Like this," he said, taking a generous gulp of the dark brown juice. He smacked his lips. "Yum-my."

A bottle blonde with a salon tan tried to squeeze between me and Jamie. She turned her body to face him then cast her doe eyes up. "Excuse me," she said with a hopefulness that he would do anything but excuse her.

That kind of thing happens only when Jamie is drinking at a bar. Or putting gas in his car. Or shopping at the grocery store. Or walking down the street. Or just standing and breathing. It didn't bother me when we dated because I was sure of his feelings for me, but I was no longer sure. We also weren't dating, so logically, I no longer had a claim on him and had no right to be jealous. So why did it feel like jealousy?

"Sure thing," Jamie said, stepping away from the bar to let her in. Then he moved around her to stand next to me again, turning his back to her. "Dennis Hopper and Seymour Cassel," he said.

"You're playing dirty."

"You'd be a lot better at this game if you had misspent your youth watching B movies and playing Galaga."

"Instead of working every night at this restaurant?"

"It boggles the mind that you never saw a single episode of *Dallas*."

247

Andy returned with the wine and poured the deep ruby liquid into an extra-large goblet. If this wine had been under lock and key in Mitch's office, it was not a wine to be gulped. I swirled the wine in the glass and looked at its legs. Jamie nodded his approval. I put my nose into the glass and inhaled the bouquet. Jamie smiled. I took a sip and closed my eyes, enjoying the elixir gliding down my throat and warming my insides. "Mmmm." When I opened my eyes, I put my hand on Jamie's arm then leaned into him and whispered, *"King of the Mountain."*

"Darn. Thought I had you."

I leaned against the back of my barstool so he could see my self-satisfied smirk. "You must have forgotten I'm a fan of Seymour's."

"Yeah, musta," he said, then pointed to my glass. "May I?"

"You may."

He went through the motions I had gone through, but he took them seriously. "Opus One," he said, then took another sip. "Nineteen ninety-seven."

"Showoff."

Jamie called Andy over to show us the label. He was right about the winery and the vintage. "Lot of cake for that wine," he said, rubbing his fingers against his thumb. "Retails for about five hundred a bottle."

Curious about what our customers paid for it, I called Andy back to us. "How much are we selling this for?"

"We're not. It's Will's private stash. He said I should share it with worthy customers." He topped off my glass. "You fall into that category, I think."

I looked at my goblet feeling more worried than worthy. How could Will justify giving away $150 glasses of wine?

248

After we ate a couple of appetizers and finished our drinks, Jamie drove me back to my car near the Driskill before heading to Emo's to play an early set with his jazz band, Zzaj. He didn't ask about my plans for the evening, so I didn't tell him I had agreed to be the pretend wife of a gay man I'm temporarily living with in order to fool an old woman into showing her son's work at an art gallery.

I had to park a few blocks away, and as I stood on the side-walk in front of Four Corners, I understood why. The huge pic-ture window framed a colorful fresco of live models bathed in soft golden light. Artists, clients, critics, photographers, and reporters flowed elegantly around the room like cursive handwriting. Sev-eral stained-glass pieces already had discrete silver "Sold" tags on them. John With was right. Four Corners was finally on its way.

When I walked through the door, I caught sight of a reporter I knew casually, and felt like a dolt. Lots of people there would know me as Poppy Markham, not Poppy Jones. I turned away, but not fast enough. "Miss Markham," she called, shouldering her way through the crowd. "Can I ask you a few questions?"

I panicked and looked around for the Johns. We needed to get this over with before my cover was blown. When the reporter reached me, I cut her off with, "Mitch is fine and Ursula is inno-cent," then found a waiter.

As I accepted a glass of white wine, John Without appeared and grabbed my wrist spilling liquid over my hand. "Hey!"

"Sorry," he said, like he didn't mean it. "John and I just got some bad news and he's not handling it very well."

"What is it? Where is he?"

"That's not important now," he said, one hand on my elbow, the other at the small of my back, guiding me through the room. "Where are you taking me?"

He took the wine glass out of my hand and handed it to a passing waitress. "You need to be my wife tonight."

My feet cemented to the very spot. "No way."

"Poppy, please," he said, pulling me, "we don't have time for this."

I wrenched my elbow away. "The deal is I'm John's wife, not yours. Even if it were an arranged marriage, no one would believe I'd marry you." This is exactly why I don't like doing favors. I knew I shouldn't have threatened him so I could use his camera. I shouldn't have even agreed to this charade in the first place.

He looked at my neck, probably sizing it up for a hand necklace.

"What's going on with John?" I demanded. "Why did the plan change?"

"I don't want to get into it now." He looked around the room, then bared his teeth into a smile at a woman walking through the crowd toward us. She was short, but moved with the bearing and assurance of a rear admiral. Rodrigo's mother, I presumed. John stood by my side and put a stiff arm around my waist. "I'll do anything you want," he said, not moving his lips. "Please just go along."

"Say please again."

He *ghrfed*, then said with absolutely no emotion, "Please."

"And take your hand off me. I might ralph on her."

When the woman stopped in front of us, John removed his hand from my waist and I thought he was going to salute her.

"Mrs. Luna!" he said, all sweet and fake excited, shaking her hand with his right and patting it with his left.

Mrs. Luna turned to me. "This must be your lovely wife." She extracted her hand from John's, who looked as pale as an uncooked biscuit, and lightly touched my arm.

I took a moment to enjoy the look of panic on his face, then said, "Poppy Smith. We're so honored to be showing Rodrigo's work tonight."

John resumed normal breathing, and Mrs. Luna and I made small conversation about her son's life's work. She took me around to see some of her favorite pieces, describing how Rodrigo set traditional Aztec images in stained glass, using old window sashes as frames. John Without stayed on me like a little boy tracking the ice cream man, making sure I didn't expose this farce to Mrs. Luna.

We stopped in front of an eight-foot-tall portrait of a man in a colorful headdress, his barrel chest and muscular legs bare, his vitals concealed behind a blink of a loin cloth. "Montezuma," Mrs. Luna announced proudly. "My Rodrigo spent two years on this."

"Incredible," I said, hoping she didn't notice that the wife of an art dealer couldn't come up with something more arty and descriptive. I turned to John. "Darling, don't you have some shorts like that?"

John Without made a sound like a Chihuahua choking on gristle, but Mrs. Luna laughed. I could tell she liked me and probably found John to be obsequious and perfidious, an accurate reading. I thought she would appreciate me putting him in his place.

Mrs. Luna led us past an Aztec calendar, then collages of doves, fish, and cats, then stopped in front of a face with large round eyes and two tusky fangs. "Rodrigo's first piece," she said. "A Tlaloc mask."

"You must be so proud of him," I said to her, then to John. "It's like looking in a mirror, isn't it darling?"

My stand-in fake husband turned a lovely shade of eggplant, then he took a deep breath and asked, "Don't you have that thing you need to get back to?" I didn't know his voice could get that high.

"Oh, no," said Mrs. Luna. "And we were having so much fun."

"John's right," I said. "I'm the assistant manager on the late shift at Wendy's and we're cleaning grease traps tonight."

John's eye began to twitch, but I saw another reporter coming toward me and didn't have time to revel in his discomfort. "I hope to see you again soon, Mrs. Luna," I said, shaking her hand quickly. Then I punched John in the arm. "See you at home, darling."

I threaded my way through the throng of art lovers, feeling a little sad about deceiving such a nice woman, and feeling a lot disgusted that she really believed I had said "I do" to that patronizing little elf.

I couldn't leave, though, not without knowing what happened to John With. I found him in the stock room lining up empty frames according to size. "Are you okay?" I asked, closing the door.

He looked up, his eyes red and puffy. My heart hurt for him. "We're losing our lease," he whispered.

"No, John," I moved toward him.

He wiped his nose with the back of his hand. "We found out today. Someone bought the whole block. They're going to build—"

"Condos."

Fresh tears started. "Everything we've worked for …"

252

"You'll find another space." I felt like an idiot for saying something so trite, especially when I knew it wasn't true. Four Corners had a sweet location with plenty of parking and similar art businesses surrounding it. It would be hard to find another space that even came close.

I put my arms around his waist and laid my head on his chest.

John touched his chin to the top of my head. "Thanks Poppy Markham."

I pulled away, still holding onto his waist, and looked up into his troubled face. "It's Poppy Smith tonight."

Then the door opened and John Without and Mrs. Luna entered just in time to hear me say, "but Poppy Jones has a better ring to it."

TWENTY-SEVEN

THE NEXT MORNING, I showered and dressed quickly so I wouldn't have to face the Johns. I had left the stock room saying, "Sorry you had to find out like this, darling." At least I had left Mrs. Luna with no doubt that the Johns were straight.

On Sunday, visiting hours at the jail flip-flopped from Saturday's hours for N through Z, so instead of waiting an entire day to see Ursula, I could see her first thing. I signed in at 7:00 AM and waited for an hour. I almost didn't recognize her when she walked in the room. Her vibrant red hair had matted into a dull penny brown, and bruise-colored circles echoed under her eyes. She looked worn out and defeated. In the kitchen, she was always in control, and always had things to be in control of. But here, she controlled nothing, not even who she talked to or when.

She snatched up the receiver. "Mom says Ari Gross is in the country and will be in town tonight. Maybe he can talk them into setting bail."

"Maybe," I said, trying to inject hope into the word. "In the meantime, I'm still working on proving that you're innocent."

"Having any luck?" She smiled with one side of her mouth, making her comment seem derisive, but I didn't hear it in her voice.

"I think so." I didn't want to overwhelm her with information, so I took things one at a time, starting with Belize and Trevor. "Did you know they were secretly dating?"

"No. But what does Trevor's dalliance with some nothing little waitress have to do with who killed Évariste?"

"Maybe nothing. But Belize is the reason Trevor threatened Évariste with a meat cleaver. Do you think something was going on with Belize and Évariste?"

She held up her hand. "Please, Poppy, the bologna is making me sick enough without that nauseating image. But to answer your question, I doubt it. If Belize was having an affair with a famous French chef, she seems like the type of girl who'd want everyone in the restaurant to know about it. And even if she was, but managed to keep it a secret, there would at least be rumors, and I've never heard any."

"Say there was something going on. Do you think Trevor was jealous enough to kill?"

"It's possible. But why would he use my knife? What good would it do to frame me?"

"Well, with Évariste gone and you in jail, he's the acting chef at Markham's."

"Belize is a money-hungry opportunist," she said, not willing to admit Trevor's possible role in this. "Maybe *she* killed that

255

French fornicator and framed me to ensure Trevor's rise to the top so she'd be dating the chef at Markham's."

I told her about Évariste offering Trevor a personal sous chef job.

"That explains their sudden coziness," she said. "Trevor's not as tough as he pretends to be. Évariste would have scalloped his potatoes within six months." She started to sound like her old self. "I've been thinking about what you said last night. Are you sure Évariste owns two percent of Markham's?"

"Now it belongs to BonBon."

"Let's hope she doesn't have aspirations to take Évariste's place in the kitchen."

"Trevor wouldn't be happy about seeing her, either," I told her about Jamie's fake interview with BonBon, and about the flash drive and BonBon's attempts to get it from Trevor. "Do you know about a deal Mitch was making with Évariste?"

She pushed lank hair behind her ear. "Just what Mitch told me about partnering with Évariste for his name."

"His name?"

"That's what he told me. Mitch was in negotiations with Évariste to rename the restaurant 'Évariste Bontecou's Markham's Grille and Cocktails' or something like that. Like Emeril does." She snorted. "Emeril probably hasn't cooked in half the restaurants his name is on. Évariste would have been like that." She traced a dirty crack in the Plexiglas with her thumbnail.

"Why didn't you tell me about this name deal before?"

She looked at me, confused. "You already knew. You said Nina told you."

When I had gone to sleep the previous night, all of the pieces of these puzzles had been tumbling around in my head, but Ursula had given me a piece I hadn't even known was missing. It seemed that Évariste was involved in two different partnerships: one with Will and his investors that gave him two percent of Markham's, the other with Mitch to use his name. That changed everything.

I called Jamie as soon as I left the jail and asked him to meet me at his office. I told him that I was standing in line for the only thing I knew would both apologize for waking him up that early and get him out of bed: migas tacos with extra cheese and jalapeños from Taco Xpress.

Taco Xpress is an Austin landmark that didn't sell out to developers. Well, it did, but it worked a deal to rebuild the restaurant a few hundred yards down the street, bigger, funkier, and more colorful. On the weekends, the place is impossibly busy. But the number of cars in the parking lot in no way indicates the chaos inside because it's within walking distance of several neighborhoods. At 9:00 AM, the line already snaked out the door.

A cross-section of Austin had descended that morning—college kids and yuppies in their orange and white UT gear, hippies in their cut-off shorts, young families whose babies were young enough to sleep through all the noise, couples sitting across from each other reading the paper. Jamie and I used to do that. If he was quietly absorbed in a story, he would tap my foot with his under the table every so often to let me know he was thinking about me.

As I neared the counter, I automatically scanned for obvious health code violations, like missing hair restraints on cooks or employees drinking from open cups instead of ones with lids and straws. I saw nothing.

Twenty minutes later, I had my hand inside a bag of warm tacos, feeling around for the extra containers of hot sauce I had requested. I drove to Jamie's office, a large open space downtown near the railroad tracks that he shared with a graphic designer and two freelance writers. Jamie hadn't arrived yet, so I sat on the stoop and rolled my idea around, remaining cautiously optimistic that I had dug long enough and deep enough, and been lucky enough, to hit something solid.

I jumped up when I saw Jamie's car, feeling a little wobbly from the anticipation of what we could discover and elation at seeing him again. Being with him the past few days had started to heal my heart. Maybe I was ready to forgive him.

He dressed in black jeans, hiking boots, and a green t-shirt. His wet hair hung in his eyes and he hadn't shaved. He looked better than I knew he felt. Early sets with Zzaj often turned into late-night jam sessions, with lots of beer to call down the muse. "Tacos, hot sauce, coffee," he said, "in that order."

I held up the bag of tacos as he unlocked the front door. He let me enter first, then flipped light switches and turned on the air conditioner. "I'll make coffee," I said on my way to the kitchen.

I returned with two steaming cups and waited for Jamie to "Heaven" and "perfection" his way through two tacos. When he had come back to life, he asked, "How's the jailbird?"

"Dirty and grouchy, but that's not why I'm here. I need you to look something up for me."

He wiped grease from his fingers with a paper napkin, then sat up in his chair. With me instructing over his shoulder, he punched in some names and addresses. We both watched as the information came up on the screen.

"Would you look at that," he said. "Las Vegas, Miami, Phoenix, San Diego. They're all there." He grinned up at me. "Nice work, Detective Poppycakes. Now what?"

"First, I want to find out how Mitch hooked up with these guys so we can figure out a way to get unhooked. Then I'll keep working on who killed Évariste." I stopped. "But I guess I'll have to wait until Tuesday when we open again to talk to Trevor. Dang. I feel like I'm so close to figuring this out."

"I could find out where Trevor lives," he offered.

"Belize too?"

"You got it." He stood and looked into my eyes. "Sally Field and Jeff Bridges."

Stay Hungry?

He wrapped his hands around my wrists and pulled me to him.

Kiss Me Goodbye.

Jamie leaned into me and I closed my eyes, excitement mixed with fright as I felt myself sliding over the cliff.

The front door scraped open. "Jamie?" a female voice called.

"You're here bright and ..." she hesitated when she saw us, "early."

The girl with bad timing was Kimberlee, one of the writers who shared his office. She dressed like she was going to meet some of her sorority sisters for Sunday brunch, which in Austin meant a Greek life t-shirt, running shorts, too much makeup, and flip-flops.

"Sorry," she said, disappointed. Was she the one?

"That's okay," I said, pulling away from Jamie, glad for this unlikely rescue. What was I thinking, anyway? I was *this close* to kissing him! No preparation, no list of pros and cons, no evaluation about whether it was a good idea, which it certainly was not. Yes, he was handsome, chivalrous, smart, and sweet, but those golden nuggets couldn't tip the scale against the lead brick of my broken heart.

"There's coffee in the kitchen," Jamie said to her. He still held my hands, but he knew he had lost the moment. "Almost nearly," he said, letting go of me.

"But not quite hardly," I finished.

He combed his fingers through his hair, which had started to dry into long, shiny curls. "I made a mistake, Poppy. One I've regretted every day for the past three months."

"I know. It still hurts, though. A lot."

"What can I do to make it up to you?"

I knew Jamie would do whatever I asked, but what could I ask? That he pay me money? What's the market price for loyalty? That he take me on a trip? In what country do facts get erased? That he give me his daily itinerary and call me every hour so I would know his whereabouts at all times? That would make me his probation officer, not his girlfriend. And it wouldn't make me feel better. No "thing" could make up for the fact that he had broken my trust.

"I just need some more time, okay?"

———

I had been traveling the triangle of my neighborhood, the restaurant, and the hospital so often that I found myself on Lamar and driving toward Markham's before I realized what I was doing.

I had intended to go to the hospital, get Nina out of the way with some raw meat stuffed with tranquilizers, then demand answers from Mitch. But since I was already at Markham's, I figured I would do a little foraging. If I could snoop around in Will's office, I probably wouldn't have to talk to Mitch at all, except when I accepted his thanks for alerting him to the grim future of his restaurant that Jamie and I had discovered.

I pulled around to the back, unlocked the door, and walked through the dark kitchen to Will's office. The door was locked, but that wouldn't stop me this time. Long ago, my brother had taught me the very necessary art of lock picking. At the time, I never thought I would have to use that skill, but it often comes in handy during my inspections.

I pulled the tools from my backpack, squatted in front of the door, and got to work. The last time I picked a lock had been a few months ago. The manager of a popular deli claimed he had lost the key to his only deep freezer, so I offered to open it for him. That time, I had worked with bright lights and no agenda, and it still took half an hour. When I opened the lid, a bloody deer carcass full of buckshot was sitting on top of the frozen lox and bagels.

The third pin had just clicked into place when I heard, "Most people like to wait at the bar."

"Will," I said, popping up like a groundhog. My tools clinked as I dropped them into my open backpack. "What are you doing here?"

"I'm running checks today, remember?"

No, I did not remember.

"I thought I made it clear that you didn't need to sign them," he said.

"You did."

"Then why are you here?" Will looked down at the doorknob to let me know he knew what I had been doing.

"I wouldn't have to break in if you'd given me a key like I asked."

Will shook his head. "As I told you before, I don't hand out the keys; Mitch does."

He unlocked the door and I pushed into the office before he could shut me out. "He trusts you to sign checks, but not to hand out keys? That's a strange place to draw a line."

"I think so, too." He closed the door, then took a seat behind the desk. "I'm only here for an hour, so what can I help you with?"

I sat across from him. "I want to know about the partnership." I saw a flicker of anger in his eyes, then he said, "Also something you need to speak with Mitch about."

"I will about the one involving Markham's," I said, "but I'm curious about the other partnerships. The ones you had with Évariste."

He placed his hands on the desk. "What about them?"

"Why did all of the restaurants close a few months after y'all invested in them?"

He looked like he had swallowed peroxide. Oh, how I love catching people off-guard. And oh, how I love being right.

Will cleared his throat then said, "Some restaurants take on investors because they want to expand, but many are in financial trouble. I'm sure you know this. My partners and I lent them money, and Évariste and I lent them our restaurant expertise." He sighed. "But in spite of our best efforts, they didn't make it."

"That makes sense. But what I'd really like to know is whether it's just a coincidence that those restaurants and the surrounding businesses are now high-rise condos owned by you and your partners."

He sat back in his chair. "Poppy——"

I pointed an accusing finger at him and raised my voice. "Is that your M.O., Will? You swoop into a dying restaurant, promising to help them with money and a famous chef, but you and Évariste run it even further into the ground so they have to close and sell to you? Is that what you were planning to do to Markham's?"

Will stared at me. I often use a calculated silence as a tactic during restaurant inspections, but I could see him calculating something in his silence. What I saw frightened me.

I changed my tone. "Mitch will never sell Markham's."

I turned toward the door, but quick as a panther, Will was around the desk and behind me. "In a few months, he won't have a choice."

I turned to face him. "What are you talking about?" He stood so close to me, I could smell the detergent on his shirt.

"That secret little side deal he tried to make with Évariste to franchise his name would have helped, but now there's no help for him." Will laughed at the shocked look on my face. "Évariste told me about it the night of the party. That silly man thought their deal would get him out of debt with us at the same time. He never did like ruining restaurants."

TWENTY-EIGHT

WILL LAUGHED. "IF THE police thought that, they would have arrested me instead of Ursula."

I reached behind me for something, anything, to stop me from crumbling to the floor. My fingers fumbled against the doorknob. Locked. "You framed her."

"There's no evidence to support that, Poppy." His voice sounded smooth and controlled, the way it had the night of the party when he wanted Évariste to speak with reporters. "Not even a flash drive."

He took a step back and started to say something else, but I jerked up my knee, grazing his groin. He only winced, but it bought me the moment I needed. I turned the lock, flung open the door, and fled into the darkness of the kitchen. I heard him slam through the swinging doors as they swung back toward him, then the lights came on. I would lose a physical fight against Will, but if I could get through the back door I had a chance.

In two seconds my chance vanished as Will's fingers wound around my wrist.

I pulled forward out of his grasp, then pumped my elbow back. I didn't connect with him, and the force of my swing knocked me off-balance. I reached for the silver prep table, but my hand slipped on the curved edge. My rump connected hard with the tile floor.

Will stood over me and extended a hand to help me stand up. Was that the hand that held the knife that killed Évariste? I scooted back and he stepped forward.

"Can you claim self-defense, Will? Did Évariste have the knife and you used it on him before he could use it on you?"

"I could say that, but the police would want to know what took me so long to remember." He looked down at me, his face unreadable. "Why would I do that anyway? Markham's was the spike in our development plans, and now it's not. Everything is going so well." He raised an eyebrow. "Except for one or two details."

I jumped ten steps past panic, and animal survival instincts took over. I pulled my knee to my chest and kicked up between his legs as hard as I could. Full contact.

Will doubled over, his face crimson with pain and rage. "Witch!" he gurgled.

I scrambled backward and around the corner of the prep table, grabbing pans from the low shelf, hurling them in front of me. They couldn't hurt Will, but they would slow him down. He said something, but I couldn't hear over the racket of metal against tile.

A few more inches and I would have what I needed. I flipped over to my belly and flung myself around the third corner. I reached into the curved well under the prep table and felt it: a bread knife I had hidden ages ago. My fingers curled around the handle as Will jerked up my ankles. I pitched forward and the knife bounced off the bottom shelf and under the table.

I reached for it, but Will dragged me back. I kicked loose of him, and threw my body forward with a grunt. The knife cut my palm as I grappled with the blade. I switched the handle to my left hand and wrapped my right arm around the leg of the prep table.

"Let go, Poppy."

I held on tighter and flailed my legs. Will kicked my right elbow to loosen my hold, then yanked hard on my legs. He pulled me through the noisy rubble of the pots and pans, my body sliding easily across the floor, leaving a red smear on the white tiles.

"Where is that blood coming from?" he demanded.

"My nose," I lied. "Belize knows about all of this, doesn't she? You going to kill her too?"

"Belize was a diversion for one of my partners. The one with the bad manners and big mouth, unfortunately. She tried to black-mail us, but I'm better at that game." He stopped and dropped one of my ankles. "She will be dealt with."

I heard the walk-in door pop open and felt a rush of cool air. I kicked back and struck his shin. He stomped my ankle, then picked it up and jerked me over the threshold. The walk-in floor felt cold and gritty.

"Another murder so soon after Évariste's and the police will know it wasn't Ursula."

"By the time someone finds you on Tuesday, you'll be frozen. An accident." He laughed. "Don't worry. We can blame Trevor for turning down the thermostat."

He held my legs and tried to turn me around so his back was to the exit, but he stumbled and dropped one of my ankles to steady himself.

I twisted onto my back, pulling my other leg free. He lunged for me and I slashed his knee with the bread knife. He howled in pain, his eyes huge from the surprise of my attack.

"That was for Ursula," I said. "And this is for Mitch." I kicked at the bleeding wound, rolled out of the walk-in, then shut the door. I scrambled up, ready for Will to make one last effort to push open the door. When I heard the catch release, I rammed the door with my shoulder. I heard a crash and hoped he had toppled that large crate of tomatoes onto his head. I still had the knife in my hand and shoved it into the catch.

Then I slid down to the floor and waited for the dry heaves to stop so I could call Jamie.

"How many stitches?" Mitch asked. He was propped up on some pillows, full of color and life, spooning tapioca into his mouth. Nina had gone to pick up Ursula.

"Eleven," I said, holding up my bandaged hand. After I had been released from the ER, Jamie and I went straight to Mitch's room. "You know my side of the story, so now tell me yours."

"It's complicated, Pene—"

"Don't Penelope Jane me, Daddy, Will Denton almost killed me. Tell me what's going on."

"Okay." He placed the empty bowl on the rolling table next to his bed. "As you already figured out, Évariste and Will and those other men were business partners. They were using Évariste in a fairly complicated real estate scam."

"We got that far," I said. "Jamie and I saw that all of their restaurant investments turned into condos. Is that what they were trying to do with Markham's?"

Mitch nodded. "If they wanted to buy a restaurant, and the restaurant wouldn't sell, they found other ways to get what they wanted. If the restaurant was in financial trouble, Will and Évariste would offer the owners an injection of cash along with free consulting services. Will took control of the front of the house and Évariste came in for a couple of weeks to work with the chef to prepare for a big debut."

"But Markham's isn't in trouble, is it?" I asked.

"Upgrading the restaurant wasn't cheap, and they offered better terms than the bank. I'm getting too old to run everything by myself, and the package they presented was exactly what I needed. Will managed everything, and Évariste's involvement guaranteed more press coverage than I'd ever get on my own." He adjusted the pillows behind him. "The deal was that if business increased by a certain percentage within thirty days, Will and his buddies would get forty-nine percent ownership and Évariste would get two percent."

"Giving up controlling interest seems pretty hefty," Jamie said.

"As I said, it was just supposed to be a temporary thing. And I didn't know their true intentions until Évariste told me, but by then it was too late." Mitch looked out the window then back at me and Jamie. "In spite of being a bad guy, Will knew what he was doing and he got the numbers up pretty quickly. It was only after they had their percentage that we started losing money."

"So that's why Will comped all that food and expensive wine," Jamie said. "He was running costs into the red to bankrupt the restaurant."

"And that's probably why he opened this weekend and let Trevor lead the kitchen," I said. "He hoped Trevor would screw up and we'd lose even more money," I shook my head. "I owe Trevor an apology."

Jamie said, "Shall I post my review of his first night?"

"Immediately, please," I said, then remembered I wouldn't be the one dealing with this trespass onto Ursula's territory. I looked at Mitch to second the motion and he nodded. "Okay, keep going with the story, Daddy."

"The deal didn't look that bad at first because they gave me the option of buying them out. But it had to be in one lump sum."

"Couldn't you take out a loan or get another investor and pay them back?" I asked.

"That's something that had to be voted on among the three shareholders," Mitch said, "which Will and his partners would never do because they didn't want their money back. After we all had our percentages and everything was nice and legally binding, Will sprang on me that because Markham's was losing money, they had decided to sell the restaurant to developers."

"Which happened to be them operating under a different name," Jamie said.

Mitch looked sad and guilty. I knew he felt foolish for getting involved in this, but he didn't deserve all the blame. Nina had taken his focus away from Markham's. "If anything came to a vote," he said, "Évariste was always supposed to vote with Will to give them a fifty-one percent majority."

"So what role does the name deal play in all of this?" I asked.

"Will and his partners had been using Évariste for years and he decided he'd finally had enough, so he told me everything. Évariste wanted to franchise his name, and over a couple of days, we hashed out a plan."

Jamie laughed. "Leave it to an old Texas hippie to bring down an international scam."

"It wasn't without its problems," Mitch said. "The first is that once Évariste defected to my side, he could also vote with me to take out a loan, which meant I could pay Will and his boys back. Will's partners had already bought up other businesses over a couple of blocks. They had too much at stake and Markham's was threatening to bring it to a halt."

"So losing Markham's meant losing millions," I said.

Mitch pointed to a cup of water, which I handed to him. After he drank, he continued. "A second, more long-term problem is that losing Évariste meant the end of their game."

"Wait," Jamie said, "I thought Évariste owed Will money. How could Évariste get out from under them?"

"Once Évariste started franchising his name, he would eventually earn enough to pay them back."

"Which they also didn't want," I said.

Mitch nodded. "The only reason they were able to invest in as many restaurants as they did was because of Évariste. The night of the party, Évariste got drunk and told Will that he wouldn't be voting his two percent to sell Markham's."

"So Will killed him," I said. "But why? At least if Évariste was alive, Will could possibly make him change his mind."

"Honey, there are two kinds of people in this world. Those who work out their problems by civilized means, and real estate developers."

Jamie and I laughed, then Jamie said, "With Évariste dead, his two percent goes to BonBon."

"Who they would make sure voted with them," I said.

"I did a little digging after you left my office," Jamie said. "The deals they made for other businesses in the area were contingent on all of the properties being sold to them. This whole thing takes Markham's off the table, I imagine, so the investors who don't go to prison can legally back out."

"Which means the Johns can stay where they are," I said. "And I'm assuming Will set fire to my house. Or hired someone to do it. That jerk tried to kill me twice."

Jamie hugged me. "I'm proud of you, Poppycakes."

"Me too, honey," Mitch said.

"Me too," said Ursula, bounding into the room. She kissed Mitch's forehead. "Mom's outside talking to the nurse. They might let you out of here today." She wore the same pants and t-shirt she had worn in the kitchen during the party.

Ursula turned to me and pulled me into a tight hug. "I owe you my life, Poppy," she whispered.

I drew back and quickly put some distance between us. "I'm sorry to be the one to tell you this, Ursula, but you stink."

THE END

© LEIGH-ANN SHRUM

ABOUT THE AUTHOR

Robin Allen holds a BA degree in English from the University of Texas at San Antonio. She worked in restaurants and bars to pay her way through college. *If You Can't Stand the Heat* is her first novel.

WWW.MIDNIGHTINKBOOKS.COM

From the gritty streets of New York City to sacred tombs in the Middle East, it's always midnight somewhere. Join us online at any hour for fresh new voices in mystery fiction.

At midnightinkbooks.com you'll also find our author blog, new and upcoming books, events, book club questions, excerpts, mystery resources, and more.

MIDNIGHT INK ORDERING INFORMATION

Order Online:

- Visit our website www.midnightinkbooks.com, select your books, and order them on our secure server.

Order by Phone:

- Call toll-free within the U.S. and Canada at 1-888-NITE-INK (1-888-648-3465)
- We accept VISA, MasterCard, and American Express

Order by Mail:

Send the full price of your order (MN residents add 6.875% sales tax) in U.S. funds, plus postage & handling to:

Midnight Ink
2143 Wooddale Drive
Woodbury, MN 55125-2989

Postage & Handling:

Standard (U.S. & Canada). If your order is:
$25.00 and under, add $4.00
$25.01 and over, FREE STANDARD SHIPPING

AK, HI, PR: $16.00 for one book plus $2.00 for each additional book.

International Orders (airmail only):
$16.00 for one book plus $3.00 for each additional book

Orders are processed within 12 business days. Please allow for normal shipping time. Postage and handling rates subject to change.